THE SPY WHO HATED ME

A JAMES FLYNN ESCAPADE

HARIS ORKIN

Black Rose Writing | Texas

ISBN: 978-1-68513-445-7
LIBRARY OF CONGRESS CONTROL NUMBER: 2024931871
PUBLISHED BY BLACK ROSE WRITING
www.blackrosewriting.com

Printed in the United States of America
Suggested Retail Price (SRP) $22.95

The Spy Who Hated Me is printed in Book Antiqua

*As a planet-friendly publisher, Black Rose Writing does its best to eliminate unnecessary waste to reduce paper usage and energy costs, while never compromising the reading experience. As a result, the final word count vs. page count may not meet common expectations.

Author Photo Credit: Laura Burke

Other Titles by
HARIS ORKIN

YOU ONLY LIVE ONCE

GOLDHAMMER

ONCE IS NEVER ENOUGH

LICENSE TO DIE

"*The Spy Who Hated Me* is a laugh out loud, action-packed thrill ride. James Flynn and his friends are off to save the world again, but this time they might not make it out alive. The action is realistic and heart-pounding, and you cannot help but root for James and his band of misfits."
–Christy Cooper-Burnett, author of *No Way Home*

"Haris Orkin creates double-0 the fun with the return of his delusional but debonaire, martini-sipping hero, James Flynn. The thrills, the action, and the quips are fast and furious as Flynn battles to save his lady love and the world from an enemy that makes Mr. Goldfinger seem like Oscar the Grouch."
–Linda Sheehan, award-winning author of *Fore Play* and *Decanted*

"A hilarious mash-up of James Bond and Don Quixote in which a psychiatric patient believes he is a secret agent and must rescue the girlfriend who doesn't want to be his girlfriend. Full of wacky characters, villains who can't quite succeed in being dastardly, and action scenes with hilarious gadgets. You will not be able to stop turning the pages or laughing."
–Carl Vonderau, award-winning author of *Murderabilia* and *Saving Myles*

I dedicate this book to my Uncle Sandy. He has been more like an older brother than an uncle as he's only thirteen years older than I am. He is always there to listen and offer me his wisdom. We have sipped a lot of good bourbon, enjoyed a lot of good food, and shared a lot of laughs over the years and I look forward to more of that in the future. I am forever grateful for his love and encouragement.

ACKNOWLEDGEMENTS

I am so grateful for all the fans who have written reviews and written me notes expressing their love of Flynn and his adventures. I wouldn't have written *The Spy Who Hated Me* without their enthusiasm and support.

I also need to thank my endlessly patient editor M.J. Moores and my energetic and tenacious literary agent, Darlene Chan, who helped to get the Flynn Escapades optioned by Avalon Entertainment this year. (Along with my agent at APA, Steve Fisher.)

I want to thank Victoria Gerken and the team at Podium Audio as well as the brilliant actor who plays Flynn (and everyone else) in the audio books, Chris Cuilla.

I'm grateful to the many friends and fellow writers who take the time to read my early drafts and offer their thoughts and ideas and endless encouragement. In particular, I want to thank Dwight Holing, Richard Procter, Jeff Fisher, Larry Kelter, Khaled Talib, Linda Sheehan, Christy Cooper Burnett, Toni Runkle, Carl Vonderau, and Lawrence Allen.

Next I want to thank Reagan Rothe and the entire team at Black Rose Writing. I will single out David King for the incredible covers he creates. (Along with an assist from my wife, Kim.)

My siblings, Mike, Lisa, and Lynne, and my Uncle Sandy are constant champions and supporters and make my life so much better just by being there.

My wife, Kim, and my son, Jakob and his wife Charlotte, patiently listen as I lay out the characters and the plot and then read much of what I write in all its iterations. They are my sounding boards and my cheerleaders, and I greatly appreciate their love and support.

THE SPY WHO HATED ME

"What man can pretend to know
the riddle of a woman's mind?"
–Miguel de Cervantes Saavedra, *Don Quixote*

CHAPTER ONE

Caitlyn Valentine hated wearing dresses and high heels. Especially tight, strapless, semi-see through dresses and four-inch-high stiletto heels. But Oleg picked this dress out for her personally. A Dolce & Gabbana. What he spent on the dress would probably feed a family of five for a year. But then Oleg Ivanov had more money than God. Even so, he wanted more. Billionaires always want more. Especially those who grew up poor. More wealth. More power. More prestige. More safety. Though safety was the one thing money couldn't guarantee. That tended to make them paranoid.

In business.

In life.

In love.

Oleg liked having Caitlyn on his arm, but he didn't completely trust her. He didn't completely trust anyone. Not even his wife, Anya. Since Caitlyn spoke fluent Russian, Oleg took certain calls on a secure line in his office. Caitlyn wasn't privy to those calls, but his London townhouse was built a hundred years previously and she discovered that sound often traveled from one room to another through the ancient air ducts. By climbing up on a priceless antique sideboard and putting her ear up to the ventilation grille in the library, she could hear the conversation in Oleg's office. One side of it anyway. That made it difficult to discern exactly what was being discussed. She did catch a few choice words, however.

Extortion.

Cyberwarfare.

Economic collapse.

Chaos.

Caitlyn heard footsteps in the corridor outside the office and hopped down off the sideboard, not easy in a skintight dress and high heels. The door opened moments after her heels hit hardwood. Oleg's wife, Anya, seemed startled to see her. The tall, striking, forty-something redhead spoke to Caitlyn in Russian-accented English. "My dear, what are you doing in here?"

"Waiting for Oleg to get off the phone."

She offered a devious smile. "It's always all business with him, isn't it?" Anya glanced at the grille high on the wall above the antique sideboard and then lowered her gaze to Caitlyn.

"But then it's all business with you too."

"I better get back to Oleg."

"Why?" She eyeballed the grille again. "Is his conversation over?"

CHAPTER TWO

Flynn maintained a discreet distance from his target. He kept her in view, but never looked directly at her. Prey can feel the eyes of a predator. Not that Flynn meant her harm. His mission was to protect her. She stopped in front of *Dancers in the Rotunda at the Paris Opera* by Edgar Degas.

Tall and slender with long jet-black hair and pale flawless skin, her blue-green eyes studied every detail of the painting, her expression inscrutable. She resembled the dancers on the canvas, her posture like that of a ballerina. Only the fine lines around her eyes and mouth hinted at her age. She moved with a confident athleticism through the various halls of the Norton Simon Museum, catching the attention of every male over the age of fifteen.

One man in particular eyed her as she ambled by. A rough character in the uniform of a security guard. Shorter than Flynn, but broad shouldered and solid. The guards at the Norton Simon carried no weapons. At least none visible to the naked eye.

The double-sided slit in the soft cashmere sweater dress showed off her shapely calves. That could account for all the attention. Or perhaps those watching her had more sinister motives. She slowed to scrutinize a bronze sculpture. Another Degas. *Little Dancer, Age Fourteen.* Eyes closed, head back, arms taut, the young dancer stood in a modified fourth position. Almost a *tendu croisè devant.* Flynn once dated a dancer in the Bolshoi, and she schooled him in the five basic positions. He then schooled her in a few more advanced ones.

His target moved on, unaware that anyone was watching her. She moved from room to room and gallery to gallery, slowing to pause and take in paintings like Botticelli's *Madonna and Child with Adoring Angel* and *Tulips in a Vase* by Paul Cezanne. Flynn stopped when she did and stared at whatever painting or sculpture stood before him. At one point, he felt her eyes on him, but didn't dare look for fear of giving himself away. When he finally turned and glanced in her direction, she was gone. He hurried to find her, but not too quickly, not wanting to reveal himself to those pursuing her.

He caught a glimpse of her outside in the sculpture garden, standing by the large, lush pond. At certain angles she reminded him of a love he had lost. Or at least misplaced. Caitlyn Valentine. Usually, Flynn was the one who did the dumping. He did it to protect himself as well as those he cared about. He couldn't afford to love too deeply. To do so would put those he cherished in great jeopardy. But Caitlyn Valentine understood the risk. She lived the same life he did. A life he promised to abandon if she agreed to do the same. Caitlyn, however, wasn't ready to settle down. Not yet. At least that's what Flynn told himself.

The Norton Simon's lush sculpture garden resembled Monet's Garden at Giverny. Flynn followed his beautiful target through the sunlight and shadow, keeping hidden behind various large bronze sculptures, cedar, and eucalyptus trees. He cut through some lavender and found her standing below a towering abstract statue by Henry Moore. As she turned, he frantically searched for somewhere to hide and found cover behind Aristide Maillol's *L'Aire*.

The statue was huge, and Flynn crouched next to the large nymph's naked buttocks. He peered over the curve of the recumbent nude's hip and caught his target looking right at him. Flynn ducked down and waited, wondering if she was looking at him or the sculpture. He crawled forward and peeked between the naked lady's hefty thighs and caught her eyes again. She grinned at him playfully and took off, disappearing into the trees.

Flynn hurried to catch up. He had no reason to be surreptitious as she'd clearly made him. He followed her back inside the museum and caught her rounding a corner. Others watched and followed as well. He had to find her before they did. He caught glimpses of her flashing him a naughty smile before disappearing around another corner. She played with him. Baited him. Was she leading him into a trap?

More people populated this part of the museum as it held a newer art installation. Flynn lost her in the crowd. He looked about frantically, desperate to find her in the throng. Then he caught sight of her mischievous face. She offered him a devilish smirk and disappeared through another doorway. Flynn followed, pushing through the crowd. He found himself in a long, empty corridor, lined with paintings from the Renaissance. There were two doors. Both locked. He raced to the far end and through an open archway into another smaller gallery with Italian paintings from the 14th century, all religious-themed, depicting Christ and the Madonna and the horrors of hell.

Flynn stood alone in the room, his target gone. *Did I lose her? Did they grab her? Have I failed her?* He turned to hurry back down the corridor. One of the previously locked doors abruptly opened. Someone grabbed him by the arm and jerked him inside. The door slammed shut, plunging him into darkness. The scent of Black Opium by Yves Saint Laurent filled his nostrils. An iPhone flashlight blinked on, illuminating her mesmerizing blue-green eyes. She stood inches away.

"You were watching me," she whispered.

"I'm not the only one."

"I was watching you too."

"Under whose orders?" Flynn demanded.

"My orders."

"Why would *you* be watching *me*?"

"Why wouldn't I be? Let's stop playing games, James. I see how you look at me. I know what you want."

"Miss Grossblatt, please…"

"Shelley. Call me Shelley."

"Shelley, listen—"

Shelley silenced Flynn with a kiss as she grabbed him by the arse. He tried to back away and bumped into the storage closet door. Her tongue forced its way past Flynn's lips. She pressed herself against him. Flynn desperately wanted to give in, but gently pushed her back until their tongues decoupled and he broke the suction created by their mouths.

"I'm not saying I don't find you attractive," Flynn whispered. "I find you very attractive. But I promised my superiors I'd refrain from dipping my pen in the company ink."

"James, look at me. Life is fleeting. We must take our pleasures where and when we can."

"I don't disagree."

"Then make love to me."

"I worry we might be in danger."

"Of course, we're in danger. Death stalks us all. But before I die, I want to live. I want to love. I'm not getting any younger. I don't want to wake up one day and discover that life has passed me by. If I don't take a chance, if I don't grab life by the balls—" Flynn flinched as she grabbed him by the balls. Not to the point of pain, but firmly and with great conviction. "Then why am I even here? Do you know what Henry David Thoreau said?"

"If a man does not keep pace with his companions, perhaps it is because he hears a different drummer."

"Yes, he did say that," she nodded. "But he also said I want to live deep and suck out all the marrow of life." She unbuttoned his button and unzipped his zipper and sank to her knees. "All good things are wild and free. There is no remedy for love but to love more." She put her iPhone face down on the floor, plunging the little closet into darkness.

. . .

Sancho Perez tried not to panic. Dr. Michaels assigned Sancho the task of monitoring Flynn and now Sancho had lost him. He'd looked away for just a moment, and Flynn disappeared. Flynn reminded him of his one-year-old son, Miguel. Once Miguel learned how to crawl, he would vanish in an instant, take off like a rocket, chasing the dog or the cat or whatever caught his interest. Flynn too often disappeared in the blink of an eye.

The higher-ups at City of Roses Psychiatric Hospital hadn't authorized an off-campus field trip for quite some time. Not since the fiasco at the paintball park last year. Dr. Michaels brought as many minders as patients this time, and Sancho was there specifically to keep an eye on Flynn. As a psychiatric nurse at City of Roses, he always anticipated the unexpected. But Flynn, who suffered from a severe delusional disorder, pushed the envelope when it came to unpredictability.

James Flynn believed that City of Roses served as a satellite headquarters for His Majesty's Secret Service, and that he operated as a secret agent with a license to kill. Sancho was an orderly when they first met. Flynn befriended him, encouraged him, and mentored him. Flynn helped him find his confidence and taught him to believe in himself and his abilities. The money he made on his adventures with Flynn paid for his college education and his house. They were like brothers, and that was why Dr. Michaels put Sancho in charge of keeping tabs on him. No one knew Flynn better than Sancho.

"*Mierda,*" Sancho mumbled as he moved from gallery to gallery, nervous sweat beading on his forehead. He searched for a glimpse of Flynn's grey Brioni suit. No other patients dressed as fashionably as Flynn. Most wore sweats or jeans or shorts. He spotted a few of them staring at various paintings and sculptures or nothing at all.

Forty-something Mary Alice had freckles, graying red hair, and anger management issues. Three-hundred-pound, twenty-something Ty used a gangsta attitude to cover up his crippling anxiety. Eighty-two-year-old self-proclaimed genius inventor Quentin Smith suffered from delusions of grandeur. Rodney, a stout, sixty-something with a Santa Claus beard, struggled with substance abuse. Bob was bipolar. Zipper, a shy schizophrenic, dozed on a bench in front of a Goya.

Where the hell did Flynn get to? Flynn wasn't under lock and key at City of Roses. He was there voluntarily and could come and go as he pleased. Yet, the outside world wasn't a safe place for him. Not in his delusional condition. Whenever Flynn ventured outside the hospital walls, he regularly found himself in insanely dangerous situations. As a young dad, Sancho couldn't afford to take the same risks he once did. His days of saving Flynn from himself were over. He prayed his old friend hadn't wandered away from the Norton Simon.

Sancho spotted Nurse Durkin standing by an Alexander Calder. *Maelstrom with Blue.* The head nurse at City of Roses was Sancho's immediate superior. At six feet tall and two hundred pounds, she brooked no insolence and took no prisoners. Sancho considered asking her if she'd seen Flynn, but that would mean admitting he lost him. So instead, he continued on into the next gallery where he spotted the hospital's other chaperones: Nurse Alvarez, Nurse Benson, and Dr. Michaels.

Dr. Michaels, the head psychiatrist at City of Roses, was balding and slender. He sported a black goatee streaked with gray and Giorgio Armani eyewear. Michaels had an imperious attitude and hesitated to approve this outing. Somehow Shelley, the new art therapist, changed his mind. They had a certain contentious familiarity. Sancho wondered if they'd worked together before.

Shelley Grossblatt was a lot more attractive than her name. For a woman in her forties, she kept herself in good shape. Tall and slim with long black hair and blue-green eyes, she reminded him of the actress Kate Beckinsale. It's probably why every male patient of City of Roses signed up for art therapy. Flynn included. She was cold and stand-offish until Flynn started charming her. She loosened up. She smiled. She laughed. She…

Shit.

Sancho didn't see her anywhere in the museum. *Did she and Flynn disappear together?* He moved faster. Room to room. Gallery to gallery. No Flynn. No Grossblatt. And then he noticed Ty standing by a hallway door, his ear pressed up against it, a stupid grin filling his face. Sancho approached him and heard what Ty heard. Moaning and groaning and bumping and squeaking on the other side of the door.

Someone bumped into Sancho from behind. He turned to see Quentin, his hand cupped over his ear as he tried to hear what was happening behind the door. Rodney stood grinning next to him. Bob giggled behind a glowering Mary Alice. She did not look happy. Sancho knew she had a thing for Flynn, and she didn't react well to other women throwing themselves at him. Nurse Durkin headed in their direction, probably to see what all the fuss was about. That caught the attention of Nurse Alvarez and Benson and, finally, Dr. Michaels himself.

Everyone stood and stared at the entrance to the storage room, listening to the intimate sounds emanating from within. Durkin pushed her way forward, shoved Ty to one side, and pulled open the door, flooding the little storage room with light.

CHAPTER THREE

Norton Simon made his first fortune in sheet metal. He used that money to buy an insolvent orange juice bottling plant in Southern California. The company, renamed Val Vita Food Products, expanded its product line to include all kinds of fruit and vegetable products. He sold his company to Hunt's Foods in 1969. That same year he married Jennifer Jones, the widow of David O. Selznick, producer of Gone with the Wind. *Later, he bought Canada Dry, Avis Car Rental, and Max Factor. At one time, he was one of the wealthiest men in America with a net worth of over 10 billion dollars. He collected 8000 works of art over 30 years, and in 1975 opened the Norton Simon Museum in Pasadena, California.*

Flynn squinted into the light. A small crowd of people gathered outside the storage closet. Most were fellow agents or support personnel from His Majesty's Secret Service. Even M was there, though out in public everyone called him by his cover name, Dr. Michaels.

They stared at Flynn, and Flynn stared at them, and no one said a word.

Flynn's pants were down around his ankles. He wore no jacket, shirt, or tie. Shelley Grossblatt had even less on. Just a pair of black Manolo Blahniks. Flynn felt sheepish, but Shelley showed no embarrassment whatsoever. In fact, she appeared proud of her nakedness. Her impertinent breasts. Her brazen behind. Her long, flawless legs. She looked directly into M's eyes and offered a defiant smile. "Darling, would you please close the door?"

"How could you do this to me?" M sputtered.

"I'm not doing this to you, darling," Shelley said with a smile as she gestured towards Flynn. "I'm doing this to *him*."

Flynn raised his hand. "Sir, I'm sorry. This might seem somewhat…inappropriate, but I do have an explanation."

M's complexion changed from light pink to red. "An explanation?"

"Several enemy agents were eying Miss Grossblatt with ill intent and closing in. Miss Grossblatt thought it best we hide from view and pulled me into the closet with her. To throw off suspicion if any of them opened the door, I thought it best we appear to be…"

"Out!" M shouted.

"Sir?"

"Out of the closet, Flynn! Out! Now!"

Flynn stumbled out with his pants still around his ankles. He nearly tripped, but Ty caught him before he could fall.

M went to close the door, but Miss Grossblatt kicked it back open, banging M in the nose. "Look at me, Tony. For once, look at me!"

"I'm looking!" M shouted as he held his injured nose.

"But you don't see me. Not really."

"*Everyone sees you!*"

"Are you even attracted to me?"

"Of course, I am."

"Then why do you ignore me?"

"Shelley—"

"Do you even remember the last time we had sex?"

"Shelley, please! Don't do this to me!"

"I wouldn't have to if you would occasionally do something to *me*!"

"This isn't the time or the place."

"Of course, it is! You ignore me at home. You ignore me at work. You barely talk to me. We're barely roommates. How else was I going to get your attention?"

Recognition slowly dawned on Flynn as he pointed at Miss Grossblatt and then at M. "Are you two…"

"Yes, Mr. Flynn! We're married. Shelley is my wife!"

"But…um…you don't have the same last name."

"Because we wanted to keep our private lives separate from our work lives!" M shouted. "We wanted a firewall to keep things professional, and then my wife set that firewall on fire!"

"Sir, I'm sorry, I had no clue that you two… that you and her…that Shelley was your—"

"Nurse Durkin, please get the patients back on the bus! This outing is over."

M stepped into the closet and pulled the door shut behind him. Muffled shouting filtered through as the argument continued. Flynn hesitated and then opened the door. "Excuse me, but could you please throw me my—" His shirt hit him in the face, and M slammed the door.

■   ■   ■

Sancho sat next to Flynn in the transport van. Dr. Michaels sat up front next to Durkin. Shelley never boarded the bus. She left in an Uber, destination unknown. Sancho knew he'd take the fall for this. He wouldn't be surprised if Dr. Michaels fired him. The ride back to City of Roses was short and uncomfortable.

After dinner, Sancho found Flynn in his room, lying in bed, staring at the ceiling, his lips pursed with anger.

"Bro, are you all right?"

"I'm ashamed of myself."

"We talked about this."

"I know."

"You're out of control."

"I had no idea she was a married woman."

"None of us did," Sancho said.

"M seemed upset."

"No shit."

Flynn sat up and put his feet on the floor. "I was just trying to keep her safe."

"You did a little bit more than that."

"I didn't seduce her, Sancho. She seduced me."

"You've been getting seduced a lot lately."

"Not on purpose."

"Bullshit. You're putting out the wounded puppy dog vibe, and women can't resist that."

Flynn shook his head. "I don't know what you're talking about."

"You're heartbroken and they can sense it. They want to fix you. Comfort you."

"How is that my fault?"

"You're using sex to distract yourself from what you're feeling."

"Don't be ridiculous."

"Caitlyn broke your heart. The sooner you admit it, the sooner you can put it behind you."

"I admit I enjoyed my time with her, but a man who does what I do can't afford those kinds of feelings."

"You told her you'd give it all up for her and she turned you down. She hurt you. Rejected you."

Flynn looked down at his shoes. His face reddened with either anger or embarrassment.

Sancho sat next to him. "I'm not trying to make you feel bad."

"I'm worried about her."

"I'm sure she's fine."

"We talked every week. Even after she moved to London. But suddenly, she stopped taking my calls. And then her number was disconnected."

"When was the last time you heard from her?"

"Not in weeks. Frankly, I'm a little concerned."

"Maybe she just moved on. Met someone else."

Flynn shook his head. "No. Something isn't right."

"Is she back with the CIA?"

"I don't know. Even if she was, she couldn't say."

Sancho nodded. "I'll see what I can find out, but you got to stop with the Don Juan shit. Keep it up and Dr. Michaels might send you somewhere else."

"Well, if he would send me on a mission, I wouldn't need to distract myself with these frivolous escapades. I'm a double 0. I need a target. A mission. A purpose. I'm fit, I'm ready, I need to be out in the world, confronting our enemies."

A sharp rap on the door ended Flynn's diatribe. Nurse Durkin filled the doorway. "Let's go, Mr. Flynn. Dr. Michaels wants to see you."

Flynn nodded and stood. He glanced at Sancho. "This might be it. Wish me luck."

■　■　■

Flynn entered the anteroom to M's office. His loyal secretary, Miss Honeywell, typed at her computer. The voluptuous African American beauty wore her hair in exotic cornrows that hung halfway down her back. Flynn sat on the edge of her desk. She didn't look up.

"Miss Honeywell, you are a sight for sore eyes."

"Uh huh."

"Have you changed your hair, Miss Honeywell? It's quite fetching."

She looked up at Flynn with a smirk. "Mr. Flynn, are you flirting with me?"

"What if I was?"

"Then I would say your little head is getting your big head in all kinds of trouble."

"So, you heard?"

"Everybody's heard."

"I had no idea she was married."

"Or who she was married to."

"No, ma'am."

"You sure stepped in it this time."

"Apparently so."

Honeywell snickered and shook her head. "Go on in. He's waiting."

"Okay then. Until we meet again."

"Uh huh." Honeywell went back to typing.

M sat behind his desk, pointing at his couch. Flynn took the hint and sat. "Sir, if I may."

"You may not."

"I had no idea you were married to Miss Grossblatt. If I had the slightest inkling, I never would have—"

"Please stop talking."

"Of course."

"I'm not angry with you, Mr. Flynn. I'm angry with my wife. But that's a personal matter, and that's the last I'll speak of it. I don't take what you did personally. You're dealing with deep abandonment issues, and the end of your relationship with Miss Valentine only exacerbated that trauma. You're acting out. It's a cry for attention. I understand that."

"Sir, if I may—"

"I'll tell you when it's your turn to talk. Right now, it's my turn."

"Of course."

"I considered sending you elsewhere, but that would be admitting failure, and I haven't given up on you yet, Mr. Flynn."

"Thank you, sir."

"But I *am* restricting you to the premises. No more outings. No more visitors. No computer access. No phone privileges. You are on lockdown."

"You're not sending me on a mission?"

"Your mission is to make yourself whole. Get better. Integrate your personality. We're going to get aggressive with your treatment, and try things we haven't tried before. You've been here for over twenty years. My predecessors failed you. I won't. It's time we made a concerted effort to get you better.

"Yes, I agree I may suffer from a certain amount of PTSD, but that goes with the territory. No one does what I do and walks away completely unscathed. However, that's not what I'm worried about. I'm worried about Miss Valentine. Worried she might be in trouble. Since you're not sending me on a mission, I'd like to fly to London and make sure she's okay."

"What did I just say, Mr. Flynn? You're in no condition to go anywhere. For the foreseeable future, you are on lockdown."

CHAPTER FOUR

In 1934, a Hungarian doctor named Ladislas Meduna came up with the concept of using one disease to cure another. He injected a drug called Metrazol to induce epileptic seizures in a catatonic patient. After a number of treatments, the patient was able to walk, speak, and feed himself. But the technique often caused severe neurological damage. Italian neurologist Ugo Cerletti thought inducing seizures with electricity might be more humane. He first perfected this technique on dogs and then, in 1938, conducted the first human trial on a schizophrenic found wandering around a train station in Rome. With the application of 110 volts, they successfully induced a seizure. After ten more treatments, they reduced the schizophrenic's outward symptoms of psychosis and he returned to his wife and job and life in the community. This technique, known as electroconvulsive therapy or ECT, later became widespread, even though it produced certain side effects like loss of memory, confusion, headaches, nausea, and even heart rhythm irregularities.

Dr. Michaels told the staff he only wanted Flynn to find his true self. To that end, he was going to try every drug, technology, and technique known to modern psychological science. His stated goal? Break Flynn's delusion.

Instead, Sancho watched as he broke Flynn.

From his course work at Cal State, Sancho knew that delusional disorder was relatively rare. Because of his affection for Flynn, Sancho read a lot of the research literature, and learned of the various factors that might contribute to the condition.

Delusional disorder often ran in families, so there was likely a genetic component. But abnormalities in certain areas of the brain or a chemical imbalance might also contribute. Losing his mother and father at age ten had a major impact on Flynn. His years in foster care. The bullying. The isolation. The fact that he felt so helpless and all alone. It was no wonder he became the most powerful person he could imagine. Someone who had no fear. Someone who could handle any situation and survive anything.

Sancho snuck a peek at Flynn's file. Dr. Michaels put Flynn into intensive cognitive behavioral therapy. Michaels wanted Flynn to take a closer look at his notions and emotions. The goal was for Flynn to unlearn behaviors, reduce negative thoughts, and confront his delusional thinking directly. To help accelerate that, Michaels upped Flynn's meds.

First-generation anti-psychotics work by blocking dopamine receptors in the brain, but the side effects were no joke. Michaels started with chlorpromazine and thioridazine. They made Flynn incredibly drowsy and slow. He shuffled when he walked, and his face lost all emotion and expression. Flynn retained water, gained weight, and developed facial tics. His hands shook. He stopped exercising, stopped socializing, and slept away most of the day.

When Sancho tried to talk to Flynn, his old friend struggled to focus and form sentences. He seemed fearful, and confused.

Second-generation anti-psychotics like clozapine and ziprasidone blocked serotonin receptors and made Flynn restless and agitated. So, Michaels prescribed tranquilizers and anti-anxiety meds. Flynn grew slower, and sleepier, and more lethargic. He even started to drool.

Sancho tried to make an appointment with Michaels, but his secretary claimed he didn't have an opening for weeks. Finally, Sancho cornered him in the cafeteria one day as they both waited in line for lunch.

"Hey, Dr. Michaels, can I ask you a question?"

"Can we do this after lunch?"

"Flynn's not looking too good lately. Are you sure all these new drugs are necessary?"

"I wouldn't have prescribed them if I didn't think so."

"Are you sure you're not punishing him?"

"Excuse me?"

"For what happened with your wife?"

"What are you accusing me of?"

"I'm just saying—"

"I know what you're saying, Mr. Perez, and I do *not* appreciate it."

Michaels picked up his lunch, found an empty table, and took a seat. Sancho followed and sat across from him. "I'm not accusing you of anything. I'm just…I'm just saying…I don't like seeing him like this."

"No one does."

"Other doctors have gone down this route before. It just doesn't work."

"That's your expert opinion?"

"Look, I know I'm just a nurse, but I've known him a long time."

"Yes, you and Mr. Flynn are very close. Too close. So close you can't be objective about this."

"I don't think that's true."

"Mr. Flynn has been a resident of this institution for over twenty years. His treatment here has not been effective. If anything, he's fallen deeper into his delusion. We are not doing him any favors by ignoring his condition."

"I'm not saying we should ignore it."

"I know my predecessor, Dr. Nicholson, made a serious effort at one point to help Mr. Flynn. He tried antipsychotics. Anti-depressants. Even transcranial magnetic stimulation. And for a time, Mr. Flynn found his way back to reality."

"Yeah, but he wasn't happy. He wasn't himself."

"He was exactly himself and if Nicholson had stayed the course, Flynn would have finally been able to live a normal life. A life outside a psychiatric hospital."

"I don't know if that's true."

"Well, I intend to find out. Monday, I'm starting him on electroconvulsive therapy."

"Shock treatment?"

Dr. Michaels frowned at the disparaging nickname for the procedure. "ECT. It's non-invasive and it's performed under anesthesia. It'll help accelerate changes in Mr. Flynn's brain chemistry. The side effects are minimal. Mild headaches. Short-term memory loss."

"Short-term memory loss?"

"It's rarely permanent."

Sancho angrily slapped his hand on the table. Everything jumped. *"I don't like seeing him like this."*

"Lucky for you, you won't have to. I'm transferring you to another facility. I'm afraid you've become an impediment to Mr. Flynn's progress. You're enabling his behavior and reinforcing his delusion."

"Transferring me? Where?"

"To a facility in Long Beach."

"Seriously?"

"Unless you'd rather leave the employ of Health Management System Services entirely."

That took Sancho by surprise. "What?"

"Think about it." Dr. Michaels stood, leaving his tray and his dirty dishes on the table. "Talk to your wife. But let me know by tomorrow."

■   ■   ■

Transferred? Sancho couldn't believe it. He'd been there six years. He had never worked at another hospital. He felt at home at City of Roses and liked everyone he worked with. Well, mostly everyone. Not Nurse Durkin. And some of the orderlies were assholes. Especially O'Malley and Barker. But most of his fellow nurses were great. He even liked most of the patients. And Flynn…Flynn was the big brother he never had. If not for Flynn, he never would have married his wife, or finished college, or owned an Aston Martin DB 9 Volante. *Shit. Maybe Michaels is right. Maybe we are co-dependent.*

Sancho decided to give Michaels the benefit of the doubt. Long Beach wasn't that much longer of a commute. Maybe he needed to stretch his wings. Try something new. Part of him felt like he was letting Flynn down. But what if it was for the best? *What if I'm holding Flynn back?*

After lunch, Sancho went looking for Flynn. Before Michaels tried to fix him, Flynn spent most days reading, researching on the communal computer in the activity room, or working out either in the hospital's exercise area or in the outdoor courtyard on the little patch of grass between the picnic tables. He was better looking than Bradley Cooper and had a physique that would put Hugh Jackman to shame. Lean. Tall. Wide shoulders. A solid six-pack. The nurses would often lunch outside just so they could watch Flynn perform his shirtless karate katas. But Sancho didn't find Flynn in the courtyard or the exercise room or even his own room. He found him in the TV room.

Flynn never watched TV, but there he sat on the sofa, squished between Ty and Rodney. His puffy face the result of all the extra pounds he put on. Probably from the anti-psychotics. Still, between Rodney and Ty, he looked relatively petite. They watched a Magnum PI rerun. Well, Rodney and Ty did. Flynn slept like a drooling, bloated, pasty-faced baby.

Normally, Flynn dressed better than any patient in the place. He had a vast collection of stylish clothes he bought from online vintage thrift shops. Designer suits from Versace and Armani and shoes from Gucci. Even his casual clothes were the best of the best. But today, someone had dressed him in gray sweatpants, plastic sandals, and a baggy yellow t-shirt decorated with the remnants of his breakfast.

A few other patients sat scattered around the room. Flynn's elderly roommate Quentin, who Flynn referred to as Q, played Uno with Doris Frawley and Mary Alice. Doris, a former 1940s pinup girl, claimed she dated L. Ron Hubbard and gave birth to the Antichrist back in 1952. Big-boned, freckle-faced Mary Alice beckoned Sancho over. She had a raspy three-pack-a-day voice and an East Texas accent. "What the hell are they doing to Flynn?"

Sancho shrugged. "They upped his meds."

"What the fuck for?"

"Dr. Michaels is trying something new."

"Are you shitting me?"

"No ma'am. Michaels wants to help him get better."

"He don't look better to me. He looks like crap."

"I don't disagree."

"He was such a beautiful man. Charming as all hell. Now look at him. It ain't fair. It ain't right. I know he had a thing for me. I saw how he looked at me. I intimidate most men. But not him. He was working up the nerve to finally make a move, and then Michaels pulls this shit? You know what anti-psychotics do to boners?"

"Nothing good, I'm guessing."

"No, sir. They are boner killers."

"He does look a little droopy."

"It's revenge, ain't it? Cause Flynn bumped uglies with his bride."

"I don't think so."

"Bullshit! He didn't even come on to her! That hussy came onto him! Took advantage of him. Because he's a man and men can't say no." Mary Alice looked up and immediately shut up.

Sancho followed her gaze. Shelley Grossblatt stood in the doorway. She wore a long, light blue linen dress that accentuated her modest curves. It was sexy without being provocative, and she likely wore it to impress the puffy couch potato who used to be James Flynn. By the look on her face, Sancho saw Flynn's condition shocked her. Eyes wide, full of tears, she glanced at Sancho. "Did my husband do this?"

Sancho played dumb. "Do what?"

She pointed. "*This* to Mr. Flynn."

Sancho tried to change the subject. "Are you teaching art today?"

"I asked you a question!"

"Of course, he did," Mary Alice replied. "And he did it because of *you*!"

Shelley Grossblatt flounced away angrily, headed in the direction of her husband's office.

Mary Alice grinned and got up. "Can we put this game on hold for a sec? I wanna stand outside Michaels' office and listen to the fireworks." As she headed off, she offered a raspy giggle. "This is gonna be good."

Sancho went to Flynn and grabbed him by the arm. "Brother, we need to talk."

He tried to pull Flynn to his feet, but Flynn was immovable, lodged as he was between Rodney and Ty. "How 'bout a hand here!"

Rodney and Ty struggled to stand up. Being as big as they were, moving from a seated position to a vertical one required some effort. They groaned and grunted and finally got upright. Between the three of them, they managed to get Flynn on his feet as well.

Sancho held his compadre by the arm and guided him down the hall. "I got something I need to say to you, and I just hope you can hear me."

Flynn grunted, then farted and wobbled as Sancho navigated him down the corridor. It took some time, but finally they reached Flynn's room. Sancho helped him onto the bed. Flynn lay flat on his back, his face slack, his mouth open, drool dripping.

"Flynn, can you hear me?" Flynn stared unseeing at the ceiling. Sancho shook him by the shoulder. "Flynn! *Flynn!*" Flynn's eyes slowly moved in Sancho's direction. "Nod your head if you can hear me!"

Flynn nodded his head.

Sancho sat on the edge of his bed. "Dr. Michaels is transferring me. He thinks I'm interfering with your treatment, and he might be right. I don't like seeing you doped up like this, but maybe it's for the best. I hope it's for the best."

"It's not," Flynn said with a strong, clear voice. He sat up.

"What the hell?"

Flynn shushed him, holding his finger to his lips, before leaning close and whispering in his ear. "I took the medication at first. I sincerely believed M wanted to help me with my PTSD. But when I started feeling the effects, it occurred to me that perhaps M had a hidden agenda."

"You're not taking the drugs?"

"I pretend to but spit them out later. I'm feigning the effects so as not to arouse suspicion."

"Are you kidding me?"

"No. Which is why I allowed Nurse Ramos to dress me in this appalling outfit."

"Well, you're doing a damn good job of faking it."

"I believe M is transferring you for the very same reason he's trying to drug me."

"What reason would that be?"

"He's working for the enemy."

"Enemy? What enemy?"

"Moscow most likely. Though it could be some international criminal cartel."

"*What?*"

"Someone got to him. Maybe they're blackmailing him with *kompromat*. Maybe they're threatening his family."

"You don't think it's about his wife?" Sancho asked.

"Maybe his wife was trying to warn me. Maybe that's why she tried to seduce me."

"*Tried?*"

"It was likely a cry for help."

"*Dude.*"

"It's not the first time His Majesty's Secret Service has been compromised."

"Look at me, man. You are spinning out here."

"Am I? Monday M intends to have me undergo ECT. Electroconvulsive Therapy."

Sancho nodded. "He thinks it might help you."

"Help me what?"

"See things more clearly."

"So, he's fooled you too?"

"What? No. I don't know."

"Well, I do. I'm going to continue to play along and see how far he takes this. I'm going to find out who's manipulating him. Find out if his handlers are the ones who took Caitlyn."

"You think someone took Caitlyn?"

Flynn stood, too upset to stay seated. "I told you, I've been trying to get a hold of her for weeks."

"Right, I know, but that doesn't mean someone took her."

"What other possible explanation could there be?"

"Maybe she's just…you know…busy."

"Too busy to let me know she's okay?"

"Maybe."

Flynn raised a finger in the air. "Or…maybe she's being held prisoner at some black site undergoing enhanced interrogation. They're probably trying to break her."

"Who?"

"Exactly! That's what we need to find out."

"*We?*"

"M doesn't want me communicating with anyone on the outside. No phone privileges. No computer access. He has me on lockdown."

"Look, if you don't like what Dr. Michaels is doing, you can go somewhere else. You're here voluntarily. You can leave anytime you want."

"How can I leave? M is my only lead. No, I need to play this out, but I'm going to need your help."

Sancho sighed. "What do you need?"

"A burner phone. Something untraceable."

"Why?"

"I need to contact Miranda Jacks."

"You want to call the FBI?"

"Perhaps she knows what happened to Caitlyn."

"I don't know if that's such a good idea."

"A burner phone, Sancho. It's the only way I can learn the truth. If it turns out that Caitlyn is okay, then that's one less thing I'll have to worry about."

Sancho shook his head and rubbed his eyes. "A burner phone. Fine."

Footsteps approached. Flynn fell back on the bed. His eyes lost focus. His jaw went slack. Drool dribbled down his chin.

CHAPTER FIVE

Sancho didn't know what to do. If he reinforced Flynn's delusion, he could send him down a rabbit hole he might never climb out of. But what if it wasn't a rabbit hole? *What if Caitlyn really is in trouble?*

From the first moment Sancho met Flynn, the man was a conundrum. Sure, he was delusional and sometimes saw treachery where there wasn't any, but other times he saw things others didn't. He had a nose for nutty schemes and wild criminal conspiracies. He had book smarts and street smarts and a knack for uncovering the grand machinations of evil cabals and supervillains.

Maybe because those supervillains were just as insane as he was.

Flynn taught Sancho things no one ever had. Flynn believed in him. Guided him. Trusted him. Yet each time Flynn discovered a mad scheme, Sancho doubted him.

But what if Dr. Michaels was right? What if Flynn was getting worse? More delusional? More paranoid?

It shattered Flynn when Caitlyn broke up with him. His cool, confident savoir faire disappeared when she did. He seemed agitated and anxious. Less sure of himself. Now he was convinced Caitlyn had been kidnapped. Flynn wanted to play the hero again. He wanted a reason to get back together with her.

Flynn was smitten. Maybe because she was so much like him. Not crazy exactly, but insanely brave. A fearless risk taker. A real badass. She knew karate and could hack any computer and looked like a cross between Trinity from *The Matrix* and Lisbeth Salander from *The Girl with The Dragon Tattoo*. A hardcore heartbreaker. No wonder Flynn fell for her.

And *she* fell for him. She understood him. Appreciated him. Maybe even loved him. But in the end, she walked away. She tried to let him down easy, and at first Flynn let her go and went on with his life, but her rejection gnawed at him. He went from calling her once a week, to once a day, to twice a day, to three times a day until finally she cut him off. That was probably why she refused to pick up for him. Why every call went to voicemail. She didn't want to encourage him. Didn't want to break his heart any more than she already had. Well, that ship had sailed. She needed to let him know she was okay.

Sancho told Flynn he'd get him a burner phone, but only to stall him. Flynn was in no condition to call the FBI. Sancho would contact Caitlyn himself. He needed to convince her to call Flynn. She needed to tell him she wasn't in any danger.

Sancho called Caitlyn's number. It had been disconnected. Having no other numbers for her, he called the CIA. They claimed she no longer worked for the agency, but refused to tell them when she left or where she might be. Sancho's next call was to Miranda Jacks, the Special Agent in Charge at the Los Angeles FBI office. He left a message.

Later that day, when Sancho was on his way home in his Aston Martin DB 9 Volante, the phone rang. The number was blocked, but Sancho answered anyway.

"Agent Jacks, thanks for getting back to me."

"Of course. You said in your message you needed to get in touch with Caitlyn Valentine."

"Yeah, the number I have for her is disconnected."

"I called the CIA, but they were not forthcoming. As you probably know, the FBI and CIA don't always see eye to eye."

"They told me she left the agency."

"They told me the same thing. And that's all the information I could get out of them."

"Did you tell them she might be in danger?"

"*Is* she in danger?"

"Flynn thinks so."

"What do you think?"

"I don't know. I doubt it. I just want Flynn to stop obsessing about it. If she can call him and reassure him, that would be a big help."

"We stayed in touch while I wrapped up that case with her and Flynn. But after that, we lost contact. The last address I have for her is in London. I can send you that if you like."

"Sure."

"Do you want me to keep poking the agency?"

"If you think it'll do any good."

"Can't hurt to try. I'll let you know if I hear anything."

"Thank you, Agent Jacks."

"Of course. You and Mr. Flynn have helped me out more than once. It's the least I can do."

■   ■   ■

When Barker and O'Malley picked him up for his ECT session, Flynn pretended to be doped up and docile: jaw slack, arms loose, legs rubbery. He flopped around and drooled as they struggled to get him out of bed and into the wheelchair. They weren't gentle, but then those two never were. Both were HMSS security masquerading as orderlies. But then everyone at the Pasadena, California field office played their parts to the hilt. The outpost masqueraded as a mental hospital, and every agent there pretended to be a patient, a doctor, a nurse, an orderly, or support personnel.

It wasn't the first time a mole infiltrated their operation. The enemies of freedom were ruthless. To fight them effectively,

Flynn knew that he, too, needed to be ruthless, relentless, and remorseless. After all, he was a double 0 and that designation required a certain amount of cold-blooded efficiency. He would play this out as long as necessary, root out the traitors, and deliver harsh justice to whoever deserved it.

As Barker and O'Malley wheeled him down the corridor, Flynn sat limply in the wheelchair, his bonce bouncing like a bobblehead. He kept his gaze on the floor but caught some of the other agents watching him out of the corner of his eye.

Arabella Durkin, the agent who posed as head nurse at City of Roses, watched him trundle by with a look of satisfaction. M's beautiful and bountiful secretary, Miss Honeywell, seemed surprised by Flynn's floppy condition. She usually feigned disinterest in Flynn, but he knew that deep down she felt great affection for him.

Finally, they arrived at the room where M would perform the procedure. Flynn had suffered and survived torture from the best of the best. Expert sadists who knew how to inflict the maximum amount of pain. A bit of shock treatment was nothing compared to other tortures he had endured. Two nurses strapped his arms and legs down, while a third attached a helmet-like device to his head. Flynn tested his restraints. They didn't budge.

Nurse Durkin came in with a rolling tray arrayed with various straps, cables, leads, suction cups and clips. It also held two large syringes. Flynn didn't know until that moment that M intended to anesthetize him. Durkin inserted an IV drip, attached leads to monitor his vitals, and secured an oxygen mask to his face. Flynn watched as she injected a syringe into his IV line and felt himself fading. Did M intend to probe his brain? Pump him full of truth serum?

Durkin told him to count backwards from ninety-nine.

Flynn mumbled into his oxygen mask. "Ninety-nine, ninety-eight…"

■ ■ ■

Flynn opened his eyes to find himself back in his room. The overhead light blinded him. A dull ache throbbed near the back of his skull. Someone held his hand. When he turned his head, Shelley Grossblatt wavered before his eyes, sitting by his bed. She smiled at him with concern. "Look who's awake."

"Thirsty," he said.

She held a plastic glass with a straw up to his lips. Flynn savored the cold water.

"I'm sorry." She dabbed at his face with a damp washcloth.

"No need."

"No, this is all my fault. I was selfish and foolish, and I never should have come on to you like I did. I'm sorry."

"I'm not."

Her eyes lit up briefly with a smile as she blushed. "It wasn't appropriate."

"Because you're married?"

"That's one reason."

"To be honest, Shelley, I prefer married women. It keeps things simple."

"But you didn't know I was married."

"A woman of your age, as beautiful as you are, how could you not be married? I just didn't expect you were married to my immediate superior."

"Well, I'm sorry for what he did to you."

Flynn wiped a tear off her cheek. "I'll be fine. It's you I'm worried about."

"Me?"

"You were trying to warn me, weren't you?"

"Warn you?"

"That he's compromised."

"I'm not sure I —"

Flynn tugged on her hand, pulling her close, lowering his voice. "Your husband."

"I know he's very angry, but—"

"How long has he been working for Moscow?"

"*Moscow?*"

"Are they blackmailing him? Have they threatened you?"

"Who?"

"Don't bother denying it, Shelley. I've seen this sort of thing before. It wasn't so long ago that 006 was compromised. It's not the first time, and it won't be the last."

"Maybe you better get some rest."

Flynn struggled to sit up, his head throbbing. Fuzzy. "I know it feels overwhelming, but you aren't alone anymore, and I'll do everything in my power to protect you."

Tears welled up. "You don't have to protect me."

"Of course, I do."

"What you think is happening isn't happening."

Flynn kissed a tear off her cheek. "You don't have to pretend with me."

Shelley leaned into him and he held her close and stroked her hair and kissed her on the forehead just as M walked in. Shelley wrenched herself away from Flynn and leaped to her feet. "It's not what it looks like."

M's face turned pink and then purple. "No?"

"No," Flynn replied. "Your wife told me everything, so let's stop pretending."

M glared at his wife and pointed at the door. "You need to leave."

"I'm sorry, I just—"

"Go. Now. *Now!*" Shelley hurried out the door and M slammed it shut. "I am at the end of my rope, Mr. Flynn."

"As am I, sir."

M stepped closer. He studied Flynn's eyes. "You haven't been taking the medication, have you? Not the anti-psychotics.

Not the tranquilizers. Not the anti-depressants. You've been feigning the effects the entire time."

"I know you've been compromised."

"*Enough!*"

"I agree. It's time we take action. I don't know how the Russians turned you, but it's time to turn you back."

M sat heavily on Q's bed, looking more exhausted than angry. "I don't know what to do with you."

"Point me and pull the trigger. We can take this situation and turn it to our advantage. We can turn you into a triple agent."

"Jesus."

"It's not too late for you, sir."

"I failed you, Flynn. I did my best, but it just wasn't good enough."

"Don't be too hard on yourself, sir."

"It's time to send you somewhere else."

"London?"

"I'm afraid not."

"But what about Caitlyn Valentine?"

"She's not your concern, Flynn."

"Are you involved with her disappearance?"

"Don't be ridiculous."

Flynn raised an impertinent eyebrow. "*I'm* being ridiculous?"

M pushed himself to his feet. "I'm going back to my office to put in the paperwork."

"What paperwork?"

"Transfer papers. Health Management System Services has another facility in La Jolla. The Cliffs. It's larger and the facilities are a little more luxurious, but I'm sure you can afford it. I know the head psychiatrist there, Dr. Miller. He's old school. A hard-ass. But I think that might be exactly what you need."

"You're reassigning me? What about my double 0 status? Are you revoking it?"

"I'm getting you the help you need."

"So that's it? I'm done here?"

"It's for the best."

"For whom? Vladimir Putin?"

"You might want to say your goodbyes. The transfer could come through as early as tomorrow."

"I don't think so."

"It's not up to you, Mr. Flynn."

CHAPTER SIX

In 1924, Nobel Prize-winning novelist William Faulkner submitted a resignation letter as the postmaster of the University of Mississippi. He wrote, "As long as I live under a capitalistic system, I expect to have my life influenced by the demands of moneyed people. But I will be damned if I propose to be at the beck and call of every itinerant scoundrel who has two cents to invest in a postage stamp. This, sir, is my resignation."

Flynn strode into the anteroom of M's office clad in a vintage three-piece Glen Plaid suit custom tailored by Mason and Sons of London. He found Miss Honeywell click-clacking away on her computer keyboard. "Take a memo please, Ms. Honeywell."

She stopped typing to glance up at him with an angry glower. "What did you say to me?"

"Take a memo, please."

"I don't work for you."

"Sir, I hereby tender my resignation from His Majesty's Secret Service, effective forthwith. Sincerely, James Flynn."

"Excuse me?"

"After you print it and I sign it, would you mind putting it on his desk?"

Honeywell sighed. "Seriously?"

"I've enjoyed our time together, Honeywell, and I wish only the best for you."

"Are you going somewhere?"

"I'm afraid so, my dear, and I suggest you do the same. Though I have no hard proof, I believe we have traitors in our midst. If you stay here, it's possible you will be tarred with the same broad brush."

"Where are you going?"

"Back to London."

"London, okay." She raised an eyebrow. "Say hi to the king for me."

"If I see him, I shall." Flynn put his hands on the edge of her desk and leaned down close to her. Their eyes met and Flynn detected a bit of sadness. "I'll miss you, Honeywell." He planted a tender kiss on her cheek. She didn't flinch or pull away. "It's been a pleasure."

Her eyes grew shiny as she turned back to her keyboard and began typing again.

■　■　■

Flynn found Ty, Doris, Mary Alice, and Q in the recreation room, watching some lady's talk show on the telly. He stepped in front of the TV to address them, and Ty waved him away. "You're blocking the view, cuz."

"Sorry, I just wanted to let you all know—"

"What the hell, yo? You make a better wall than a window."

"I just wanted to say—"

Ty pushed himself to his feet and pushed Flynn sideways, before plopping back down on the couch. His three hundred plus pounds bounced Q and Doris into the air. Mary Alice angrily crossed the room and turned down the TV. Ty slammed his fist on the armrest. "What the hell, Mary Alice!"

"James is trying to tell us something," she said.

"So what?"

"So stop being such an asshole!" She turned to Flynn, smiling sweetly. "Okay, James. What did you want to say?"

"I've tendered my resignation and I'm returning to London."

"You're what?"

"It's been an honor to work with each and every one of you, but I fear there's something rotten in the state of Denmark and I can't root it out from here."

Ty looked perplexed. "Denmark? Thought you were going to London."

"It's a figure of speech."

Mary Alice looked gobsmacked. "You're leaving?"

Flynn nodded. "Watch your backs. Stay alert. I have no definitive evidence, so I hesitate to make concrete accusations, but all isn't what it seems."

Ty looked at Q. "What the hell's he talking about?"

Q shrugged.

Mary Alice threw her big, freckled arms around Flynn and hugged him tight, crushing him with her massive bosom. Doris hurried over to wrap her bony arms around Flynn as well. Ty got up, but only to turn up the TV. Q refrained from joining the group hug and motioned for Flynn to follow him.

After extricating himself from Doris and Mary Alice, Flynn followed Q back to the room they shared. Flynn's clothes and other belongings were already packed to go. Q opened his closet and pulled out a cardboard box. Inside he selected a few objects that he laid out on the bed. "I have two new inventions I'd like you to test out for me."

"Of course, your ingenious gadgets have come in quite handy in the past."

Q picked up a three-inch-long black plastic object with a mouth hole on one end and three holes on the other. "I call this the Sonic Blaster. It's invisible to metal detectors and packs a sonic punch that can stun and disable any attacker."

"So, it's a…whistle of sorts?"

"This is a whistle like a slingshot is a laser cannon. Each ten-point increase in decibels equals a tenfold increase in sound intensity. Sounds above one hundred and twenty decibels can cause immediate harm to your hearing. This tops out at one hundred and fifty decibels. Which is why you need to use these reusable silicon earplugs to protect yourself. Used up close, it can take an opponent to his knees. Have you heard about the mysterious sonic weapon the Soviets used in Havana to create mental confusion, nausea, and hearing loss?"

"This thing is *that*?"

"The effects are similar." He then picked up a tiny white spray bottle with a plastic cap. "Looks innocuous, does it not? But don't let this tiny spray bottle fool you. A single spritz can incapacitate an entire squad of enemy combatants within seconds."

"Is it some kind of nerve agent?"

"No, it's non-lethal. A military grade putricant."

"A what?"

"It deploys an appalling stench so powerful it can induce fear, panic, violent nausea, and projectile vomiting."

"It makes people spew?"

"Yes, but this particular stench has never been tested in the field. So use it only with the utmost caution." Q handed both devices to Flynn.

"Thank you, Q."

"Of course."

"I'll say hello to your old team at headquarters if you like."

Q raised a confused eyebrow. "Headquarters?"

A knock at the door ended the conversation. Sancho walked in. "You order a limo?"

"I did indeed," Flynn replied.

Sancho pointed towards the luggage and boxes. "You sure you want to do this? It's not too late to change your mind."

"I'm not doing this on a whim, my friend. I believe Caitlyn is in grave danger and we are dealing with enemies from within. I'll call you from London."

"You flying out today?"

"Tuesday. It's the first flight available."

"Do you even have a passport?"

"Of course, I do. Not a UK passport, of course, as I'm here in America incognito. I obtained a U.S. passport some months ago. Arranged by the solicitors who handle my trust."

Sancho shrugged. "Okay, fine, but where are you staying until then?"

"I took a cottage suite at the Langham Hotel in San Marino."

"Fancy."

"It'll do."

Sancho picked up one of the cardboard boxes packed with clothes. "Can I at least give you a hand?"

"Of course."

Between the two of them, it took five trips to cart out all of Flynn's luggage and boxes. The driver loaded it all in the boot. Sancho stood at the curb by the circular driveway as the chauffeur opened the limo door.

Flynn reached out and they shook hands. "Be well, my friend."

"I'm here whenever you need me, brother. You have my number. Call me anytime."

. . .

Sancho looked on as Alyssa gave little Miguel a bath. She kneeled by the edge of the tub and held their boy steady as she washed him with a tiny washcloth. "How could they just let him leave?"

Sancho sighed. "They can't make him stay if he doesn't want to. He's there voluntarily."

"I know, but Flynn listens to you."

"No, he doesn't."

"Maybe you can find someone to go with him?"

"That's what I've been trying to do, but I haven't had any luck."

"What about Alessandra Bianchi?"

"She just had knee replacement surgery."

"Oh, no…Is she okay?"

"Yeah, but she's laid up for the next six weeks."

"What about Bettina?"

"She's working on some big story. Chloe's shooting a movie in Toronto. Her brother, Tyler, is back in Wisconsin, taking care of their sick mother."

Alyssa looked over her shoulder at Sancho. "Can you watch him for a second? I left his hooded towel in the laundry."

Sancho nodded and put his hand on baby Miguel's shoulder as Alyssa hurried away. "How's my big boy doing?"

Miguel laughed and splashed soapy water into Sancho's eyes. Momentarily blinded, Sancho grabbed a towel and lost his grip on little Miguel. His son's slippery baby body tipped backwards and Sancho barely caught him before he went under.

"You are hard to hold on to, *mijo*!" Miguel abruptly stopped laughing and Sancho recognized the dreaded poop face. It often happened in the tub. The warm water relaxed all of his muscles, including the ones down below. Sancho lifted him above the water and Miguel let go with a long and surprisingly loud fart. His poop face turned into a happy face and Sancho grinned back. "Okay, false alarm. Feel better?"

Alyssa came in with his hooded towel, wrapped it around little Miguel, and wrinkled her nose. "Was that you or your daddy?"

"I thought he was gonna drop a depth charge."

"Wouldn't be the first time." Alyssa took Miguel from Sancho and carried him across the hall. Sancho followed and watched as she put him on a changing table.

"Wanna hand me a diaper?"

Sancho pulled a disposable diaper out of a large bag and handed it to her. "I even called Wendy Zimmerman."

Alyssa had the diaper on Miguel in seconds, and Sancho handed her a onesie. "Is she busy too?"

"She just got engaged. And she's working for Google now."

"Good for her."

"Yeah, but not for Flynn."

"You tried to talk him out of going. You tried to find someone to go with him. What else can you do?"

"Well, I guess I could go with him."

"You?"

"It's just for a few days."

"What? Just up and leave your job?"

Sancho handed two miniature socks to Alyssa. "I have a bunch of vacation days banked. I can use those."

Alyssa slipped the socks on Miguel's tiny feet. "I thought you were saving those days for us."

"I am. I was. I won't use them all. Look, if not for Flynn we wouldn't even be together. We wouldn't have this house. I wouldn't have my degree. I owe the guy. I care about him."

"So do I. You *know* I do. But you're a father now. You have responsibilities. Miguel needs you. *I* need you. "

"Look, I'm sure Caitlyn's doing fine over there. Once Flynn figures out she's okay, we'll probably take the next flight back. "

Alyssa sighed and shook her head. "Why does it have to be you?"

"If I let him go on his own and something bad happens, I'm never going to forgive myself."

Alyssa nodded. Her face softened. "I get that."

"It'll be okay. If things start getting crazy or dangerous, I'll come right home."

She looked at Sancho hard. "You promise."

"I promise."

CHAPTER SEVEN

Many ancient civilizations had rituals around bathing in natural hot springs. They considered the 'fire of the earth' a gift from the Gods. The Greeks, the Romans, even the Vikings healed themselves in geothermal springs. But it was Roy Jacuzzi who invented the first self-contained whirlpool bath system. The Jacuzzi family immigrated to Oakland, California from Italy in 1907. They became bricklayers and telegraph operators, and eventually early aerospace engineers. When one of their own developed rheumatoid arthritis, Roy created the first Jacuzzi hydrotherapy apparatus. It became ubiquitous when given as a prize on the TV show 'Queen for A Day.' The company went public in the 1970s, and the family made millions by making tens of millions pruney.

Bubbles and hot water pummeled Flynn's muscles as he enjoyed the Langham Hotel's communal Jacuzzi. Steam rose into the cool evening air, slightly obscuring the beautiful blonde in the tiny bikini who sat across from him. An Asian man, as skinny and desiccated as a piece of turkey jerky, sat on his left, the bubbles buffeting him about. On his right, a pale and plump suburban mom wore a large, floral one-piece bathing suit with a ruffled top. A yellow chiffon bathing cap sat atop her head as she sucked on a pink cocktail in a plastic glass.

Flynn caught the eye of the blonde. She smiled flirtatiously through the billowing steam. A dimpled knee bumped into his. It belonged to the tipsy suburban mom.

"You ever try a pink squirrel?" She held up her plastic glass filled with what looked like Pepto-Bismol.

Flynn detected a Minnesota accent. "I don't believe so."

"Vanilla ice cream, Crème de Cacao, and Crème de Noyaux. Put it all in a blender and voila!"

"Looks tempting."

She slid closer until her entire body was pressed up against Flynn. "Try it."

"Thank you, no."

"Don't be such a party pooper." She held the thick, striped straw up to Flynn's lips.

Flynn acquiesced and took a sip. The cloyingly sweet milkshake-like drink gave him an instantaneous brain freeze.

He winced and pushed the plastic cup back in the suburban mom's direction. The Asian man floated away from his seat and bobbed around in the middle of the hot tub. Flynn gently pushed him back to where he started. The blonde watched all this with amusement.

"So? What do you think?" the lady with the pink squirrel said.

"Interesting."

"Is that a real British accent?"

"It is indeed."

"I'm Tammy."

"James."

"James? Wait. I know you. You're that famous crazy secret agent guy! I read all about you!"

"Excuse me?"

"You're even better looking in person."

"I think you might have me confused with someone else."

The Asian man floated into the middle again and bumped into Tammy. She nudged him away and he drifted into the blonde and then bobbed around in a circle before Flynn guided him back to his seat.

Flynn didn't realize how tall and slender the blonde was until she climbed from the Jacuzzi and toweled herself off. Her long, well-muscled legs matched the rest of her athletic frame. She caught Flynn's eye and, not wanting to stare, he moved his gaze left.

That's when Flynn saw him.

He sat on a chaise longue under a white umbrella and held up his phone as if taking a picture. A big man in jeans and a black leather jacket, taller than Flynn, and broad across the shoulders, lowered the phone when he caught Flynn watching and took off.

Flynn stood and quickly climbed from the Jacuzzi.

"Getting too pruney?" Tammy asked.

"A pleasure to meet you, Tammy."

Flynn slid his feet into his sandals and headed after the man in the black leather jacket. He maneuvered through the pool area and across a small wooden bridge painted with pictures of early California, before ending up in a garden courtyard. Malibu lights illuminated the shrubbery. The man in leather? Nowhere to be found.

Flynn hurried up and down the stone pathways, past rose gardens, private rooms, and suites. He scanned the parking lot and then headed back into the hotel's courtyard.

"James!" Tammy waved and rushed up to him. Remnants of pink squirrel decorated her upper lip.

"Tammy."

"Are you here all by your lonesome?"

"I am indeed."

"Me too. I'm here from Minnesota for a Neonatal Nursing Conference."

"Oh?"

"I work with new moms and newborns."

"Sounds fascinating."

"Have you had dinner yet?"

"Dinner? Um? No, I haven't, but…I was…um…"

"Having dinner with me." The voice had a sexy rasp. Flynn turned to see the blonde from the hot tub. She wore a sheer white sarong over the bottom half of her swimsuit.

Tammy looked put out. "Really?"

She smiled. "Uh huh."

"When did he even ask you?"

"Not ten minutes ago."

Tammy frowned. She looked back at Flynn. "Maybe another time, then?"

Flynn nodded. "You never know."

Tammy offered Flynn a tight smile, and the blonde an angry glare, before heading off down the walkway, her flip-flops slapping the ground with irritation.

When Tammy was out of earshot, the blonde said, "You don't actually have to have dinner with me. I just wanted to—"

"Come to my rescue?"

"I guess so."

"So, you're not really interested in dinner?"

A shy smile. "I am if you are."

"Are you asking?"

"I guess I am." She grinned.

"I understand the Royce is quite good."

"So is the room service."

"Room service?"

"I need to shower first. What's your room number?"

"I'm staying in the Clara Vista Cottage Suite."

"I'll be over in an hour." She offered her hand. "I'm Bree, by the way."

Flynn took it and shook it. "James."

"I know." Bree gave Flynn the same flirtatious smile he saw in the Jacuzzi and headed off across the courtyard.

■　■　■

Flynn finished his hot shower with a cold one. The ice-cold spray pounded his back and sharpened all his senses. He considered warm baths to be unhygienic and believed cold showers offered health benefits that helped offset his somewhat unhealthy lifestyle. Studies had shown they improved circulation, lowered blood pressure, boosted energy, and burned fat by raising the metabolic rate. They even mitigated stress by releasing endorphins into the bloodstream. Mainly, though, Flynn found them invigorating.

As he grew older, he paid more attention to his health and well-being. He stopped smoking years ago and hardly ever had a drink. Never when stationed at headquarters. Every morning he did one hundred press-ups as slow as possible. Then one hundred leg raises, followed by toe touches and burpees.

The amenities at the Langham allowed him to vary his routine as each morning he took advantage of the well-appointed fitness center. Each evening, he enjoyed an expertly mixed martini in The Tap Room (shaken, not stirred) followed by a half dozen oysters, and either a bone-in ribeye or the grilled branzino in the Royce Wood-Fired Steakhouse.

But not this evening.

Tonight, he would have a visitor, and he made preparations. In this day and age, women often resented men who ordered for them. They didn't like someone stealing their agency and dictating the evening's repast. But Flynn was old-fashioned that way. Besides, he wanted the food and drink to arrive with his guest.

He called room service and ordered Thai lobster bisque for two, a dozen oysters, and two wagyu steaks, medium rare. For sides he selected roasted wild mushrooms, sauteed brussels sprouts, and truffled French fries. He also ordered a Chateau Montrose 2019 Saint-Estephe Bordeaux, and a bottle of Dom Perignon to keep on ice for later.

Room service arrived at 6:55 and Bree arrived at 7pm on the dot, dressed in a silk, navy blue cocktail dress with a plunging neckline and high slits.

"I see you dressed for dinner."

Bree smirked. "I see you didn't."

Flynn wore soft, grey Tom Ford jeans and a black Tommy Bahama twill shirt and no shoes. "I already ordered. I hope you don't mind."

"That was presumptuous of you."

"I hope you like your steak medium rare."

"Steak?"

"Wagyu."

She grinned. "I'm a vegetarian."

Flynn sighed. "I took you for a carnivore."

"I guess I'm not who you think I am."

Flynn smiled. "I wouldn't be so sure." He motioned to the large Spanish-style double doors. "I did order some side dishes you might enjoy."

"Lead the way." Flynn led her to the patio and pulled out her chair. She sat and glanced at the label on the wine. "Red?"

"A nice Bordeaux."

Bree frowned. "Red wine gives me a headache."

"Luckily, I also have champagne. Or don't you indulge in alcohol?"

"I love champagne."

Flynn grinned, uncorked the Dom Perignon, poured her a glass, and sat across from her. Candlelight illuminated their faces. Italian lights twinkled on the hedges surrounding the patio. Flynn dished her some wild mushrooms, brussels sprouts, and steak frites, and did the same for himself. He then poured himself a glass of red.

The wagyu was perfectly prepared. Charred on the outside. Juicy on the inside. "This wagyu is exceptional."

"I'll take your word for it."

"Last time I had wagyu I was in Japan. Kobe beef is the finest wagyu. Grown to very strict standards in the prefecture of Hyogo. Kobe is the capital. Hence the name."

"What makes it so special?"

"How it's raised. They're obsessive about the selection, care, and feeding. They use special feed mixed with beer and sake and massage each animal every night with a local Japanese spirit called *shochu*."

A smile curled Bree's lips. "Is it true?"

"Is what true?"

"Are you the famous James Flynn?"

"Let's talk about *you*. Are you here on business or pleasure?"

"I'm here for a wedding."

"Are you in the wedding party?"

"I am."

"Why aren't you out with your friends tonight?"

"I don't know. I guess I needed some time alone."

"Yet, you're not alone."

A seductive smirk. "No, I am not."

Flynn watched her intently. "Why don't you tell me why you're here."

"In your room?"

"Yes."

"I liked how you looked at me. I liked how you made me feel."

"Why don't you tell me who you *really* are."

"I told you who I am."

"Who sent you?"

Bree smiled. "No one sent me."

"Don't lie to me."

"Why would I lie?"

"Do you work for the Russians?"

"I'm a realtor. I live in Glendale."

"Are you an assassin?"

"Excuse me?"

"Are you here to kill me?"

"*What?*"

"Look at me, Bree. If that's even your name. I'm no one to trifle with. But then you know that, don't you? Up until my resignation from the British Secret Service, I held a double 0 designation."

"Oh. *Oh!*" Bree's eyes lit up. "I get it."

"Get what?"

"This. You. All of it. I love it."

"Love what?"

"Role-playing. I used to do it with my ex. He'd be a refrigerator repairman and I'd be the housewife. Or I'd be the teacher and he'd be the student. Or…" Her voice grew husky. "Or he'd be the priest and I'd be the nun."

"What are you talking about?"

"Right, you don't want to break character. Fine. I'll be the assassin and you be the spy."

She scraped back her chair, stood, and lifted a steak knife off the table. She grinned and slowly moved toward Flynn. He was up in an instant, grabbing and twisting her arm until the steak knife fell from her grasp. She gasped with pain and grinned and kissed him hard on the mouth and then bit his lower lip. Flynn instantly released her and backed away, tripping over his chair.

She raced back into the cottage proper, and Flynn wondered if she had a gun in her clutch. He snatched the steak knife off the ground and crept into the cottage, weapon at the ready. He saw no trace of Bree.

Did she flee? Or was she lying in wait?

The door to the bedroom was closed but unlocked. Flynn pushed it open and stood to one side. No gunshot.

Bree called to him from the bedroom. "Are we doing this or what?"

Flynn dove into the room, executing a perfect shoulder roll before landing on his feet, steak knife in hand, ready to wreak havoc. He found Bree in bed. She didn't have a gun. Or a knife.

Or a dress. Or underwear. Flynn stepped closer and she grabbed him by the wrist. "Are you going to kill me now? Or seduce me?"

"What are you doing?"

"What are *you* doing?"

The reality of the situation finally dawned on Flynn. "Are you really a realtor?"

"No, no, *no*, stay with the fantasy. You're a secret agent and now you're going to take me. Turn me." She whispered the last sentence. "Make me a double agent."

Flynn stabbed the knife into the wall, and Bree shuddered with excitement. She grabbed him by the arm and pulled him into bed. She ripped open his shirt, popping the buttons as she whispered sweet nothings with a Russian accent. "Touch me. Kiss me. Yes. *Yes. Yes, my darlink.*"

They made love for hours. Bree seemed insatiable. Finally, her need overwhelmed Flynn's desire and he needed a breather. He fell back, slick with sweat, and closed his eyes. He must have dozed off, because when he opened his eyes, Bree stood above him, stroking his face. She was fully dressed and silhouetted by the light of the doorway. "I have to go. Today's the big day."

"What's today?"

"My wedding day." She kissed him on the cheek and then on the lips and then left without another word.

CHAPTER EIGHT

Flynn walked past a yoga class on his way to the fitness center. A dozen women in yoga pants posed with their bottoms in the air as they executed downward-facing dog. Tammy, the pleasantly plump suburban mom with the penchant for pink squirrels, caught Flynn's eye and gave him a grin.

The plush Chinese-themed spa and exercise center offered a vast array of wellness treatments. Everything from hydrating facials to hot stone massage to Himalayan salt saunas and elemental mud wraps. Perhaps a massage would do him good after his workout.

The luxurious spa reminded him of one he visited back in England. All the cigarettes, martinis, and hard living weren't doing Flynn any favors, so the powers that be arranged a stay for him at a health farm in Sussex. There, he stumbled upon a diabolical plot to blackmail the world. Someone even tried to murder him there.

Flynn's enemies were everywhere, so he never let his guard down, even in the most serene and seemingly benign settings. One could never predict when an old adversary bearing a grudge might seek revenge.

Flynn found a few more men in the fitness center, but far more were of the fairer sex. The skinny Asian man who bobbed around the Jacuzzi the previous evening trudged on a treadmill with a built-in TV. Flynn also observed the big man by the pool who snapped his picture and then hurried away when caught red-handed. Today he wore black shorts and a tank top as he worked out on a weight machine. When Flynn caught him staring, he glanced away.

Flynn knew a predator when he saw one. This wasn't some insurance salesman. The width of his shoulders and the size of his arms and legs indicated years of hard training. Rather than confront him and create a scene, Flynn waited him out and started his workout by warming up on the elliptical machine.

The reflection in the mirror on the wall across the way allowed him to monitor the big man, and anyone else who might come up behind him. Flynn didn't bother turning on the little TV and instead, turned up the intensity. He stepped high, he stepped hard, he worked his arms, his breath quickening, his legs pumping, enjoying the exertion. Something caught his attention in the periphery of his vision. The big guy now occupied the elliptical on his left.

Flynn lowered the intensity to prepare for combat. He glanced over to see the big guy smiling right at him. "Hi!"

The happy greeting momentarily stunned Flynn and he had no reply.

The big guy continued; his voice surprisingly high-pitched for someone so massive. "I'm sorry about last night. I should have asked your permission before I took your picture, and I don't mean to interrupt your workout, but you're him, aren't you?"

"Who?"

"James Flynn. I'm a big fan."

"I think you have me confused with someone else."

"Really? You look just like him."

"I'll take your word for it."

"You two could be twins. Tall. Lean. Muscular. Ruggedly handsome. Very much in the David Gandy mold."

"Who?"

"David Gandy. Only one of the top male models in the world."

"Who are you?"

"Mike Adams and I'd really like to shoot you."

"I bet you would."

"I'm a fashion photographer here on assignment and you are just what we're looking for."

"Who is we?"

"GQ."

"So, by shoot me you mean—"

"A photo shoot."

Flynn glimpsed the medicine ball in the mirror an instant before it crashed into the back of his head. The impact slammed his face into the elliptical's control panel. A hand grabbed him by his collar and pulled him off the machine. Flynn hit the ground hard, knocking the wind out of him. A dark-haired man in his twenties loomed above. He held the medicine ball high over his head and slammed it down on Flynn's solar plexus.

Flynn couldn't breathe. The pain incapacitated him. All he could mumble was "who" before the young man picked up the medicine ball and slammed it down again. This time on his twig and berries. Flynn gasped for air. The agony all-encompassing. He rolled over on his knees to shield himself.

"Bree's mine, you son of a bitch!" A kettlebell to the side of the head knocked Flynn sideways. "Today was supposed to be our wedding day!"

Mike Adams hopped off his elliptical to come to Flynn's aid and caught the same kettlebell in the balls. He sank to his knees and cradled his naughty bits. Flynn crawled behind him, desperate to keep the angry young man at bay. "You're engaged to Bree?"

"Yeah, that's right, asshole. I followed her to your cottage last night. I would have confronted you right then and there, but…" Tears filled the young man's eyes. "But she crushed me, man. She destroyed me. I couldn't bear it. I couldn't…stand to see her in someone else's arms." A heart-wrenching sob escaped his lips.

"I didn't know."

"What? That she was my soulmate? The love of my life?"

Flynn used a weight rack to pull himself to his feet and finally got a good look at his assailant. Late twenties. Five foot ten. Slightly handsome. A little chubby. Clearly not an apex predator. "I'm sorry," Flynn said.

"I'm sorry too. How can I compete against someone like you? Rich. Handsome. Charming. *Famous.* You fucking saved the world! And that accent! Jesus! I'm just a goddamn dentist."

"Clearly, you love her."

"And you don't. You don't even know her. You don't know how special she is. How smart she is. How amazing! Everyone can see how beautiful she is, but she's just as beautiful on the inside. In her heart." His voice broke. "*In her soul.*"

"Todd?" Bree stood in the entrance to the fitness room wearing faded jeans and a light blue silk shirt. "Do you really mean that?"

"What did you hear?"

"Everything. All of it. Why don't you ever say that kind of stuff to *me*?"

"You know how I feel."

"I don't know. You never tell me. You keep it all inside."

Todd wiped away a tear. "I'm sorry."

"Did you come here to defend my honor?"

Todd nodded. "Stupid, huh?"

Bree shook her head. "No one's ever done that for me before."

"I'll always fight for you." Todd crossed to Bree. He took her hand. "You are everything to me. *Everything.* I can't lose you. I love you."

"I'm so sorry. I just…I guess I didn't trust what we had. I thought…I don't know…that we'd end up like my parents. That you'd hurt me. Leave me."

"So, you left me first?"

Bree sobbed. "I love you, Todd." She pulled him close and hugged him tight.

"Will you marry me today?"

"Of course, I will."

Everyone in the fitness center applauded, except for the elderly Asian man whose eyes remained locked on his tiny TV.

Todd and Bree left the fitness center hand in hand.

Mike Adams limped up next to Flynn. "Oh, my God, that was amazing."

"I'm glad they worked things out."

"With your help."

"Hardly."

"So, what about my proposition? Can I take a few pictures? Can I put together a proposal?"

"As flattering as your proposition is, I have more pressing matters at hand. A good friend of mine is in trouble half a world away. I can't just abandon her on a whim."

"Well, think about it. Perhaps when you return, we can arrange something."

"Doubtful. But I appreciate the offer."

■　■　■

Flynn used a bit of spit to place a hair on the door of his cottage suite before he left for the fitness center. A somewhat primitive early warning system. One he had used before in other dangerous places. The door was still locked. The *Do Not Disturb* sign hung from the knob. Even the hair was there. But Flynn sensed danger and he trusted his intuition.

Flynn eased open the door and crept inside, scanning the large sitting room with the high wood beam ceilings. He tip-toed across the hardwood floor and checked the patio doors. They were open. Unlocked. He stepped outside. No one. He backtracked to the master bedroom and peered inside, half-expecting an assailant to come rushing from the closet. No one did. Then he noticed the bathroom door was shut. As he approached, he heard the whoosh of a toilet and water splashing into a sink. The door opened. Flynn grabbed the intruder and tossed him through the air with a sweeping hip throw. The trespasser hit the floor hard, flat on his back. Flynn put his foot on the man's throat before he recognized the terrified face.

"Sancho?"

"What the hell?"

"Sorry, old friend, but you know how dangerous it can be to surprise me."

"I had to pee. I hopped the hedge and came through the patio."

"It's a good thing I wasn't armed."

"Can I get up now?"

Flynn helped him to his feet. Sancho, red-faced and flustered, sat on the edge of the bed. He noticed the bruises on Flynn's face. "What happened to you?"

"A misunderstanding. What are you doing here?"

"I'm here to help."

"Help? How? You know I resigned. We no longer work for the same organization."

"I took a bunch of vacation days."

"To what end?"

"To come with."

"To London?"

Sancho nodded. "I thought you could use a wingman."

"M is okay with this?"

"Michaels doesn't need to know. What I do with my free time isn't really any of his business."

"I appreciate your loyalty, but I can't ask you to put yourself at risk. You have a family now. A wife. A son."

"Alyssa's okay with it. She understands."

"She's a good woman."

"She cares about you, man. I do too."

Flynn nodded. "All right. I suppose it wouldn't hurt to have someone watching my back. I believe I'm already being followed."

"You've seen someone?"

"It's more of a sense. A sixth sense I have about such things."

"I'll keep an eye out."

"Good. Though I insist on paying for your ticket and lodging. It's the least I can do."

"I appreciate it."

"Of course. Our flight leaves at 1:45pm tomorrow. LAX. British Airways."

"Okay, cool. I'm going to go home and pack."

"Get a good night's sleep, my friend. Tomorrow, the adventure begins."

CHAPTER NINE

They demolished the tiny hamlet of Heath Row in 1944 to make room for London Airport. The airport's name was changed in 1966 to Heathrow to differentiate it from Gatwick. It's now officially the world's busiest airport. Eighty airlines fly over two hundred thousand passengers a day. Billionaires, movie stars, world leaders, rock stars, and commoners who don't mind running up their credit cards can avoid the unwashed masses and the main security gates with a VIP suite. A VIP concierge team takes care of their check-in and luggage while they relax in a private lounge. They're then whisked directly to the plane in a BMW Limousine. The only requirement is the purchase of a first-class ticket and an additional three thousand pounds.

Sancho had never flown to Europe before and found the experience both annoying and confusing. He took an Ambien to knock himself out. When that didn't work, he took a Benadryl. And then another one. He sat squished in his economy class seat next to a lady with a crying baby. She kept apologizing and the baby kept shrieking and Sancho wanted to cry too. He was totally exhausted, yet painfully wide awake and ready to jump out of his skin.

Flynn sat in first class, but the section was sold out. So, the only seat available to Sancho was in coach. He sat on the aisle where the flight attendant's cart smacked him every time she wheeled by. The seat back in front of him had a personal TV. Sancho scrolled through the selections. *The Great British Bake Off* was prominently featured and, having never watched it, Sancho checked out the first episode. Over the course of the next ten hours, he watched all ten episodes and became very invested in the outcome. Even as the baby next to him screamed like a banshee, he rooted for Maggie, the retired nurse and midwife, to bake a better caramel tart than Chigs, the sales manager, and Jürgen, the physicist. In the end, Maggie got the boot and Chigs took the grand prize. Fifteen minutes later, the Boeing 777 touched down at Heathrow.

Sancho lost Flynn seconds after they exited the plane. His compadre disappeared into the crowd and Sancho hurried to keep up with the stampede of arriving passengers. He didn't know where he was going and searched for signage as he wobbled forward on stiff, achy legs. His back felt weird, and his neck hurt. Not because he slept on it. He didn't sleep for one single, solitary second.

He glimpsed Flynn ahead in the crush of bodies and tried to pick up the pace, but it was like wading through molasses. Sancho yawned. Groggy. Spacy. Not a feeling he enjoyed, but if he could stay awake all day and go to sleep at his usual time, he'd avoid some of the inevitable jet lag heading his way.

Between light blue walls, the speckled-gray linoleum tile floors, and fluorescent lighting, terminal five at Heathrow didn't feel all that different from LAX or SFO. *Have I really crossed a continent and an ocean?* He rode down three long escalators to reach the shuttle to baggage claim. Before he stepped into the shuttle, he first had to hit the *loo*. That's what they called it here according to Flynn. Though the signs in the airport used the word toilet. He finally found one, rushed inside, and fumbled to pull out his equipment. Once he started, he didn't think he'd ever stop peeing. Three different travelers arrived to use the urinal next to his before he finished. He washed his hands and hurried out and caught the next shuttle.

Sancho found Flynn and together they waited in what Flynn called a *queue*. "It's good to be back on the old sod," Flynn said.

"You look like you got some sleep."

"I did indeed. Slept like a baby after two martinis. You, on the other hand, look a bit knackered."

"Uh huh."

"Last time I was here I had to interface with a passport control agent. But these automated Eurostar terminals make the whole process so much smoother. They use facial recognition software to check your identity against your passport."

Sancho knew for a fact that this was Flynn's first time in the UK. As part of his delusion, he'd fabricated an entire imaginary history of which Sancho knew every detail. Flynn believed his father was Scottish and his mother Swiss. Born abroad, he traveled everywhere with his adventurous parents. At age eleven, they tragically perished in a climbing accident. His father's sister took him in, and he lived in Kent until he went to Eton. Expelled after some "girl trouble" with a maid, he later attended Fettes College in Edinburgh, his father's alma mater. Upon graduation, Flynn entered the military and joined the Special Air Service where he distinguished himself in special operations and counterterrorism. He later joined the Special Branch before being recruited by Her Majesty's Secret Service.

In truth, Flynn was born in Burbank, California. His parents died in a car accident when he was ten and none of his relatives wanted to take him in. He ended up in the foster care system. Nine foster homes over seven years. Bullied, terrified, and all alone, he became an obsessive fan of 1960s espionage films. Over time, he developed an imaginary persona based on the most famous of those fictional characters. Someone who had no fear and could handle himself in any situation. That imaginary persona eventually became a full-blown delusion.

As they shuffled forward, Sancho struggled to stay focused. Finally, they passed the Eurostar terminals and headed for baggage claim one floor down. After a quick trip through customs, Flynn led the way toward ground transportation. Two dozen men stood in the terminal and held up signs with names on them. Flynn approached a burly man in a black suit. His sign read Rudolph Svensky.

"That's me," Flynn said.

"Good to meet you, sir." The burly man had a bald head and some kind of middle eastern accent. "Follow me, please."

A flustered Sancho frantically whispered to Flynn, "You're not Rudolph Svensky."

"It's an alias. It's the name I used to order the limo. I gave you a cover name, too."

"You what?"

"Norton."

"Excuse me?"

"That's your cover name."

"*Norton*?"

"Norton J. Johnston."

"Are you serious?"

"It's just for the limo company and the hotel. Didn't want to raise any unnecessary red flags." They followed the driver outside to a gleaming silver Rolls Royce Phantom. "I didn't want to take the tube," Flynn explained. "Our enemies are everywhere."

"I'll take your word for it."

The burly driver tossed their luggage into the trunk and opened the rear passenger door. Sancho climbed in, followed by Flynn. "Claridge's in Mayfair, driver."

The driver grunted and nodded and pulled out into traffic.

Sancho settled back into the plush leather seat. "Nice ride."

"The Bentley was booked, but I figured this would suffice. I used to own one, you know."

"A Rolls?"

"A Bentley. A battleship gray convertible coupe. A 4 ½ liter with the Amherst-Villiers supercharger. I restored it myself."

"No kidding."

"Unfortunately, it was totally destroyed on a mission to save London from complete destruction."

A glass partition separated the chauffeur from the passengers. Sancho caught the driver watching them in the rearview mirror. His eyes were flat. Hard. Cold. Sancho recognized that look from his old Boyle Heights neighborhood. Gangbangers who'd been to prison looked at you like that. Or maybe Flynn's paranoia was getting to him. Maybe the driver was just having a shitty day.

Heavy gray clouds dropped a cold drizzle. Sancho marveled at the weather. Rain like this was a rarity in Los Angeles. Sancho followed their route on his iPhone. He signed up for an international pass before they left, and his phone worked just like it did back home. But driving on the left side of the road was an odd sensation. It made Sancho uneasy.

Traffic was stop-and-go once they hit the A4. Insecurity clouded Flynn's eyes. "I know it's been a while since I've been here, but I hardly recognize anything. The city has changed so drastically."

"Memory can play tricks, mano."

"I used to know London like the back of my hand. Now it's almost as if I've never been here before."

Normally, Flynn moved through the world with a crazy confidence untethered to reality. That unshakable self-assurance made people believe in him. Made him believe in himself. But that self-assurance only *seemed* unshakable. When hard reality collided with Flynn's fantasy it sometimes shattered his delusion. Sancho had seen it before. When he lost his protective armor, James Flynn became fat, frightened, bullied, timid twelve-year-old Jimmy.

By the time they reached South Kensington, Flynn recognized some familiar buildings and landmarks and that helped bolster his confidence. He pointed out places as they passed. "The Victoria and Albert Museum. Harrods Department

Store. Now I know where we are. Knightsbridge hasn't changed a bit." Sancho knew that actual memories and scenes from movies were often interchangeable for Flynn. "On our left is Hyde Park. That's the famous Speaker's Corner, where nutters, radicals, crackpots, and geniuses stand on fruit crates and hold forth. Wellington Monument is to your left and behind that long wall on your right is Buckingham Palace."

Sancho matched their route with the map on his iPhone and noticed they were off route. He tapped on the glass separating the driver from the rear. "We're heading to Claridge's Hotel, right?"

"Yes, sir," growled the driver over the intercom.

According to Sancho's map, they weren't heading in the right direction. But maybe the driver had a different route in mind. Or maybe there were one-way roads to contend with. Or road construction.

"Last time I was here, the world was a different place," Flynn mused. "Back then, it was still *Her* Majesty's Secret Service. The queen reigned for seventy years. Guided us through the Cold War and the dissolution of the British Empire as India, Ghana, Malaysia, and Jamaica all became independent. Even Hong Kong is no longer under our purview. Under her watch, we joined and left the European Union and saw the fall of the Berlin Wall. She lived a long life. A life of service. I was proud to call her my queen. And now that her son wears the crown, my oath is with his majesty. King and country. That's why we're here."

Sancho peered out the window. They crossed a bridge. Vauxhall Bridge according to his iPhone. Sancho knocked on the partition window again. "Where are you taking us?" The driver ignored Sancho and kept his eyes on the road. Sancho knocked again and raised his voice. "Hey!" He lifted his phone to show him the screen. "I got Google maps. Where the hell are you taking us?" The driver pushed a button on his dashboard and the glass partition grew opaque. "What the hell?"

"It's electrochromic glass," Flynn said.

The rear door locks clicked down and Sancho couldn't unlock them. The driver also locked the tinted windows. "What the hell?"

"I'm beginning to believe that this isn't the driver I hired," Flynn mused.

"No shit!" Sancho pounded on the glass. "Hey! HEY!"

"That's ballistic glass, my friend. We have no way to break it and no way to escape. Sit back and enjoy the ride. There's nothing we can do until we arrive at our destination."

CHAPTER TEN

Flynn suspected the driver from the start. He'd refused to look Flynn in the eye and loaded them into the Rolls without a word. This wasn't the first time an enemy had met him at an airport, posing as a driver. It happened when he arrived in New York for a mission back at the beginning of his career. It happened in Jamaica twice. If whoever grabbed him wanted him dead, he would be. Clearly, his abductor wanted him alive. His arrival apparently rattled someone's cage.

Good.

Sancho pounded on the partition glass. "Where the hell are you taking us?"

Flynn tried to calm Sancho with a hand on his shoulder. "Conserve your energy, my friend. We'll know soon enough."

"I didn't think anyone was really after us! I thought you were just being paranoid, man!"

"It's not paranoia if someone's really out to get you."

"Yeah, no shit, but who?"

The Silver Shadow entered an underground parking garage, took a couple of hard turns, and came to an abrupt stop. The passenger doors unlocked with a click and the door nearest Flynn opened wide. The burly driver held an Uzi as he motioned for them to exit the rear of the Rolls.

Flynn climbed out. A frightened and sweaty Sancho followed. Flynn tugged his sleeves and straightened his jacket as he took in his surroundings. Fluorescent lights flickered above.

Besides the Silver Shadow, he saw only one other car. A black Range Rover with dark tinted windows.

Flynn directed his gaze at the driver. "From your accent, I assume you're Israeli. And from your physique, I assume you served with Shayetet 13."

Flynn heard slow clapping behind him. "Very good, Mr. Flynn."

Flynn turned to find a familiar face. "Mr. Ohana. It's been a long time."

"Two years."

Ohana wasn't as wide as the driver, but taller and leaner. His hair was longer and lighter, and so was his beard. He wore jeans, a black t-shirt, and a black leather jacket. He held a Benelli semi-automatic combat shotgun and rested the barrel on his right shoulder. Flynn glimpsed a shoulder holster with a Glock 19 dangling under his left armpit.

The wiry operative next to Ohana held a SIG-Sauer P229. A Compact Bullpup hung from a sling across his back.

"Avi. Frisk him."

Avi crossed to Flynn and Sancho. "Hands on the car! Spread your legs." Flynn and Sancho complied, leaning forward as they put their hands on the hood of the Silver Shadow. Avi patted them down, emptied their pockets, and put the contents on the hood of the Rolls. Wallets, iPhones, passports, keys, a pack of Extra gum, and a pair of reusable silicone earplugs. Also included were Q's black Sonic Blaster and the clear two-ounce spray bottle full of military grade putricant. Flynn carried both on the plane and TSA didn't have a problem with either one.

Flynn eyed Q's two new gadgets and considered making a play, but knew the odds weren't in his favor. He needed to lower Ohana's guard and lull him and his men into complacency before making a move. Perhaps Sancho could create a distraction. Flynn offered Ohana an ironic smile. "Do you still work for Black Star?"

"Not since you made me persona non grata with the U.S. government."

"I'm assuming Mossad wouldn't take you back."

"No."

"Because you're wanted by Interpol?"

"That's one reason."

"So, my arrival here in the UK offered you an opportunity?"

"You were out of my reach and now you're not."

"Did you kidnap Caitlyn to lure me here?"

"Who?"

"Caitlyn Valentine."

"No, I did not. I did read all about your stupid adventures though. How you're still alive is a mystery."

"So, you don't have her?"

"Isn't that what I just said?"

"How did you know I was coming?"

Ohana grinned. "Goldhammer."

"Goldhammer?" Sancho sounded skeptical. "He's in San Quentin."

"He still has resources, and he still keeps tabs on you."

"Of course, he does." Flynn foiled the billionaire's dastardly plot two years previously and apparently the man still held a grudge. "Did he hire you to kill me?"

"He did. Though I would have done it for free. You ruined my life. You ruined his."

"And how many lives have you two ruined?"

"I will not be lectured to by a *meshuggeneh*!"

Flynn smiled at that. "You think I'm crazy?"

"Everyone thinks you're crazy!"

"If that's true, then how is it I so easily defeated you?"

Ohana lifted the barrel of the Benelli off his shoulder and leveled it at Flynn. "Because nothing you do makes any sense! No one can predict what you'll do next!"

"I call that using the element of surprise."

"Well, today's the day I surprise you. Today's the day, you pay for what you did to me."

"If today's the day I die, so be it, but Sancho had nothing to do with what happened to you. He doesn't need to be any part of this."

"I disagree. He helps you. He enables you. He needs to die too."

Flynn glanced at his old friend. A growing wet spot spread over the front of his jeans. Flynn looked back at Ohana. "Well, I must admit, you have us at a disadvantage."

"Yeah, that was intentional."

"But not very sporting."

"Because this isn't a goddamn game."

"Of course, it's a game." Flynn picked up the ear plugs and put them in. "A game where we make up the rules as we go."

The world went silent, but Flynn read Ohana's lips. "What are you doing? Are those earplugs?"

Flynn picked up the Sonic Blaster, put it up to his lips, and blew. Even with the earplugs, the shrill, ear-splitting shriek set him back on his heels. Yet still he continued to blow.

Sancho covered his ears with his hands and dropped to his knees. Ohana's face contorted with pain as Avi jammed his fingers in his ears.

The driver attacked Flynn like a panicked animal and slapped the Sonic Blaster out of his mouth, ending the auditory assault. Flynn's ears continued to ring as the angry driver grabbed him by the hair and slammed him face first into the hood of the Silver Shadow.

Flynn snatched up the tiny spray bottle with the military grade putricant and spritzed the driver square in the face. The driver gasped and let Flynn go, choking and gagging like a cat trying to cough up a hairball. The smell hit Sancho, still on his hands and knees. He gagged and dry heaved as Flynn spritzed Ohana and Avi.

They both reacted physically as the foul miasma engulfed and overwhelmed them. Both gagged. Avi spewed. Ohana tried to fire his weapon at Flynn, but slid on Avi's puke and fell back, blasting the ceiling.

Flynn and Sancho grabbed their belongings off the hood of the Silver Shadow. Flynn blew the whistle once again, staggering Ohana and his men.

The driver slipped in the vomit as he squeezed the trigger in Flynn's general direction but shot Avi in the leg. Avi fell and continued to retch as Flynn slid behind the wheel of the Silver Shadow. Thankfully, the driver left the key fob in the center console.

Sancho hopped into the passenger seat.

Flynn fired up the Rolls.

■   ■   ■

Sancho flew forward as Flynn shifted into reverse and hit the gas. Ohana's Benelli boomed as the rear bumper sent the ex-Mossad agent flying. Flynn shifted into drive. The tires squealed as the Rolls tore through the parking structure and crashed through the drop gate. Flynn took a hard left and kept the pedal to the metal.

"Wrong side!" Sancho shouted. *"Wrong side!"*

Flynn swerved to the left, the oncoming car horn blaring, the driver screaming. He veered back into the right lane, directly into the path of another oncoming car. The driver changed lanes at the last second and Flynn leaned on his horn. *"Learn how to drive!"*

Sancho pointed frantically at a truck bearing down on them. *"Left! Left!"*

Flynn swerved left, banging into another car, sending it crashing into a bus bench. He swerved back to the right lane and glanced in the rearview mirror. "I don't think they're following us."

Sancho pointed straight ahead. "*Yo! Yo! You're on the wrong side of the road!*"

"What?"

"*Wrong side of the road!*"

"Hmm?"

He swerved around more oncoming cars and Sancho pulled out the earplug plugging Flynn's left ear. "*You're on the wrong side of the pinche road!*"

"You don't have to shout."

"I'm just saying—"

"Ah, yes, of course." Flynn moved back to the left. "It's been quite some time since I've been back to the Big Smoke. Driving on the left feels rather wrong."

"Yeah, but it's right."

"Right?" Flynn started to veer.

"No! Left! *Left!*"

Flynn grinned and stayed in his lane. "Just busting your balls, as they say in Brooklyn." He plucked the plug out of his right ear. "Fish your iPhone out of my pocket and find us a route to the Connaught."

"I thought we were staying at Claridge's?"

"So does everyone else, apparently. I thought we'd change our hotel and keep the competition guessing."

Sancho grabbed his phone and found the correct directions. "Okay, okay, make a left at the next light."

"Got it."

Flynn made a left but ended up in the right lane, directly in the path of a Black Cab. He swerved, banged into a van, clipped the front of the cab, bounced up onto a sidewalk and crashed into a red post box.

CHAPTER ELEVEN

Mayfair got its name in 1686 when King James II granted permission for a fair to be held on a large, undeveloped muddy field on what is now the site of Shepherd's Market. In 1710, the Earl of Scarborough built Hanover Square on that same site and so began what eventually would become Mayfair. The wealthy aristocracy left their cramped and outdated houses in Soho and Whitehall to move west to new mansions and townhouses. Minor royalty vied for the best habitations and decorated them lavishly. Construction on Buckingham Palace began in 1703 and wasn't finished until 1853. By then, the most sought-after mansions in London were located in Mayfair.

Sancho and Flynn unloaded their luggage and lugged it up the street, away from the scene of the crash. Sancho didn't want to be there when the police arrived, so he called an Uber, and thirty-seven minutes later they arrived at one of the most exclusive hotels in Mayfair.

The Connaught.

Flynn booked Sancho a suite on the fourth floor and a premiere suite for himself on the sixth. The Eagle's Lodge had a wrap-around terrace that offered incredible views.

Sancho marveled at the vista. "Bro, this is crazy."

"It's very comfortable, but I have to say, I'm sorry I gave up my old flat in Wellington Square."

"Where?"

"I can't even remember the last time I was there." Flynn stood at the railing and looked over the city with a wistful expression.

"You okay?"

"Right as rain."

"So, are we going to talk about what happened?"

"Hmm?"

"With Ohana!"

"What about it?"

Sancho couldn't believe Flynn's blasé attitude. "He just tried to take us out!"

"But he didn't succeed, did he?"

"But he's still out there!"

"And a little worse for the wear."

"He knew we were coming! Knew when. Knew where. Knew what limo service you ordered."

"I wonder if Goldhammer enlisted M in his little scheme. M wouldn't do it for the money. Perhaps he's blackmailing him."

"M? You mean Dr. Michaels?"

"We already know he's compromised. The question is who is pulling the strings?"

"Seriously?"

Flynn nodded. "We probably should inform Interpol."

"I don't think Dr. Michaels had anything to do with this."

Flynn held up his tiny spray bottle. "I'm just glad we were well provisioned."

"What the hell is that anyway?"

"A military grade putricant."

"A what?"

"It produces a harrowing, assaultive stench so foul it can cause some people to spontaneously spew."

"And that whistle. Jesus."

"Parting gifts from Q."

Sancho sighed. "I can't believe Goldhammer's still after you."

"It's a hazard of the profession. I've made a lot of enemies over the years."

"How 'bout we don't make any more?"

Flynn raised an eyebrow. "What are you suggesting?"

"I'm suggesting we get on the next flight back home! It ain't safe here, man."

"Of course, it's not safe. If it was safe, I wouldn't be needed here."

"I'm just saying…"

"It's a dangerous world we live in, my friend. Many have tried to end me, and I've survived each and every attempt. So, I understand better than most that nobody lives forever."

"I don't have to live forever, but another forty or fifty years would be good. You wanna stay? Stay. Me, I'm booking the first flight back."

"I totally understand. You have a family who needs you. But I doubt there are any flights available tonight. Book yourself a return flight for tomorrow and I'll buy you dinner. First, though, I suggest you shower and change those trousers."

Sancho looked down at the drying wet spot on his pants. "Good idea."

"No shame in pissing yourself. It's perfectly natural. Completely instinctual. In dogs, they call it submissive urination. It's how they acknowledge another dog's dominance."

"What about Ohana? He's still out there. What if he makes another try tonight?"

"He won't. He'll need to lick his wounds. And then he'll need to suss out where we're staying. But make no mistake, he will be back. Of that, I have no doubt."

■ ■ ■

Sancho felt underdressed in his jeans and flannel shirt. The Connaught Grill, one of the hotel's high-end restaurants, had a modern yet very elegant decor. They didn't have a dress code, but everyone dressed pretty damn well, including Flynn, who wore a suit and tie.

Sancho ordered the Heirloom Tomato Salad and the Welsh Rack of Lamb with a side of mashed potatoes. Flynn went for a dozen oysters and the Dover Sole. He also ordered a fancy bottle of wine. Sancho asked for a beer, Pilsner Urquell. He began to relax after the second bottle. From nursing school, Sancho knew that alcohol had a biphasic effect on the brain, increasing dopamine levels, and inhibiting neurotransmitters. He knew his anxiety would shoot back up as soon as the alcohol wore off. But he enjoyed the short break from constant worry until he realized he couldn't find his passport.

"Perhaps you left it in your room."

"No, I think it's back at that garage. It probably fell on the floor when that pendejo bounced your head off the hood."

"It's possible. We *were* in a hurry."

"Not your fault, bro, but I can't book a return flight without it."

"I was planning to go to the U.S. Embassy tomorrow. It's not far. Come with me and you can apply for an emergency passport while we're there."

"Why are you going to the U.S. Embassy?"

"To see the CIA's chief of station. I'm hoping he can point me towards Caitlyn."

"I thought she quit. Isn't that what Miranda said?"

"That's what the CIA told Miranda, but of course, that's what they *would* say."

"So, you think Caitlyn still works for them?"

"That's what we need to find out, and the American Embassy is the best place to start. Plus, we can let the local FBI legal attaché know that Ohana is here in London. They can inform Interpol and MI5."

Sancho nodded, ate one last piece of lamb, and pushed his plate away. "Goddamn that was good."

"What do you say we retire to the Connaught Bar? I understand their bartender is one of the best in the city."

"Oh, man, I'm pretty tired."

"One nightcap?"

Sancho sighed and smiled. "Fine."

■ ■ ■

Flynn ordered the Number 11, a variation on the classic martini with Gray Goose, Ambrato vermouth, Amalfi lemon oil, and a distillation of five bitters. He requested it to be shaken, not stirred. The bartender grumbled but did as Flynn asked. Before Sancho could order another beer, Flynn steered him towards a craft cocktail. A Vintage Negroni.

Flynn raised his Number 11 in a silent toast and tasted it. He nodded in appreciation to the bartender. Sancho took a sip of his Negroni. His face puckered up.

Flynn smiled. "What do you think?"

"Not what I expected."

"Better?"

"Different. Tangy." He tried another taste and made another face.

Flynn heard a high-pitched squeal behind him. He recognized it as the excited sound certain women make when they greet each other in public.

"Oh, my goodness! Mr. Flynn!"

Flynn turned to see a pale, slightly plump brunette with a giant smile and lipstick on her teeth. She seemed awfully familiar, but Flynn couldn't quite place her.

"It's me! Tammy Torkelson! From the Langham in Pasadena!"

She wore a big beige sweater dress with buttons up the front, but he didn't really remember her until he saw the pink squirrel. "Tammy. Of course."

"What are you doing here?"

"What are *you* doing here?" Flynn countered.

"I'm here on vacation. Traveling with AAA of Minnesota. The Best of Britain Tour."

Flynn set down his Number 11 and searched Tammy's eyes. "And you just happen to be staying at the same hotel?"

"Isn't that a crazy coincidence?"

"It is." Flynn felt his hackles rise. *Too crazy.*

"Well, maybe we can all get together for dinner one night!"

"Maybe."

"I know you're probably busy, but if you have time, I would love to buy you dinner. What room are you in?"

"I'm in 408," Sancho said. "James is in the Eagle's Lodge on six."

Tammy grinned and laughed. "I'll call you!"

Flynn smiled politely as Tammy left the bar. He shot Sancho an angry glare. "You shouldn't have told her what rooms we were in."

"Why not?"

"We don't know why she's here."

"She told us why she's here."

"First, I see her at the Langham, and then I see her here?"

Sancho shook his head. "Crazy, right? What are the odds?"

"Exactly. This can't be happenstance."

"She probably wouldn't walk up and start talking to you if she was doing something shady."

"Or perhaps she thinks I'll think the same thing you're thinking. That an assassin would never reveal themselves in such an obvious way."

"Dude, look at her. You really think she's a hired killer?"

"If she wanted me to believe she wasn't, this is exactly how she'd present herself. A zoftig suburban lady on vacation with AAA."

"You can't be serious?"

"Once is a coincidence. Twice is a pattern."

Sancho drained the rest of his Negroni and made another Negroni face. "I think you need to get some sleep. I know I do."

Flynn nodded. "I agree. But don't let your guard down. The best assassins are those who look like someone no one would ever suspect."

CHAPTER TWELVE

Savile Row, known worldwide as the place to purchase the finest bespoke suits, was once occupied exclusively by military officers and their wives. In 1846, Henry Poole, creator of the tuxedo, opened a store at 37 Savile Row. Other tailors soon opened their establishments on the street. In 1870, the Royal Geographical Society made 1 Savile Row their new headquarters, where they planned expeditions to Africa and the South Pole. The fictional Phileas Fogg of "Around the World in Eighty Days" lived at 7 Savile Row. Today, 44 exclusive fine clothing stores call Savile Row home. Anderson and Sheppard opened their doors in 1906. Nutters opened their doors in 1969. Tommy Nutter himself made suits for The Beatles, Mick Jagger, and Elton John.

Flynn had a 9 a.m. fitting at Gieves and Hawkes at 1 Savile Row. A ten-minute walk from the Connaught. He brought Sancho along to have him fitted as well.

As they rounded Berkley Square, Sancho expressed his skepticism. "I appreciate the gesture, but I really don't need a new suit."

"Nonsense. Every well-dressed man needs a fine bespoke suit."

"I'm not a well-dressed man."

"You know what Edith Head said?"

"Who?"

"Eight-time Academy Award winner for costume design."

Sancho sighed. "What did she say?"

"You can have anything you want in life if you dress for it."

"I thought we were going to the U.S. Embassy?"

"We are indeed, but our appointment is at 1300 hours. So there's more than enough time for us to get fitted."

"How much is this going to cost me?"

"Not a pence. This is my treat."

"Dude—"

"Don't argue. I'll have it shipped to you when it's finished."

Sancho shook his head. "Fine."

"Being perfectly well-dressed gives one a feeling of tranquility that religion and, might I add, psychoanalysis, is powerless to bestow."

■   ■   ■

Sancho and Flynn stood side by side as their tailors measured every inch of their very different bodies. Lean and powerfully built, Flynn had broad shoulders and a six-pack that would make Chris Hemsworth jealous. Sancho, on the other hand, had the classic dad bod. Though he had that same bod before he was a dad. So being a new papa had nothing to do with his short legs, his paunch, or the lack of definition in his upper body.

Sancho's tailor stretched the measuring tape uncomfortably close to his package. He found the whole process completely embarrassing. Flynn seemed so at ease, joking. Relaxed. The tailors shouted out the measurements and note takers repeated them back.

"Eighteen and a half."

"Eighteen and a half."

"Thirty-two."

"Thirty-two."

"Forty-Three."

"Forty-Three."

Sancho's tailor eyeballed the front of his jeans. "Which side?" he asked.

"Hmm?"

"Do you normally dress left? Or right?"

"Umm?"

Flynn jumped in with an explanation. "He's asking you where you normally put your twig and berries."

"My what?"

"Your bait and tackle. Your meat and potatoes."

"Oh. *Oh.* Umm…"

"On the left or on the right?"

"Haven't really thought about it. They just kind of go where they go."

"Let's try the right side, then. That's where I keep mine."

"Fine," Sancho mumbled.

Flynn caught his tailor's eye in the mirror. "Benjamin?"

"Yes, sir."

"As I mentioned earlier, I'd like my two-piece single-breasted in a classic navy-blue hopsack material."

"Of course, sir."

"My friend here, I believe, wanted something in charcoal grey sharkskin."

Sancho's tailor nodded. "Yes, sir."

"Good. Now I do have a special request. Beyond looking and fitting perfectly, they also need to be practical. We need the ability to move freely. For instance, would the crotch of my suit hold if I executed a spinning back heel kick?"

"It will if we reinforce the seams and add a little material for a fuller cut. Of course, you'll need to wear them high. That's the key. We wouldn't want the crotch to be too baggy or hang awkwardly. We want what I call practical elegance."

Flynn nodded. "Excellent. Same with the shoulders. Will I be able to hang off a ledge without tearing out my shoulder seams?"

"We'll make sure the armholes are high enough to accommodate that kind of movement and extra stitching."

"Excellent. Now, how soon can we get these?"

"The process from beginning to end takes approximathly eight to twelve weeks."

"That's fine. You can't rush perfection. We'll have them shipped to us when they're done. In the meantime, we'll also need something sooner. In ready-to-wear. Tailored, of course."

"Of course."

"We would need to put a rush order on those. Money is no object. We'll pay whatever is necessary to make that happen."

Sancho raised an eyebrow. "*We'll* pay?"

"I'll pay," Flynn said.

"Of course, sir. How soon would you need those?"

"The ready-to-wear? Ideally, tomorrow."

■ ■ ■

After the fitting, they still had a little time before the American Embassy meeting. Flynn decided to pop over to headquarters to let them know he was in London. Even though he formally resigned from the service, he felt obligated to let them know that the head of the satellite office in Southern California might be compromised.

They climbed from their cab and stood on the edge of Regent's Park. The London headquarters of the Secret Service masqueraded as a fictional global export company. He couldn't quite remember the address, but was sure he'd recognize the building once he saw it. So much time had passed. Many years. Perhaps that was why nothing seemed familiar. Flynn felt a momentary flash of anxiety. *Could this be some sort of temporary amnesia?* He had been beaten unconscious more times than he could remember. Perhaps he suffered from that condition that afflicts American footballers, chronic traumatic encephalopathy, CTE.

He shivered. The weather in London was quite a contrast to Southern California's desert-like climate. The damp cold penetrated his unlined leather jacket and chilled him to the bone.

Sancho tapped him on the shoulder. "You all right?"

"Yes, just getting my bearings."

They walked the circumference of the park. Flynn searched for the once familiar building. He had walked through those doors so many times. He scrutinized the map on his iPhone and saw a number of buildings and businesses surrounding the park: Madame Tussauds Wax Museum, the Sherlock Holmes Museum, the Royal College of Physicians. He couldn't quite remember the cover name for the company and googled *Global Exports*. The only listing was for a company in New Jersey.

Sancho looked at him with concern and, for some reason, that angered Flynn. "*What?*"

"Nothing."

"It was right here. Right on the park. I know it was."

"You okay, bro?"

"Of course, I'm okay. Why wouldn't I be?"

Sancho shook his head. "No reason. Just asking."

Flynn looked all around in each direction. Not one thing looked familiar. "Bloody hell!"

"How 'bout we put a pin in this and head over to the American Embassy? We can figure this shit out later."

. . .

Sancho called an Uber and put the U.S. Embassy down as the destination. Meanwhile, Flynn continued to freak out. Anxiety radiated off him in waves. It was hard to predict how Flynn would act when reality slammed up against his delusion. Sometimes he found a rationalization to explain the clash between fact and fiction, but sometimes he just blew a gasket. That was why Sancho came along for the ride. To be there just in case Flynn had a fit. But as much as he wanted to help Flynn out, Ohana was nobody to fool around with. He needed to convince Flynn to fly back to L.A. with him. ASAP.

The drive took twenty-five minutes, and when they climbed from the car, Sancho once again caught the confusion on Flynn's face. The embassy stood on the banks of the Thames. A towering twelve-story translucent crystalline cube plopped in a park-like setting with grassy knolls, oak trees, and a semi-circular pond that looked a little like a moat.

"The former embassy was in Mayfair," Flynn said. "Grosvenor Square. It was massive. The largest American Embassy in Europe. This one here in Nine Elms seems just as large and just as striking, though far more modern."

They entered through the South Pavilion and had to pass a security checkpoint. They took a ticket from a kiosk and a seat in the waiting area. Forty-five minutes later, a fresh-faced young brunette wearing black slacks and a blue blazer greeted them. "Mr. Perez?"

Sancho raised his hand and stood. "That's me. And this is a…friend of mine…Mr. Flynn."

"I'm Julie Howard. I'm a consular officer and I'll be helping you today."

"Thank you."

"Follow me, please." They followed her through a maze of corridors to a tiny windowless office. Julie sat behind her desk and motioned to the two chairs facing it. "Did you download the forms online and fill them out?"

Sancho handed her the printed pages and took a seat. "I can email you pictures of my stolen passport. I have them on my iPhone."

"Great."

Flynn didn't sit, but rested his hands on the back of the chair. "Would you mind contacting the Deputy Chief of Mission and tell him that James Flynn would like to speak to him?"

"Is he expecting you, sir?"

"Not at all."

"Well, he's a very busy man and you'll need to make an appointment with his staff. If you like, I can give you his assistant's number."

"Perhaps you can put me in touch with the FBI Legal Attaché, then."

"Excuse me, who are you again?"

"James Flynn. I'm Mr. Perez's colleague. Or I was until a week ago when I resigned from Her Majesty's Secret Service. *His* I mean. It was *hers* for so long, it's been hard to make the adjustment. But now I'm simply a concerned private citizen who knows the whereabouts of a dangerous international fugitive."

Julie Howard looked at Sancho. He smiled sheepishly. "I can explain."

"Yosef Ohana," Flynn continued. "A former special op with Shayetet 13, who worked for Mossad and later for a man by the name of Goldhammer. He's currently on the FBI's most wanted list. Interpol has a Red Notice on him."

"Yosef who?"

"Ohana. But that's not my only concern. There's a CIA agent I believe may be in grave danger. If you can't put me in touch with the Deputy Chief of Mission, perhaps I can speak with the Chief of Station for the CIA."

Julie Howard offered Flynn a tight smile. "Would you mind showing me your passport?"

Flynn handed her his passport. "I'd explain why I have an American passport, but I'm afraid that information is classified."

Unease crept over Julie Howard's face as she looked over Flynn's passport. "So you're *not* an American citizen?"

"Again. That information is classified."

"I see."

She stood up. "Can I make a copy of this?"

"Absolutely."

Julie Howard left with Flynn's passport, and they sat in her tiny office, waiting for her return. Fifteen minutes later, she showed up with a lanky man in his mid-thirties. Flynn rose to shake his hand. "James Flynn."

"Ed Murphy. I'm a special agent with the DSS."

"Diplomatic Security Service?"

"I understand you have information about a fugitive."

"Yosef Ohana. He attempted to assassinate us yesterday, but we managed to escape. He is armed and extremely dangerous."

"Can you follow me, please?"

Sancho raised his hand. "What about my emergency passport?"

"I'll get the paperwork started," Miss Howard said. "But it may take a day or two. In the meantime, why don't you go with Mr. Murphy. I'll text you when it's ready for pick up."

SA Murphy led Flynn and Sancho to a different floor and a different office, where Sancho and Flynn waited for almost an hour.

Murphy returned with a stocky Hispanic man in his forties. "Gentlemen, I'm Agent Fuentes and I'm the legal attaché for the FBI."

Flynn rose to shake his hand. "I'm—"

"I know who you are, Mr. Flynn. One of my colleagues in Los Angeles let us know you might be coming."

"Miranda Jacks?"

"She told me *all* about you, sir."

"So, you know I'm here undercover, then?"

Fuentes tried hard not to smirk as he caught Murphy's eye. "I understand you believe you saw Yosef Ohana yesterday?"

"I didn't just see him. He tried to kill me. In an underground garage in Lambeth."

Fuentes looked at Sancho. "Did he try to kill you, too?"

Fuentes' smirk pissed Sancho off. "He sure did."

"So why aren't you dead?"

"Because I utilized Q's gadgets to fight back," Flynn explained.

"Q's gadgets?" Again, the smirk.

"A military grade putricant and a Sonic Blaster."

Sancho bristled as Murphy suppressed a snigger.

"Then what happened?" Fuentes asked.

"Then we escaped."

"I see."

Fuentes and Murphy traded another snarky look as both struggled to keep a straight face.

"Dude, he's telling the truth," Sancho said.

Fuentes threw Sancho a pointed look. "What about you? Are you telling the truth? Do you know it's a felony to lie to an FBI agent?"

"Why does it feel like you're not taking me seriously?" Flynn asked.

"We're taking you very seriously, Mr. Flynn," Murphy said. "I'll put in a call to MI5 and Interpol as soon as you're on your way."

Flynn looked pissed. "I'd like to have a word with the Chief of Station."

"I'm afraid that's not going to happen."

"What about Caitlyn Valentine?"

"Who?"

"She's why I'm here. Why I came to London. She works for the CIA."

Fuentes glared at Sancho. "I think we're done here."

Flynn looked incensed. "Have you not heard a single word I've said?"

"Every single one and now it's time for you to go." Fuentes stood.

"She could be in great danger."

"Who?"

"Caitlyn Valentine!"

"Fine. I will write a note to the Chief of Station with this information, and someone will get back to you."

"When?"

"As soon as they can."

"I'm afraid that's not good enough."

"I'm afraid it'll have to be. Good luck, Mr. Flynn." Fuentes backed out the door, leaving Flynn and Sancho alone with SA Murphy.

Flynn stood, angry. "Let's go, Sancho. I think we've gotten all the help we're going to get here."

CHAPTER THIRTEEN

Whitehall Court, the original building that housed the Secret Intelligence Service, was built in 1884 as a block of luxury apartments in Westminster. Residents included William Gladstone and George Bernard Shaw. The SIS moved to 54 Broadway in 1924. The brass plaque outside the door identified it as the offices of the "Minimax Fire Extinguisher Company." Sir Stewart Menzies, chief of the SIS, often entered via a tunnel that connected directly to his private residence in Queen Anne's Gate. Though the address was classified, every taxi driver, tourist guide, and KGB agent in London knew its location. The SIS moved to the Century House in 1964 and in 1985, the National Audit Office declared that location irredeemably insecure. Probably because the mainly glass building had a gas station at its base. In 1987, Margaret Thatcher approved the construction of a far more secure building and in 1995, MI6 moved into 85 Albert Embankment in Vauxhall. The new headquarters stretched far below street level with numerous underground corridors. Rumor is one such tunnel extends beneath the Thames and stretches all the way to Whitehall.

Flynn googled MI6 to discover they had moved to a new building. Obviously, that bit of information had completely slipped his mind. Clearly, all the hits to the head over the years had taken their toll. That combined with the jetlag and that ECT session back at City of Roses must have affected his recall.

Flynn and Sancho cabbed it from Nine Elms to Vauxhall Cross and climbed out at 85 Albert Embankment. The new headquarters was a massive steel, stone, and glass structure inspired by industrialist modernist architecture as well as ancient Mayan and Aztec temples. The color scheme was khaki and aquamarine, and it sat right on the Thames. Tall steel fences ringed the building. Graffiti tags marred some of the stone walls. In his day, any young hooligan who had the temerity to tag SIS headquarters would find himself at the bottom of the Thames.

Sancho tugged on Flynn's sleeve. "Bro, maybe we should call ahead first."

"Not necessary."

A heavy metal door in the solid steel fence restricted access to the front entrance. Flynn examined the door entry intercom system. Sancho motioned to a large rectangular sign and read it aloud. "No unauthorized access. This is a protected site under Section 128 of the Serious Organized Crime and Police Act of 2005. Trespass on this site is a criminal offence."

"Of course, but they don't mean *us*. Once they realize who we are, they'll welcome us with open arms." Flynn hit the button on the intercom system. "Hello!"

"Come on, man. I really think we should call ahead and come back later."

Flynn pushed the button and shouted once more into the speaker. "Hello! Is someone there? *Hello!*"

A blue and yellow police SUV pulled up at the curb and two police officers stepped out. Both wore black body armor, a holstered sidearm, a Taser, a baton, handcuffs, and a radio. One approached Flynn with a smile. A black circular patch on his chest identified him as a member of the specialist firearms command. "Afternoon, sir."

"Afternoon," Flynn replied.

Simultaneously, a security officer from the building appeared. He too wore tactical gear, though he also carried a Heckler & Koch MP5 submachine gun on a sling. "Can I help you, gentlemen?"

"I certainly hope so." Flynn tugged on his cuffs. "I'd like to enter the building and report in."

"Can I see some identification?"

"Of course." Flynn produced his passport and handed it to the security officer.

"Mine was stolen," Sancho said. "I just applied for an emergency one at the American Embassy."

"You're both Americans?"

"He is," Flynn nodded to Sancho. "But I'm a British citizen traveling incognito as an American."

"Excuse me?"

"I'm not sure how high your security clearance goes. Until I know, I can't tell you who I am or why I'm here. Just know this. The people inside know exactly who I am."

"Sir, this is the headquarters of MI6."

"Yes, I realize that."

"Then you probably understand that we're concerned with terrorist threats. So, anyone we see acting suspiciously in this area will likely draw attention from law enforcement."

"I understand that, but if I can just go inside—"

"Not until you tell us who you are and what your business is."

Sancho cut in. "Officer, we should have called ahead. I'm sorry." Sancho grabbed Flynn by the arm. "James, come on, man, let's go. We'll make an appointment and come back later."

"We're here now."

"*Dude.*"

"Would you two mind if we frisked you?" asked the security officer.

"Yes, we *would* mind," Flynn replied sharply.

"Well, sir, I was trying to be polite, but now I must insist."

The two police officers took Flynn by either arm as the security officer frisked him. Flynn looked furious, but Sancho held up both hands, palms out. "It's okay, bro. Stay cool."

Sancho raised his hands higher as they frisked him as well.

"Officer, this is outrageous. When the higher-ups hear about this, it won't go well for you. That I guarantee."

The security officer handed Flynn back his passport. "If you can't tell us who you're here to see, I'm afraid this is as far as you go."

Flynn sighed. "Fine. I'm here to see C."

"C?"

"The chief of the SIS."

The cops and security officer traded troubled glances. "Do you have an appointment?"

"I don't need an appointment. Look, just go inside and tell whoever is at the front desk that James Flynn is here. Tell them I'm a former double 0 operative most recently attached to the satellite branch in Pasadena, California."

The security officer barely suppressed a smirk. "A double 0? Wait, you're *that* James Flynn?"

"You know who I am?"

The security officer addressed the police. "He's that nutter from California who believes he's a British spy."

"That's my cover story, yes, but as you can see, I'm far from crazy and I have news C will want to hear. Vital information about a double agent who has infiltrated the highest reaches of our organization."

"Bro," Sancho interjected, grabbing his arm. "Let's just go."

Flynn shrugged Sancho off. "No!" He addressed the security officer directly. "Use your radio and let them know we're here."

"Sorry, sir, but your friend is right. Anyone who isn't an employee needs an appointment and a pass to enter."

"But I was, until recently, a very important employee. And this gentleman still is."

"But I'm not stationed here," Sancho said. "We need to call ahead. Follow the protocol. These guys are just doing their jobs, man."

Flynn sighed and shook his head. "All right. Fine. *Fine.*" He turned on his heel and headed up the sidewalk, mumbling. "Bureaucratic nonsense..."

"It is what it is."

"Or perhaps the powers that be sent those police officers to send me packing for another reason."

"Yeah?"

"Yes. Perhaps they're afraid I'll blow my cover by showing my face here. That's not an unreasonable worry. And to be honest, to show up like this unannounced was rather reckless."

"That's what I'm saying."

"It's just that I'm very concerned about Caitlyn and sometimes I let my emotions get the better of me."

"It's okay."

"Of course, we still need to let them know M has gone rogue."

A heavy sigh from Sancho. "Of course."

"But first things first. Let's check out Caitlyn's last address here in London. If she's still living there, we can sort this out quickly. If she's not, perhaps we can pick up her trail."

CHAPTER FOURTEEN

Dozens of manor houses were built in Hoxton in the 1500s to provide ambassadors, courtiers, and minor nobility a bit of fresh air. By the end of the 17th century, many of those estates were sold off piecemeal. A few of the larger houses became schools, hospitals, or insane asylums. In the 1930s, the Hoxton Mob ruled the neighborhood with an iron fist. A few years later, the Blitz left the borough burned out and covered in rubble. The Kray Twins took control in the 1960s and, twenty years later, artists and other poverty-stricken bohemian types moved into the dilapidated district and squatted in the abandoned buildings, turning many of the lofts into trendy apartments. Today, it's a pricey area with many parks and green spaces, popular restaurants, clubs, and cafés.

Caitlyn's one-bedroom flat was on the second floor of a luxury apartment building called The Cube. Located on Wenlock Road, it sat sandwiched between Regent's Canal and Shepherdess Walk. Flynn called their leasing office and pretended to be interested in renting an apartment. Caitlyn's furnished second-floor flat apparently rented for £2,340 per month. Appropriate, Flynn thought, for a senior analyst and consultant with degrees from Stanford and the London School of Economics.

Flynn arranged for a tour of the flat with the resident apartment manager, Ms. Farley. Sancho tagged along. They rang her up on the apartment intercom by the front. She appeared almost instantly, opening the door with a smile.

"Mr. Flynn?"

"Ms. Farley?"

"Welcome to The Cube." She looked to be in her late thirties. A very attractive black woman with a public-school accent.

"This is my friend, Sancho. He's visiting from California."

"California. Brilliant. It's a pleasure to meet you."

"Good to meet you too," Sancho said.

They took an elevator to look at the loft Flynn requested and she showed them around the spacious, well-appointed flat. "As you can see, the views are quite spectacular. High ceilings. An open plan living room. The bathroom suite has recently been updated, along with the fully-fitted kitchen." She slid open the door to the balcony and let in the sounds of the city. "You can have your tea or coffee out here in the morning."

"Looks perfect," Flynn said. "My friend Caitlyn loves it here."

"You know one of the residents?"

"Yes, Caitlyn Valentine. I told her I'd pop in when I came by."

"Your friends with Caitlyn?"

"We used to work together, but I haven't seen her in weeks. In the off-chance she's working remotely today, would it be all right if I knocked on her door?"

"I don't see why not."

"Do you mind if I meet you back at your office?"

"Not at all."

Flynn and Sancho got off the elevator on the second floor and knocked on Caitlyn's door. As Flynn suspected, no one answered. He pulled out a lock picking tool and got to work on the knob. The pins quickly clicked into place. Sancho followed him inside, easing the door shut. Flynn methodically searched the flat. The closets were empty of clothes and shoes. There was no luggage. Nothing in the bathroom. Nothing in the kitchen. Not a scrap of paper or a post-it note anywhere. No indication that she had ever been there at all.

"Are you sure this is her apartment?" Sancho said.

"204."

"Looks like she moved out."

"It certainly does."

"And she's still paying rent on this?"

"Apparently so."

"Weird."

"I agree."

Flynn and Sancho stepped back into the hallway and closed the door.

"What are you two doing?"

Flynn turned to a round-faced man peering at him through his partly opened door. A security chain kept it secure. "Visiting a friend."

"Caitlyn?"

"That's right."

"But she's not home."

"No, she is not."

"Then how'd you get in?"

Flynn grinned. "I have a spare key."

"I see." The man narrowed his eyes suspiciously. "You her boyfriend?"

"We used to work together."

The man continued to stare. Flynn found his pale blue eyes disturbing. "Kind of a cold fish, isn't she?"

"Excuse me?"

"I tried to chat her up. Asked her out for coffee and she gave me the cold shoulder."

"Recently?"

"When she first moved in. I was trying to be friendly."

"That's very kind of you."

"A wasted effort. A girl like that."

"What kind of girl would that be?"

"One that goes for the money."

"What are you implying?"

"When she first moved in, she'd go out every night. I'd hear her door open around eight and I'd peep through the peephole, and she'd be dressed to the nines. Dressed to go clubbing. Hot as hell. Clearly on the pull. After a few weeks, a limo started showing up for her. It's no secret who it belonged to. I recognized the license plate. VIP 1."

"Who'd it belong to?"

"Oleg Ivanov. A Russian Oligarch. A real wanker."

"You sure?"

"It was in all the papers a few years back. The ponce paid out the arse for it. It's the same license plate the Pope used on the Popemobile when he visited Ireland."

"When was the last time you saw her?"

"Caitlyn? Not for couple weeks. One day, she just didn't come home. Haven't seen her since. She's probably shacked up in Red Square with that tosser."

"Red Square in Moscow?"

"Belgravia. All those Russian billionaires have houses there."

"Thank you for your help, Mr. —".

The round-faced man abruptly shut his door.

CHAPTER FIFTEEN

Sancho poked at his phone as he picked at his *Toad in the Hole*. Flynn tucked into a steak and kidney pie with relish. Since Sancho couldn't decipher any of the pub's menu items, Flynn ordered for him. They were having *Spotted Dick* for dessert and, luckily, it didn't appear to be dick related, but instead looked like some sort of tiny Bundt cake. Flynn referred to it as a pudding, but it didn't look very pudding-like to Sancho. Knowing his amigo's love for Negra Modelo beer, Flynn ordered Sancho a pint of stout and something called an Americano for himself. Sancho found the stout a little heavy for a late lunch, but maybe it would help fortify him for the night ahead.

According to the menu, the Wenlock Arms opened as a public house in 1835 and survived the Blitz totally intact. A horseshoe-shaped bar took up half the room. The other half consisted of tiny tables with benches and stools topped with worn, red leather upholstery. Flynn and Sancho sat at one such table as a few dedicated day drinkers stood belly up to the bar.

Sancho pointed at Flynn's drink. "What's in an Americano?"

"Campari, sweet vermouth, and Perrier. It originated in Milan and was popular with Americans in Italy during prohibition. Hence, the name. Traditionally, it's served with a slice of orange peel. But I prefer lemon." Flynn took a sip. "Any luck tracking down Ivanov's address?"

"I found pictures of it in the Mirror and the Daily Mail. 70 Eaton Square. He paid thirty-five million pounds for it in 2003."

"It must be one of those Georgian townhouses."

"Thirty-five million for a townhouse?"

"It's probably a big one."

Sancho continued to read. "No shit. It's eleven thousand square feet. It has a 40-foot indoor swimming pool, a gym, a steam room, a movie theater, and an indoor winter garden with a sliding glass roof." He looked up at Flynn. "What the hell's a winter garden?"

"They started back in the 18th century. European nobility and the very wealthy would construct large glass-enclosed conservatories to house tropical and subtropical plants."

"Some people just have too much money."

"Like Oleg Ivanov."

"Exactly."

"All right, well I propose we stake it out and wait for Ivanov to show his face. We'll brace him and see if he's seen Caitlyn."

"He probably has a security detail," Sancho said.

"Probably so, and I'm guessing most of them are ex-Spetsnaz."

"Ex what?"

"The special operations unit of the GRU. They are the Russian version of Navy Seals."

"Are you serious?"

"Ohana is ex-Shayetet 13. Israeli Special forces. We handled him and they're even better than Spetsnaz."

"Dude, let's talk about this."

"Isn't that what we're doing?"

"Look, I just don't want to get in over our heads."

"Which is why I did an intelligence assessment."

"You what?"

Flynn held up his phone. "I googled him. Apparently, Ivanov's married to a former model and Russian pop star." Flynn scrolled his phone and read aloud. "Her name is Anya, and it says here she posed for Russian Playboy back in 1999. A redhead. Quite attractive. She looks like Ann-Margret. Only taller."

"Who?"

"A movie star from the sixties."

"I was thinking Christina Hendricks."

"Who?"

"*Madmen.*"

"Hmm?"

"Doesn't matter."

.   .   .

The black hackney dropped them off right in front of 70 Eaton Square. No one stood guard outside. Flynn found that curious. The elegant five-story white Regency-style townhouse had white Corinthian columns that framed the three stairs leading to the grand front door. The doorknob sat in the center, and a large brass knocker with a lion's face sat below the more modern addition of a peephole.

Before Flynn could knock the knocker, the door opened partway and a very large man in a black suit filled the gap. A graying goatee was the only hair decorating his head. His deep-set eyes regarded Flynn with suspicion. "*Da?*"

"I'm here to see Oleg Ivanov."

"And who would you be?" He had a thick Russian accent.

"My name's Flynn. James Flynn." Flynn noticed a telltale bulge under the man's jacket, indicating some kind of weapon. Flynn also knew that concealed carry was illegal in the UK for civilians. In fact, not even bodyguards could own firearms. "Is Mr. Ivanov home?"

"Nyet."

"Do you know where he is?"

"Nyet."

"Do you know when he'll be back?"

"Nyet."

"You're not very helpful, are you?"

"Nyet."

The man closed the door in Flynn's face. An inner deadbolt clicked shut. "Well, at least we know one thing."

"What's that?" Sancho asked.

"We have the right address."

Flynn stood on the sidewalk and waited at the curb for traffic to slow. When a break appeared, he crossed the street and headed through a wrought iron gate into Eaton Square Garden. Flynn found a bench with a good vantage point of Ivanov's front door and sat by the perfectly manicured formal lawn, surrounded by Yew hedges and flower beds bright with spring blossoms. A bower of clematis vines climbed a pergola that shaded the bench.

Sancho took a seat next to him and yawned. "So that's your plan. Watch his house?"

"Do you have a better one?"

"How long do you want to sit here?"

"As long as we need to. He has to come home sometime."

"What if he's already home?"

"Then we'll wait for him to come out," Flynn said with a smile.

"You got an answer for everything, don't you?"

"Ask a question, get an answer."

"Okay. Here's one. Why's the money look so funny over here? It's all different colors and all different sizes. It looks like monopoly money."

"Why's American money all one color? All one size? UK currency is much easier to sort. A twenty-pound note is purple. A fiver is green. A ten-spot is orange."

"Who's that lady on the front?"

"Our queen. Elizabeth. Though she did recently pass. Now her son, Charles, is in charge."

"Charles in Charge?" Sancho laughed.

"Why do you find that amusing?"

"Do you know who Scott Baio is?"

"Who?"

The door to Ivanov's townhome opened, and a woman emerged. The guard with the massive bald head grabbed her by the arm and pulled her back inside. "Noooooo!" she screamed. *"I said no! You let me go!"* She spoke Russian-accented English with a UK elocution.

Flynn recognized her from her old centerfold in Russian Playboy. She wore an elegant black cocktail dress with a revealing slit up the side and a long black cape. Her curly red hair framed her face and cascaded over her shoulders. Twenty-five years older, but no less striking.

The bald man blocked her way forward as another large man came up behind her and gently guided her back inside. She shrugged him off and tried to push past the bald man, but he proved immovable.

"Get out of the way!"

"Your husband said—"

"I don't care what he said! *You are not my keeper!*"

The large man behind her tried to take her by the wrists and she elbowed him in the gut.

"Get your bloody hands off me!"

She grabbed the lapels of the man in front of her and kneed him in the balls. He crumpled and she shoved him backwards, down the three short stairs. As he fell, she vaulted over him and bolted into the street in her thigh-high, grey suede boots. Tires squealed as cars slammed on the brakes to avoid hitting her.

The two guards hurried after her. She pushed through the gate into the park and raced past Flynn and Sancho with the men close behind. Flynn put out his foot and the big bald one tripped and hit the sidewalk hard.

The man on the ground pointed at Anya as she desperately tried to climb over a wrought iron fence in her designer dress. The second man caught up and grabbed her by the arm. He wrestled her off the fence and dragged her back across the park.

She struggled to twist away, spitting at him and swearing in Russian.

The man Flynn tripped was now on his feet and glaring at him. "You did that on purpose!"

"Did what?"

"You *know* what!"

"I assure you, it was entirely unintentional." Flynn smiled.

"Bullshit! Get up!"

"Excuse me?"

"On your feet!"

Flynn rose as the second man arrived with Anya, roughly pulling her along.

"Get off me!" she screamed.

"Perhaps, you should listen to the lady." Flynn tilted his head by way of a greeting.

Anya offered Flynn a surprised smile. "Gallantry. You don't see much of that lately."

The bald guard poked Flynn hard in the chest. "This has nothing to do with you!"

Flynn addressed his next question to Anya. "Is he hurting you?"

"Yes."

He then confronted the man who held her arm. "Let her go."

"Or what?" The bald one grabbed Flynn by his tie and pulled him close. "We work for woman's husband. We are protection detail."

"Yes, but who's protecting her from you?"

The man head-butted Flynn. His knees buckled, the pain blinding as he fell back on the bench. "I see you again, I won't be so gentle." The Russian growled.

As the man turned to go, Flynn put his foot out again. The Russian tripped and toppled and smacked face first into the cement. Flynn stood up, his foot on the man's neck. The one who held Anya released her wrist to deal with Flynn. Anya could have fled, but she didn't. Instead, she took a step back and kicked the guard in the balls from behind with the silver tip of her grey suede boots. The thuggish guard grabbed his gonads and sank to his knees.

Anya grabbed Flynn by the hand. "Come on!"

She raced across the park, pulling Flynn along. Flynn glanced back. Sancho hurried after them. "*Yo, what the hell?*"

They passed through the garden gate, and Anya hailed a passing black cab. She pulled open the door and jumped inside. Flynn climbed in after her, followed by Sancho. As the cab moved away from the curb, Flynn glanced back at the two security men limping after them.

CHAPTER SIXTEEN

Horse-drawn carriages for hire, or hackneys, filled the streets of London since Tudor times. In the 1890s, many modernized those hackneys with electric engines nicknamed Hummingbirds because of the sound they made. In 1897, vehicles for hire started using internal combustion engines, as they were faster and more reliable. By 1910, gas-powered motor cabs outnumbered horse-drawn hackneys. Eventually, black hackneys became an iconic symbol of London, as ubiquitous as the red phone box, and the double-decker bus.

Anya pulled out a stylish black vape pen and took a puff, letting out a massive cloud of strawberry-nectarine scented vapor. She glanced back out the rear window. "Arseholes."

"No smoking," the hackney driver said. He was balding and looked to be in his late sixties. He had jowls, a tidy mustache, and an East End accent.

"It's a vape."

"Vapes are prohibited too."

"What if I give you a 50-pound tip?"

"Then I'll need you to crack your window a bit."

She opened the window a few inches, took a big drag, and blew the vapor cloud out into the wind.

The driver watched her in the rearview mirror. "Do you have any particular destination in mind?"

"Les Ambassadeurs Club."

"*Les A*? You got it."

Flynn caught Anya's eye. "What's at *Les A*?"

"My husband."

"And who would he be?"

"Another arsehole. But you already know that, don't you? I heard you at the front door, asking for him. Why? You obviously don't work for him."

"No."

"Are you law enforcement?"

"No."

"MI6?"

Flynn smiled. "Even if I was, I couldn't really say."

"So, you are. Okay. You're not very good at this, are you?"

Sancho chuckled at that, and Flynn shot him an irritated glance before turning back to Anya. "Why were they holding you prisoner in your own house?"

"Because, apparently, I am an embarrassment."

"To whom?"

"Oleg, of course. I made the mistake of living past my expiration date. He likes his women young, and I am on the far side of forty."

"You're still an exceptionally beautiful woman."

"Kind of you to say, but you should have seen me twenty years ago."

"You're hardly an embarrassment."

"Yet, he loves to humiliate me by stepping out with his young paramours. So, I return the favor by confronting him wherever I find him. I make a scene. I cause a ruckus. I make him as miserable as he makes me."

"So, he keeps you locked up?"

"He tries."

"Why not divorce him?"

"Because I signed a stupid prenup on our wedding day. I was eighteen. What did I know? If I leave him, he leaves me nothing."

"But if you keep embarrassing him, won't he divorce *you*?"

"Yes, and that's exactly what I'm hoping for. Because if he leaves me, it's a different story. I'll get a settlement. Not a huge one, but much better than nothing."

"But he *won't* divorce you?"

"No matter what I do." She blew vapor out the window.

"Why not?"

"Because he has a tiny penis." She held up her thumb and forefinger and held them an inch apart to illustrate. "Like an itty-bitty mushroom. A wee nubbin."

"You lost me."

"I had an affair last year. My first one ever. With my yoga instructor." She smirked. "A cliché, I know. Please don't judge me."

"The heart wants what the heart wants."

"So do the lady parts. But not until that moment did I realize how tiny Oleg's penis actually was. Well, he found out about my indiscretion and that proved to be a great insult to his masculinity. You see, he can fool around all he wants, but not me. I have one affair and his fragile ego is mortally wounded. He can't stand the idea of me with another man. He'd rather lock me away."

"I see."

She blew another blast of strawberry-nectarine vapor out the window. "What about you? What's your story?"

"I'm looking for someone who was last seen in your husband's limo."

"Who?"

"Can I show you a picture?"

"Yes, but only if you agree to do something for *me*."

"What would you like me to do?"

Her aquamarine eyes dazzled as she offered Flynn a seductive smile. "Be my escort this evening. Help me humiliate my husband."

"You want to use me?"

"I do."

"Can I use you in return?"

"I certainly hope so." She offered her hand. "I'm Anya."

Flynn shook. She had a very firm grip. "James. And this is Sancho. He'll be joining us, by the way."

"Two boy toys. Even better."

Sancho offered her a little wave.

She leaned in close to Flynn. "So, who exactly is this person you're looking for?"

Flynn found Caitlyn's picture on his iPhone and showed it to her. Anya nodded with recognition and narrowed her eyes with consternation. "Caitlyn Valentine."

"You know her?"

"She's my husband's latest *inamorata*."

Flynn's eyes widened with surprise. "*Inamorata*?"

"Yes, though he claims she's only his bodyguard." A grim chuckle. "As if I'm that stupid."

Flynn looked nonplussed. Anya noticed his dismay. "Oh, this isn't business to you, is it? This is personal. Who is she to you?"

"Just a colleague."

"By the look on your face, I would say she's more than that."

"At one time, but no longer. Now we are simply…" Flynn searched for the right word.

"Fuck buddies?"

"Friends."

"With benefits?"

"Sadly, no."

She patted Flynn on the knee. "If you two are going to accompany me to *Les A*, you'll need to change into something a little more formal. Should we make a stop at your hotel?"

"Actually, we both have new suits waiting for us at Gieves and Hawkes."

Anya rapped on the Plexiglas partition. "Driver, we have a new destination. 1 Savile Row."

CHAPTER SEVENTEEN

Sancho felt himself falling down the Flynn rabbit hole. Flynn would get pulled into some weird conspiracy or insane plot, and Sancho would find himself sucked into the vortex. He recognized the signs. Flynn was a fool for a damsel in distress, and Anya ticked off all the boxes. Beautiful. Dangerous. Sexy. Psycho. These *mamis* were always involved with a world-class sociopath, and those *pendejos* always came after Flynn. Sancho too if he was standing next to him. Last time, they even threatened his family.

Coming to London was a huge mistake. His emergency passport wouldn't be ready for another day, so Sancho just had to stay alive for a little while longer. They already had one stone-cold killer after them. Now they were about to make enemies of another. A Russian Oligarch worth billions.

Could Caitlyn really be banging that billionaire? It seemed out of character for her, but you never know. She *was* locked up in a loony-bin. That can mess up anyone. Flynn still held a torch for her, so who knows how he might react to that.

Sancho stood in front of the three-sided mirror and admired himself in the glass. He had to admit it. That Gieves and Hawkes suit looked damn good on him. No wonder Flynn swore by designer suits. They even made short, dumpy guys like him look slimmer and more elegant.

Flynn stood at a three-way mirror a few feet away and admired his reflection, turning this way and that to see how the suit fit.

Anya sat on a leather settee a few feet away and admired them admiring themselves. "You both look beautiful, but I'm wasting away here. I didn't have lunch today and I am starving."

Flynn caught her eye in the mirror. "Where would you like to go?"

.   .   .

Six Hamilton Place served Chinese and Lebanese food. Sancho found the menu confusing. Even in his new suit, he felt underdressed. The art deco décor was dramatic and elegant. They had fancy Asian Fusion places in L.A., but Sancho never went to them. He didn't make enough to spend two hundred dollars on dinner.

Flynn ordered the roasted black cod with asparagus. Anya went for the steamed Chilean Sea bass with black bean sauce. Sancho settled on the chicken kebabs, though on the menu they were called Shish Taouk. After conferring with Anya, Flynn called over the sommelier. "Sir, we'd like a bottle of the Dom Pérignon 2013."

The sommelier nodded. "Very good, sir."

Flynn glanced at Anya. "I hope you like champagne."

"I adore champagne."

Sancho raised his hand. "Can I get a Heineken?"

"Of course, sir."

Flynn had a vast knowledge of wines and fine dining, but Sancho knew his food and wine knowledge was mostly theoretical. Flynn read books on travel and studied magazines like *Bon Appetit,* but unless he was out in the world on one of his adventures, he mainly ate what they served in the cafeteria at City of Roses. In fact, most of what Flynn knew was academic. His knowledge of weapons and firearms, martial arts, international criminal syndicates, fast cars, and high-tech gadgets was gleaned from books and magazines and whatever he could find online.

The sommelier returned with the champagne. Flynn tasted it and approved, and the sommelier poured flutes for Flynn and Anya. Sancho sipped his Heineken. Anya raised her glass. "To a night we will never forget."

Flynn clinked her flute and took a sip. "Is *Les A* a regular haunt of your husband's?"

"He spends nearly every other evening there."

"He's a gambler?"

"In everything."

"What's his game?"

She sipped a little champagne. "Baccarat."

"Why am I not surprised?"

"Do you play, Mr. Flynn?"

"I do."

"Are you any good?"

"Well, since baccarat requires no real skill, I'd say I'm very good."

Anya smiled at his bravado. "It might not require skill, but it does require a certain amount of nerve."

"No one's ever accused me of lacking in that department."

"I believe that. And if you're willing to play against my husband, I'd be more than happy to stake you."

"I can pay my own way."

"Cocky too. I just want you to beat him. He loves to be the big man and show off. To his friends. To his bimbos. This new one, Caitlyn, is especially impressive, but then you probably already know that, don't you? Ex-CIA. Thrown into a mental institution where she meets…" Recognition slowly dawned as a huge smile lit up Anya's face. "Oh, my God! You! She met you! You're him. James Flynn!" Anya clapped her hands once and laughed. "Oh, my God! This is *delicious*. To have you be my new boy toy! To have you beat Oleg at Baccarat? That is perfect!"

Flynn looked a little uncomfortable as he sipped his champagne. "I'm just a humble civil servant."

She laughed again. "Hardly humble." Anya looked at Sancho. "Are you his keeper?"

"Excuse me?"

"Are you with the hospital? Are you a psychiatrist?"

Sancho sighed. "Psychiatric nurse."

"But that's only his cover," Flynn explained. "As is my status as a psychiatric patient. But I've already said more than I should. We are here incognito, and the reasons why need to remain confidential."

Anya could barely contain her delighted smile. "I won't say anything to anyone. You have my word." She pretended to zip her lips.

"Thank you."

"You are quite the complicated hero, aren't you?"

"I don't know what you mean. I just…do what I do."

"Do you do dessert?"

"I do."

Anya raised a finger to get the attention of their waiter. "They make a delicious dark chocolate hazelnut cake. It's obscene how good it is."

CHAPTER EIGHTEEN

In 1955, it cost £100 to join Les Ambassadeurs Club. The equivalent of £2000 today. Now a membership goes for £25,000, making it a very exclusive club indeed. "Les A," as it's referred to by its members, has been welcoming the rich and famous and royal since the early 19th Century. The Georgian-style structure was designed and built by Thomas Leverton in 1810 and remodeled in the Venetian Renaissance style for Leopold de Rothschild in the 1830s. The interior features a dramatic circular staircase in oak with an intricately carved balustrade. The oval ceiling fresco in the Marble Room was painted by Edmond Paris. Polish-born soldier and businessman John Mills opened "Les A" as a private casino in the 1950s. Notable celebrity guests have included Humphrey Bogart, Elizabeth Taylor, Frank Sinatra, Brad Pitt, and Angelina Jolie. Sir Christopher Lee famously kept a bottle of gin with his name on it at the club.

Flynn escorted Anya up the stairs, past the white stone portico, and under the red awning. Two burly well-dressed doormen opened the double oak doors. Unlike casinos in Vegas, Flynn wasn't assaulted by a cacophony of noise. No ringing, dinging, clattering slot machines with loud electronic music. The excited murmur of a crowd greeted him, but compared to Vegas the hubbub was more restrained and elegant. Perhaps that was due to the soft carpeting and heavy, blood-red drapes that kept out the lights of the city.

The women wore evening gowns and elegant cocktail dresses, and the men dressed in dark suits and tuxedos. No garish shorts, loud Hawaiian shirts, blue jeans, flip-flops, tube tops or ridiculous t-shirts were permitted at *Les A*. The scent of expensive perfume mingled with excitement, fear, greed, and sex. But no cigarette smoke. Even so, it all brought back memories of another time. Of danger and exhilaration, elegance and excess, the frisson of adrenaline, and the sweet anticipation of victory. Flynn felt electric and alive.

He was sure he'd been in Les Ambassadeurs Club before, though he couldn't say when. He remembered the walls paneled in dark wood, the high ceilings, and the crystal chandeliers. Cigarette smoke hung heavy in the air back then. He remembered playing Chemin de fer at a green baize table, sitting across from a voluptuous woman in a red dress, her dark hair piled high in a bouffant. She had eyes the same color as Caitlyn's. Emerald green with a splash of gray. Her name was Sarah or Sasha or something else that started with an S. Her lips were the same color as her dress. She raised the limit, and they played head-to-head until he had to excuse himself. The woman followed him. Flirted with him. He had to beg off to answer a call from headquarters. Later that night he found her in his flat, playing with his putter, dressed in nothing but gold high heels and one of his pajama tops.

Anya nodded to various people as they moved through the room. She caught the attention of every man present as she sashayed by. And Flynn noticed most of the women noticing him. Sancho hurried to stay at Flynn's side, eyes wide, mouth open, stunned by all the opulence.

Flynn patted him on the shoulder. "You cut a fine figure in your new suit."

"It's a little tight."

"That's the style now. A slimmer silhouette. Very European."

"You got the build for it, bro. I don't."

"We just have to get you to the gym more often."

Sancho sighed. "Great."

"Keep an eye out for Caitlyn, and don't let your guard down. As benign as this place seems, there are sharks everywhere."

Flynn followed Anya as she went to the cashier to buy some plaques. He stayed with her as she made a beeline for the baccarat tables. Elegant art deco-style hanging lamps in gold leaf and olive-green glass illuminated each gaming table. Anya stopped without warning. Flynn bumped into her. She kept her hand by her side as she pointed surreptitiously towards a table just ahead. "There." Most everyone playing was Asian or Arabic. All except for one.

"That's your husband?"

"In the Brioni."

Oleg was nothing like Flynn imagined. He expected to find a short, fat, balding Russian with a neck beard and several unattractive moles. Instead, Oleg looked fit, handsome, and tall with a thick head of silver hair. He wasn't a pretty boy. He had a toughness about him. A swagger.

Caitlyn stood just behind him, hovering over his shoulder. Her raven black hair fell longer than the last time he'd seen her. It brushed the tops of her bare shoulders, framing her flawless oval face. Her black sleeveless cocktail dress showed off her athletic figure. The gown had a slit up the side that gave her freedom of movement and displayed her well-toned legs. Her shoulders and arms had even more definition than before. She looked just as beautiful and formidable as he remembered.

She had nowhere to hide a gun, but then bodyguards couldn't carry concealed weapons in the UK. She had to rely on her fists and feet, but they were just as lethal as any firearm. She kept a sharp eye out for any imminent threats. Her gaze scanned the room and then stopped abruptly when they landed on Flynn. He caught the surprise and irritation in her eyes. Flynn offered her a subtle smile. She didn't smile back. He hadn't seen her in almost a year. He missed her terribly, but didn't realize exactly how terribly until they locked gazes. The sensation was physical. It hit his gut. His heart. His soul.

Anya whispered in his ear. "Your lady friend is looking very attractive this evening."

"Colleague."

"Of course." She handed Flynn a handful of square plaques of various denominations in a variety of colors. "100,000 pounds. My monthly allowance. Try not to lose it all at once." She took Flynn by the hand. "Come." She led him across the floor towards her husband's table.

Oleg did not look happy to see Anya. He offered her a tight smile. His voice cold, flat. Like his wife, his Russian-accented English sounded a bit British. "Darling. What are you doing here?"

"The same thing you're doing, *darling*. I'm here to have a little fun."

He looked at Flynn. "I see you brought a friend."

"As did you."

"Miss Valentine's my bodyguard."

Anya rested her hand on Flynn's shoulder. "And Mr. Flynn is mine."

"Flynn?" Oleg's eyes widened. "James Flynn?"

"At your service," Flynn replied. Caitlyn glared at him, but Flynn kept his gaze locked on Oleg. "Do you mind if I join your game?"

Oleg sighed. "By all means." He glanced back at Caitlyn. She looked mortified. Both her cheeks turned hot pink.

Flynn had no idea why Caitlyn would find his presence embarrassing, but for now he needed to clear his mind of all emotion and focus his attention on his opponent. Not that baccarat required a lot of deep concentration. It was stupidly simple. Especially when compared to the complexities of poker. Unlike poker, there was no skill required. No bluffing. No psychological warfare. It was purely a game of chance. The only real tactics had to do with betting. He had read *Scarne on Cards* and knew all the various strategies.

Baccarat was played with eight decks of cards shuffled by the croupier, cut by the player, and inserted into a shoe. In days past and in other casinos, the shoe was passed from player to player, so everyone had an opportunity to be the banker. But at *Les A* that wasn't the case. The casino acted as the house and dealt the cards. The player's only role was to bet on one of the two hands dealt by the croupier. One hand for the players. One hand for the bank. The players placed their wagers before the hands were dealt. They could bet on the banker, the player, or on both hands being equal. *Egalité.* Tens and court cards were worth nothing. An ace was worth one. All other cards were worth their numerical value. The winning hand was the one nearest to nine. The first and third cards went to the player. The second and fourth went to the banker. Strict rules dictated whether another card would be drawn. The formula was complicated and rather arcane. A player betting for or against the bank was paid even money. Betting on a tie paid nine to one, but the odds of that happening were extremely slim.

Flynn preferred poker as it required more skill, but he did have a betting system for baccarat based on a couple of classic strategies. Because of the odds, Flynn never bet *Egalité.* Instead, he usually wagered with the banker, as the banker's odds were infinitesimally better. Even with the tiny percentage paid to the house.

The croupier, a forty-something Frenchman with longish black hair slicked back with product and tied into a tiny ponytail, shuffled the eight decks expertly and offered Ivanov a red plastic square to cut the deck. He did and the croupier inserted the deck into the shoe. Flynn noticed that the dealers and croupiers spoke very little at *Les A.*

Ivanov laid a five-thousand-pound plaque on the banker square. Flynn decided to play against him and bet the player hand, just to get under his skin. He too wagered five thousand pounds. The banker drew a natural nine and the player hand? An ace and a five. The croupier paid Ivanov his even money with Flynn's five-thousand-pound plaque.

Ivanov flashed a satisfied smile. Not at him, but Anya, standing behind him.

Flynn doubled his bet to ten thousand pounds and Sancho whispered in his ear. "What are you doing?"

"I'm using the classic Martingale Strategy of doubling one's bet after a loss."

"Every time?"

"Until you win and then you go back to square one."

Another hand was dealt and Flynn lost again and, once again, he doubled his bet to twenty thousand pounds.

"Whose strategy is this?" Sancho grumbled.

"Martingale. It's been around for centuries. Designed by Paul Pierre Levy, a French mathematician."

"So why isn't it called the Levy Strategy?"

"Because it was popularized by London casino owner, John Henry Martingale. In 1891, a man by the name of Charles Wells used it to break the bank at Monte Carlo twelve times."

The dealer dealt another two hands. A king and an eight for Flynn and a ten and a queen for the bank, where Ivanov had his bet. As the bank had zero, the croupier drew a third card.

A nine.

Anya gasped and Sancho said, "Jesus," as the croupier scooped away Flynn's plaques and paid Ivanov his winnings.

Flynn doubled down with a forty-thousand-dollar bet.

Sancho tugged on his arm. "*Dude.*"

"I'm sorry, sir," the croupier said. "But the maximum bet on Baccarat is twenty thousand pounds."

"Is there a way to raise the limit?"

The croupier motioned over a pit boss, and they quietly conferred before turning to Ivanov. "Sir, would it be all right with you if we raised the limit to 40,000 pounds?"

"No, it would not," Ivanov said. "I would like it raised to two hundred thousand pounds, and as someone who has spent millions of pounds here, I believe I deserve that courtesy." He looked at Flynn. "Would that work for you, Mr. Flynn? Just so we don't have to keep asking permission."

"A two hundred-thousand-pound limit?" Flynn kept a steady gaze.

"Or is that a little too rich for your blood?"

Anya's hand rested on his shoulder. "Not at all," Flynn said.

The dealer dealt Flynn a ten and a four. And dealt himself a four and a two. This time, Flynn received the third card. An ace. Oleg Ivanov smiled smugly. Flynn didn't turn to look at Anya's face, but her hand did tightly grip his shoulder.

"Shit," Sancho blurted as the dealer scooped away Flynn's plaques. "You might want to rethink your system."

"It was originally designed for roulette, but it works just as well with baccarat."

"You call this working well? You're down seventy-five thousand, ese."

"Sorry, James, I can't really afford to give you anymore," whispered Anya. "You're going to have to make do with what you have left."

"Not to worry. I anticipated this." Flynn reached into his jacket pocket and pulled out a slim wallet. He selected a black credit card and addressed the pit boss. "This is an American Express Centurion card. I'd like to purchase ten plaques worth ten thousand pounds each."

"Of course, sir. But I'll need to see some ID."

Flynn handed him his passport along with the card and the pit boss headed for the cashier.

Sancho's eyes about popped from his head. "Are you serious?"

"In for a penny, in for a pound," Flynn said.

"*One hundred thousand mother-loving pounds!*"

"The secret to being successful with the Martingale Stratagem is to have enough cash to cover your losses."

The pit boss returned and handed Flynn ten gold-plated £10,000 plaques. Flynn counted out eight of them and put them on the player square. The last twenty he put with his last twenty-five thousand pounds.

Anya's hot breath heated up his neck as she whispered, "I like a man with nerves of steel." She looked across the table at her husband as he matched Flynn's eighty-thousand-pound bet with one of his own on the banker square.

The dealer dealt the player a five and a three. He dealt the banker a queen and an eight.

The dealer rapped the table. "*Egalité.*"

A tie.

Anya sighed with relief. Sancho continued to hold his breath.

Both Ivanov and Flynn let their bets stand.

The dealer dealt the player an ace and a jack. He dealt the banker an eight and a one.

"*Neuf naturel,*" the dealer said and scooped away Flynn's eight gold-plated plaques and gave them to Ivanov.

Sancho whispered, "*Hijo de puta.*"

"Motherfucker," Anya growled.

Caitlyn looked stricken. Flynn caught the pity in her eyes.

Oleg grinned with delight. "I think I've done enough damage to you tonight, Mr. Flynn. Perhaps you should step away. I really don't want to see you lose any more of your money. I'm starting to feel a little sorry for you."

Flynn tamped down his anger and pushed the last of his plaques into the player box.

Sancho grabbed his wrist, "Bro, that's forty-five thousand—"

But Flynn jerked away from his friend and finished placing his bet.

An interested crowd now surrounded the baccarat table. The same kind of rubberneckers who slow down to check out a terrible car accident.

Oleg once again matched Flynn's bet on the banker's square. "You've made me a lot of money this evening, Mr. Flynn. Perhaps you should start betting on me?"

Flynn glanced at the croupier. "Deal."

He dealt the banker a queen and a two and the player a seven and an ace. Flynn's palms began to sweat. An unfamiliar sensation for him. He watched as the dealer dealt the bank its third and final card. A seven.

"Neuf," mumbled the croupier.

The crowd gasped in unison as the croupier took the last of Flynn's plaques.

Flynn tried to catch Caitlyn's eye, but she wouldn't look at him. Oleg looked a little embarrassed.

Anya grabbed Flynn by the arm, her voice sharp. "Let's go."

An elderly Asian lady, sitting on Flynn's right, slid one of her two-hundred-pound plaques over to him. She spoke English with a Chinese accent. "Buy you and your friends drinks and a nice dinner. Get a good night's sleep. Life will look better in the morning."

"I already had dinner," Flynn said as he put the two-hundred-pound plaque on the player square.

Oleg laughed and put down a bet of his own for the same amount. "You know what the definition of insanity is, don't you? Doing the same thing over and over again and expecting a different result."

The dealer dealt the banker a queen and an eight and the player a king and a nine. "Neuf Natural," the dealer said to Flynn with a smile.

"Better quit while you're ahead, bro," Sancho said.

Flynn let it all ride.

And he won the next hand.

And the next one.

Sixteen hundred pounds now sat on the player square in front of Flynn.

"Yo, take it and run." Sancho grabbed him by the arm.

"I thought I made it clear. I'm following a strategy."

"Yeah, you told me. The Martingale!"

"But I've combined it with the Paroli system to create one of my own."

"A system where you always double down? Win *or* lose?"

Flynn won.

Again.

Now thirty-two hundred pounds sat on the player square. "I've tried them all, Sancho. The Labouchere System. The Fibonacci. The D'Alembert. But I found my own to be the most effective." The dealer dealt and Flynn won. He let the sixty-four hundred pounds ride and Oleg matched Flynn's bet with his own. "I call it the Flynn system. Odds are, eventually you're going to win. If you last long enough. If you keep your nerve. If you don't give in to negativity, eventually you will find victory."

"Bullshit." Sancho tried to pry him off his stool, but Flynn held tight.

"How many times have I told you how important positive thinking is?"

"There's a fine line between positivity and stone-cold crazy. Denial is not just a river in Egypt, amigo."

Flynn won five hands in a row and turned those sixty-four hundred pounds into two hundred and four thousand pounds.

It happened so fast, Anya couldn't catch her breath. She squealed with delight every time Flynn won. And each time Oleg's face turned a little more purple. Flynn knew Oleg wouldn't back down. He'd faced many men like him before. Narcissistic sociopaths who never wanted to admit defeat.

Sancho took Flynn by the arm and tried to ease away from the table. "Okay, man, you proved your point. You made your money back. Anya's too. Time to go before your luck changes."

"There's no such thing as luck." Flynn put two hundred thousand pounds on the player's square.

An angry Oleg matched his bet, but on the banker's square.

Flynn won. Four hundred thousand pounds worth of plaques teetered in a pile in front of him.

"Again," Oleg insisted and wagered the two hundred thousand pound maximum.

Sancho nearly peed his pants as Flynn matched his bet.

And won.

"*Again!*" Oleg slammed down the last of his plaques, betting them all. Seventy thousand pounds.

And lost.

"*Blyat!*" He scraped back his chair and pushed away from the table. "*Enough!*"

"I agree," Flynn said. "You do know what the definition of insanity is, don't you? Doing the same thing over and over again and expecting a different result."

Anya laughed and grinned at Flynn as he handed her two hundred and fifty thousand pounds in plaques. "Your initial stake and then some," he said.

"You are a very good investment, Mr. Flynn."

"It's been a pleasure."

"One we must revisit."

He handed a ten-thousand-pound plaque to the dealer, a fifty-thousand-pound plaque to the Chinese lady who staked him and a fifty-thousand-pound plaque to Sancho, keeping the rest for himself.

Oleg stepped around the table and put his finger in Anya's face. "We need to talk!"

"Not with your bimbo watching."

Oleg clenched his jaw and turned to Caitlyn. "We'll be in the smoking garden. I'll text you when I'm ready to go."

Caitlyn nodded.

Oleg grabbed Anya by the arm. She shrugged him off and headed away with an angry Oleg hurrying to catch up.

Flynn turned to find Caitlyn glaring at him.

"We need to talk too," Flynn said.

"No shit."

CHAPTER NINETEEN

Stepping into *The Library* at *Les A* was like stepping back in time. The large ornate room served as the casino's most elegant cocktail lounge. Flynn assumed it looked much like it did when it first opened its doors to the cream of London society during the reign of Queen Victoria.

World-renowned Florentine artist and designer Chevalier Rinaldo Barbetti created the intricately carved wood paneling that adorned the walls and ceiling. Persian carpets covered much of the original marble floor. The Victorian-style sofas and chairs were huge and inviting. Flynn sat on a sofa and patted the plush brown leather upholstery, expecting Caitlyn to sit beside him. She instead sat in a matching chair directly across from him.

A tuxedo-suited waiter instantly appeared. "Can I interest either of you in a cocktail or a glass of champagne?"

"Do you know how to make a Vesper Martini?" asked Flynn.

"Educate me."

"Three measures of Gordon's Gin, one of Belvedere vodka, a half measure of Lillet Blanc, and few dashes of Angostura bitters. Shake it well until ice cold, then add a large thin slice of lemon peel."

"I will convey your instructions to the bartender."

"Thank you."

Flynn glanced at Caitlyn, who sighed with exasperation as she looked up at the waiter. "A double bourbon on the rocks."

"Any particular brand?"

"Whatever. I don't really care."

The waiter nodded and headed for the bar.

Flynn caught Caitlyn's eye and offered her a smile. "You seem a bit on edge."

"What are you doing here?"

"I missed you too."

"I thought I was pretty clear when I left L.A. Whatever we had is over. We can *never* be together."

"Yes, you made that very clear."

"Then what the hell are you doing here?"

"I was worried."

"About what?"

"You."

She narrowed her eyes, mystified. "Why?"

"I couldn't get a hold of you."

"I'm sorry, but I've been busy."

"You couldn't have called to tell me you were okay?"

She spoke through a clenched jaw. Something she always did when she didn't want to lose her composure. "Why wouldn't I be okay?"

"You don't seem okay."

"I'm great. I'm perfect. I couldn't be better.

"Why'd you leave the agency?"

"Who told you that?"

"The CIA."

"You called the CIA?"

"Miranda Jacks called them on my behalf."

"Jesus." She shook her head.

"What?"

"What if I did leave the CIA? What's it any of your business?"

Flynn nodded. "So, it's true?"

"After what they did to me? I tried to put it behind me, but I just couldn't."

"Even though the people responsible are in prison?"

"A lot of people who weren't *directly* responsible either turned the other way or went along with them. Enabled them. Allowed it to happen! If just one person would have stood up and stood by me…I…I do *not* want to have this discussion right now."

"Are you sleeping with him?

"Who?"

"Ivanov."

"*What?*"

"His wife thinks you are."

"Because she's a jealous, needy, insecure bitch!"

"That's a little harsh."

"What are you even doing with her?"

The waiter returned with their drinks, and Flynn took a sip. He raised his glass to the server. "My compliments to the mixologist."

"Thank you, sir."

Flynn set down his cocktail, reached into his jacket, and fumbled through his large clattery stack of plaques. Some fell to the floor. Some landed on the table. He sorted through the pile, finally found two one-hundred-pound plaques, and offered them over. "One for you and one for the bartender."

"Not necessary, sir, but much appreciated."

As the waiter left, Flynn turned his attention back to Caitlyn. She glowered at him with unmitigated animosity. "You are such an asshole."

"So, you're not sleeping with him?"

"I can't believe you have the balls to ask me that."

"He's not an unattractive man."

"He wanted a bodyguard who didn't look like a bodyguard."

"So, you left the CIA to babysit a Russian billionaire?"

"The U.S. government used me and abused me and didn't pay me shit. At least now I'm making some money."

"So, it's just about the money?"

"It's about me taking control of my life. Making enough to do what I want, where I want, and with who I want. I'm tired of people telling me what to do."

Flynn raised an eyebrow. "Doesn't Ivanov tell you what to do?"

"He pays for the privilege, and I can quit anytime I want. But I don't want to. I'll tell you this, he treats me with a lot more respect than my bosses at the CIA ever did."

"You still haven't answered my question."

"What question is that?"

"Are you sleeping with him?"

"*Stop asking me that.*"

"Why won't you give me a straight answer?"

"Why won't you leave me the *hell* alone?"

"Because I care about you."

Caitlyn drained the rest of her drink and stood. "You need to go. You need to leave London and never contact me again. We are done. Over. I don't *ever* want to see you again." She walked away. Flynn rose to follow, but Caitlyn stopped, turned and pointed her finger at him. "What did I just fucking say? Stop following me. Stop calling me! Stop texting me! Stop stalking me!"

Flynn sat back down. He sipped his Vesper. He didn't understand what was happening. Why wouldn't Caitlyn give him a straight answer about Ivanov? Was she embarrassed to tell him the truth? She had every reason in the world to hate the CIA, but would she really be with a man like Ivanov? Caitlyn seemed savvier than that. Perhaps what happened to her damaged her more deeply than he realized. He wanted to honor her wishes and leave her be, but he couldn't let her ruin her life.

"Mr. Flynn?" The waiter stood with an older man and two younger, larger men.

Flynn stood and the older man offered his hand. Flynn shook. "Mr. Flynn, I'm John Wentworth and I'm one of the managers here at *Les A*. I'm afraid I'm going to have to ask you to leave.

"Excuse me?"

"You entered as a guest with Mrs. Ivanov and she has left for the evening along with her husband. This is a private club, and as you're not a member, I can't really have you on the premises."

"I see."

"My men will escort you to the cashier who will write you a check in exchange for your plaques, but then I'm afraid you'll have to go."

"What if I'd like to join?" Flynn pulled out a hundred-pound plaque.

"There's a whole application protocol, and the process is confidential. Our membership is quite exclusive, and it could take some time for you to be deemed suitable. So, for now…"

"You need me to leave."

"Please."

■　■　■

Flynn found Sancho sitting on the curb outside. Apparently, they had removed him from the premises as well. Flynn tapped him on the shoulder and offered his hand to help him to his feet.

Sancho dusted off the seat of his new suit. "How'd it go with Caitlyn?"

"Not well."

"Is she in danger?"

"Apparently not."

"I guess that's that then."

"I guess so."

"Okay then, amigo. Time to go home."

CHAPTER TWENTY

In 1815, the year Napoleon lost at Waterloo and the British empire reached the apex of its power, a pair of Georgian-style houses near Grosvenor Square became the Prince of Saxe-Coburg Hotel. During WWI, the owners changed the Coburg name to something that sounded less German. They used the title of Queen Victoria's favorite son, Prince Arthur, the first Duke of Connaught. Right before WWII, a Swiss entrepreneur, Rudolph Richard, became the hotel's general manager and ran it like an English private estate. He insisted on the highest standards of comfort and service, and since then many famous luminaries have enjoyed the hospitality of The Connaught. Everyone from King Edward VII to Charles de Gaulle to Princess Grace and Gwyneth Paltrow has slept between their 800 thread-count Sateen weave Egyptian cotton bed sheets.

Sancho watched London speed by from the back seat of their black cab. He looked at Flynn sitting next to him. His sad face pressed up against the window glass as the city zipped past. Sancho had no idea what to say as Flynn's imaginary persona slipped away. It sometimes happened when harsh reality collided with his delusional ideation. James would lose his cocky confidence and joie de vivre and become Jimmy, the shy, fat, lonely little boy who lost his family. The doctors believed if they could break James down to Jimmy, they could remake him into someone who didn't live in a delusional fantasy. From there, they could build him up, boost his confidence, and make him into the man he was supposed to be. Someone living in our shared reality. A valuable member of society.

Sancho wasn't so sure. He patted Flynn on the knee. "You okay, bro?"

Flynn nodded, but kept his face turned to the window. His eyes shiny with tears, reflected in the glass.

"How many times have you told me that a man like you doesn't have the luxury to fall in love? A relationship like that would be a vulnerability. One your enemies could use against you. You said it happened to you before and you wouldn't ever let it happen again."

Flynn rubbed his tears away and nodded. "I did, didn't I?"

"We need to get back to L.A. and you need to get back to doing what you do."

"Maybe you're right."

"You know I'm right. Caitlyn has her own issues, but she's not in any real danger. She's just trying to find her way."

"As misguided as that path might be."

"You did your due diligence, dude. Give her some room. Some shit you just gotta figure out on your own."

Flynn nodded and patted Sancho on the knee. "Thank you, Sancho."

"No worries, ese. The trip wasn't a total loss. You won enough to pay for our flight here and our hotel. Not to mention my kid's college education. That's not nothing."

. . .

Back at the Connaught, Flynn and Sancho rode the elevator in silence. The doors opened and Sancho exited on four. "I'll meet you in the lobby at seven, bro. Are you gonna need a wake-up call?"

"I'll be fine."

"Sleep well, amigo. See you in the AM."

The doors closed and Flynn rode the elevator to the top floor. He leaned against the side of the elevator and yawned, exhausted from the long day and night. The doors opened and Flynn headed down the plush carpeted corridor to his premiere suite.

The Eagle's Lodge.

A different top designer decorated each premiere suite. Guy Oliver wanted the Eagle's Lodge to look like the luxurious cabin of a 1930s yacht. The one-bedroom suite fanned out like the prow of a ship. Every piece of furniture was bespoke, and every detail conjured up the casual elegance of the previous century. Oil paintings of sailing ships filled the walls, and the wraparound terrace offered stunning views of Mayfair's rooftops.

Flynn immediately noticed that the telltale hair he licked and left on the door was missing. He pulled out his sonic whistle and used his key card to carefully let himself in. He found a table lamp turned on in the foyer. When he left, it was off. *Did the maid leave it on for me? Is she the one who caused the hair to fall?* He slipped off his shoes to move silently, and eased open the door to the living room. Another light glowed. He stopped. He listened. Flynn flicked off the light in the living room and detected a sliver of light under the door that led to the bedroom. Flynn put the whistle in his mouth, picked up a vase to use as a weapon, carefully turned the knob and threw open the door to find…nothing. The room was empty.

"James?"

Startled, Flynn spit out the whistle and dropped the vase directly on his foot. "Bloody hell!" He hopped around and turned to see an amused Anya watching him from the bathroom doorway.

She had wrapped her curly red hair in a towel and wore one of the hotel's terry cloth robes…and apparently nothing else. "I hope you don't mind, but I borrowed your shower."

"Who let you in?"

"The front desk. They know me here and I told them I wanted to surprise you."

"Mission accomplished." Flynn sat on the edge of the bed and massaged his injured foot.

"I ordered champagne, blinis, and caviar. I hope I did the right thing."

"You did the right thing. But you picked the wrong moment. I need to get some sleep. I have an early flight."

"You're leaving London?"

"First thing in the morning."

Anya sat on the bed beside him. Her robe fell partly open. She didn't rush to close it. "That's a pity."

"Mrs. Ivanov, does your husband know you're here?"

"Probably. His men follow me everywhere."

"Perhaps you should go home."

She shrugged. "Perhaps I should, but I felt I should warn you."

"Warn me about what?"

"My husband. He's a very dangerous man. Violent. Vindictive. Not soft like so many of the *oligarkhi*. And if you care for your friend at all, you need to show her who he really is."

"She's not naïve. I'm sure she already has a good idea."

"Putin made him rich, but Putin also takes, and takes, *and takes*. Oleg would like to be free of him, but he also knows that those who reject him don't live very long. You see, Oleg is former GRU."

"Military intelligence."

"He works directly with Glavset, the Internet Research Agency."

"The ones who tried to influence the 2016 American presidential election?"

"Tried?" She laughed. "They *succeeded*. Oleg operates troll farms that push out propaganda to every country on the planet. He also owns one of the largest cybersecurity and software companies in the world. Ivanov Antivirus markets their software internationally. As part of that, he has an entire lab dedicated to creating the most dangerous computer viruses in existence. He claims he's creating them so he can defeat them, but in the meantime, his malicious code has infiltrated every major corporation and government in the world. And now he is planning his biggest operation yet. Something catastrophic."

"What?"

"I don't know. Not exactly. But I worry what will happen if he can pull it off."

"Why are you telling me this?"

"Because someone needs to stop him. Someone who can't be frightened or bought off or blackmailed."

"You've been with him a very long time. Why the sudden concern?"

"Not so sudden. I've only kept quiet because I didn't have the courage to do the right thing."

"And now you do?"

"Now that I've met you." She leaned in closer, her robe fell further open. "Your friend is ex-CIA. She knows things. He can use those things. And once he's done using her and no longer needs her, he will get rid of her."

"Caitlyn is very strong-willed. She is not easily manipulated."

"Don't be so sure. She is already under Oleg's spell. He does that to women. He did to me. He can be so charming. So confident. So powerful. It's intoxicating. But make no mistake. She is in great jeopardy. As am I. Even more so now."

"You want him out of your life?"

"While I still have one, yes. For me to be free of him, there's only one way. Someone needs to stop him."

Flynn finally understood exactly what she wanted. "You want me to kill him."

"Don't you have a license for that kind of thing?"

"I did, but I've since resigned. Besides, I never used it willy-nilly. Only as a last resort. And only for king and country."

"This *is* for king and country. And you don't even have to pull the trigger. All you have to do is stop him from doing whatever he's planning. Show the world who he is. Make Putin believe he is a liability. Do that and Putin himself will do what needs to be done. Do you know how many oligarchs have met mysterious ends in the last twenty years? They commit suicide by hanging themselves or shooting themselves in the head. They have strokes or heart attacks or drown on holiday or fall off the roof of a twenty-story building. And that doesn't even include the ones poisoned with Polonium-210."

"You're asking me to trust you."

"I am. And I understand why you wouldn't, but please. You're my last hope. But not just mine and not just Caitlyn's, but the last hope for everyone and anyone who loves freedom."

She took his hand and held it against her rather impressive left breast. She kissed Flynn passionately and when they parted, Flynn kissed her on the cheek and on the neck. A sharp knock on the door stopped him from reaching the sprinkle of freckles deep inside her cleavage.

Anya ran her hand through his hair. "That's probably our champagne and caviar."

Flynn left Anya sitting on the bed and crossed the living room into the foyer. He peered through the peephole to see a smiling young man in a jacket and bowtie. Flynn opened the door a crack with the security chain still attached. "Yes?"

"Room service, sir."

A cart covered with a pristine white tablecloth, champagne in a silver ice bucket, a crystal caviar service, and oyster platters topped with gleaming steel covers stood beside him.

"One second." Flynn closed the door to unlatch the security chain. Just as he opened it, someone kicked it wide. The door smacked Flynn in the face, staggering him back. A man dressed in black stepped over the unconscious body of the young room service waiter. The intruder, his face hidden behind a balaclava, aimed a Glock 19 directly at Flynn's heart.

Anya brought a closed black umbrella down on his hand. The Glock discharged. A bullet tore into the floor at Flynn's feet. She swung again, this time for his head, but the man caught it and slammed the base of the umbrella back into her face, sending her reeling.

Flynn went for the man's gun, twisting the Glock to get it away from him. It fired again, shattering the window that overlooked the wrap-around terrace. Flynn wrenched the gun free, and it flew across the foyer. The man lunged for it. Flynn kicked it into the living room. As the man dove after the weapon, Flynn tackled him.

They wrestled on the floor, but the attacker used his superior size, strength, and jiu-jitsu skills to flip Flynn face down into the carpeting. Flynn turned his head to find Anya unconscious. The intruder reached over and pulled her bathrobe tie free in one motion and wound it around Flynn's neck. He put his knee in Flynn's back and pulled the tie tight around his throat, cutting off the oxygen to his lungs, and the blood to his brain.

Flynn's vision blurred as he struggled not to panic. Flashes of light filled his field of view. He couldn't reach back. He couldn't break away. He couldn't do anything but die.

A loud clunk and a grunt came from the man as the bathrobe tie loosened and he removed his knee. Flynn gratefully sucked in a lungful of air and flipped over onto his back. Tammy, the suburban mom with the proclivity for pink squirrels, loomed over him, brandishing an unbroken champagne bottle in one hand and an oyster fork in the other.

"James, are you okay?"

"Behind you!" Flynn shouted.

The assailant leaped to his feet and flicked open an expandible baton. Tammy threw the bottle of champagne at his head with the practiced form of a tennis player performing a serve. It smacked him square in the face, stunning him before bouncing off the carpeting, still unbroken.

Blood streamed from the man's nose as Tammy crossed the room in five fast steps and stabbed him in the head with the oyster fork. He kicked her in the stomach, sending her stumbling back. Flynn came at him with a small potted plant and smashed it into the oyster fork, driving it into his skull.

The attacker roared like an angry bear and shoved Flynn across the room, pushing him through the floor to ceiling window and onto the terrace. Dizzy and bleeding, Flynn grabbed the balustrade and pulled himself to his feet. The killer kept coming, the fork still sticking out of the top of his head. Flynn tried to grapple with him, but the attacker lifted him into the air, intending to throw him over the edge. Tammy, wielding a metal plate topper from the room service tray, hammered that oyster fork deeper into the killer's skull.

Flynn wriggled free and fell to the terrace. Tammy hit him again and again. The intruder pushed her away as he retreated and flipped backwards over the railing. Flynn looked down to see him bounce off an awning and crash-land on the roof of a parked car, setting off its blaring alarm.

Tammy joined Flynn at the balustrade, followed by Anya, holding her loose robe together. The man lay motionless on top of the dented car roof, the oyster fork still sticking out of his head.

Flynn glanced at the two women, staring over the edge. "I owe you both a debt of gratitude."

Tammy pointed a thumb at Anya. "Where'd she come from?"

"The bedroom," Flynn replied.

Anya put out her hand and her robe fell partly open. "I'm Anya."

Tammy scowled and didn't deign to shake. "Maybe you should go put some damn clothes on."

Flynn looked back down. The car was still there. So was the dent. But the man was not.

CHAPTER TWENTY-ONE

Tammy wouldn't leave until Anya did. Flynn called hotel security, but only to apologize for what he claimed was a "raucous party." He promised to pay for the two broken windows that resulted from the over-the-top frivolities. They didn't ask him any further questions. Luxury hotels like the Connaught were nothing if not discreet.

Flynn didn't want to tell them about the attempt on his life. He knew they'd call Scotland Yard and he'd spend the next three days sitting in police stations. Besides, he didn't want Scotland Yard delving too deeply into his private business. Everything he did was on a need-to-know basis, and Scotland Yard didn't need to know.

Flynn met Sancho for an early breakfast. Their previous plan was to stop at the U.S. Embassy on the way to the airport, but that was before Anya told him about her husband's dangerous and mysterious new operation.

And before someone tried to kill him.

They breakfasted at *Jean-Georges at the Connaught*. Flynn ordered scrambled eggs with oak smoked salmon, wheat toast, and black coffee. Sancho went for the buttermilk pancakes with seasonal berries and bananas. The floor to ceiling windows filled the elegant room with cheerful morning light. But Sancho didn't look very cheerful when Flynn told him he wasn't going to Heathrow.

"What do you mean you're not coming?"

"Caitlyn's in danger, whether she knows it or not. I told you about Anya's suspicions. I told you about the attempt on my life. How can I possibly leave now?"

"By getting your ass in a cab and going to the airport with me."

"You know I can't do that."

"You don't even know who tried to kill you. It could be anybody."

"Exactly, which is why I need you to leave town. It's not safe here for you."

"It's not safe here for *you*!"

"Yes, but that's the life I've chosen. You have a child. A family. You can't afford to live a life of danger."

"Please don't do this to me. Just come with me, man. We can figure out our next moves once we're back in L.A."

"I wish I could, but I have to see this through."

"See *what* through? How do you know Anya's not lying to you?"

"She probably *is* lying to me. But every lie hides an underlying truth."

"What does that even mean?"

"It means it's time for you to go home, amigo."

■ ■ ■

The doorman hailed Sancho a hackney. "Where to, sir?"

"The U.S. Embassy," Sancho said.

The doorman addressed the cabbie as he loaded Sancho's luggage in the trunk. "Nine Elms, driver."

Sancho climbed into the back and barely strapped himself in before the hackney took off. He pulled out his cell and placed a call to his wife.

Alyssa picked up on the second ring, her voice hushed and thick. "Hello?"

"Sorry, babe, did I wake you up?"

"It's okay."

"What time is it there?"

"1:00 a.m."

"Shit. Sorry."

"What's up?"

"I'm on my way to the airport."

She couldn't hide the excitement in her voice. "You're coming home?"

"Yep. My flight gets in at 10:30 tonight. United flight 935. Though it'll probably take me an hour to get through customs."

"You want me to pick you two up?"

"It's just me."

"Just you? What about Flynn?"

"He wants to stay."

"Why aren't you staying with him?"

"It's not safe."

Alyssa's voice went up an octave. "*Not safe?*"

"I tried to get him to come with me, but he's so damn stubborn."

"Did you find Caitlyn?"

"We did, and she was *not* happy about it. She told Flynn she never wanted to see him again."

"Poor James."

"Yeah, but he won't let it go. Won't let *her* go."

"Are you two in danger?"

"Of course we are. Flynn's like a damn danger magnet. But I promised I'd come home if things got dicey, so that's what I'm doing."

"So, you're just going to leave him there?"

"Now you want me to stay?"

"No! Not if it's not safe. Of course, I want you to come home. Maybe Miranda Jacks can get someone from the FBI to keep an eye on him."

"I already called her and told her the situation. I'm sure they'll do what they can."

"Are you okay?"

"I will be once I get home."

"I love you."

"Love you too. See you soon. Kiss Miguel for me."

Sancho hung up and eyed the Thames as they crossed Chelsea Bridge. From there they passed Battersea Park to reach Nine Elms. The black cab pulled over near the South Pavilion. Sancho opened the door and glanced at the driver. "Can you wait for me? I'll be right back. It shouldn't take long. Then we'll be heading to Heathrow."

The cabbie, a fifty-something East Ender with graying red hair, nodded. "Certainly, sir."

As Sancho climbed out, a white panel van pulled up. A smiling East Indian woman stepped from the van. She wore jeans, a turtleneck, and a long black braid. "Sir, would you be willing to give me a hand?"

"Excuse me?"

"My mother's in a wheelchair." She moved to the side of the van to reach for the handle. "Could you help me lift her out?"

"Sure." Sancho put down his suitcase and approached the side door. The woman slid it open to reveal not an elderly lady in a wheelchair, but two strapping men who grabbed Sancho by either arm and dragged him into the van. Sancho struggled and looked back to see the smiling woman slide the door shut. Someone held a piece of cloth soaked with something sweet and medicinal over his mouth. He tried to shout for help, but all that came out were unintelligible grunts. The last blurry face he saw belonged to Yosef Ohana, right before someone pulled a black sack over his head, plunging him into total darkness.

. . .

Flynn couldn't return to The Eagle's Lodge as workers were installing new windows to replace those shattered by the assassin. Instead, he headed to Grosvenor Square Park, two blocks away, to walk off his breakfast. He felt eyes on him, but couldn't catch anyone following him. A tall wrought-iron fence surrounded the perfectly rectangular park with its lush, green lawn dotted with oak, maple, and beech. In the center sat a large, oval garden surrounded by a holly hedge. Flynn traversed the gravel paths and found a bench near the Memorial Garden for British victims of 9-11.

He checked his iPhone. Five bars. Not bad. There had to be a cell tower nearby. Flynn checked his digital phonebook and found the number of his old friend, Bettina O'Toole-Applebaum, investigative reporter *extraordinaire*. She lived in Brooklyn and worked as an editor-at-large for Rolling Stone magazine. She'd grown up in Chicago, the precocious daughter of an interracial, interreligious couple who baptized her as a baby but then raised her as a Jew. She won the Pulitzer Prize for a piece on James Flynn, and from that moment on they continued to help each other out with stories, scoops, and even life-saving heroics.

Bettina picked up on the first ring. "James?"

"Bettina, how are you?"

"Busy, but good. How are you?"

"I've been better."

"Are you calling from Pasadena?"

"London."

"England?"

"Yes, the old sod itself."

"What are you doing there?"

"Getting into trouble. As usual."

"No doubt." She laughed. "What can I help you with?"

"Oleg Ivanov. What do you know about him?"

"Russian oligarch, but then you probably already know that. Former GRU. He was instrumental in organizing those Russian troll farms that continue to spew propaganda all over the world. He started as a computer programmer. A pioneer in cybersecurity. His anti-virus and anti-spyware software was ubiquitous before the FCC classified his company as a national security risk."

"That's how he made his billions?"

"His first few, but then he diversified into everything from real estate and mining to media, finance, and transportation. He has his fingers in everything. Including ransomware."

"Ransomware?"

"There are ransomware gangs that use the former Soviet Union as a safe haven. I've been researching the subject for over a year now. They're digital extortionists attacking governments, corporations, school districts, hospitals, power grids, transportation networks. Anything that uses software…which is everything. Putin claims he has nothing to do with them, but Ivanov is his conduit."

"How much money do they make from this?"

"Trillions. As long as they don't attack Russia, Putin gives them free rein for a piece of the pie. And Ivanov takes a nice slice as the intermediary."

"How does it work exactly?"

"They use a malicious data-scrambling code to kidnap an organization's files. Then they demand a huge ransom to restore them. If victims fail to pay up, they publish that unscrambled data on the open internet."

"And no one fights back?"

"No one knows how. These gangs are slippery. The whole team works remotely and disguises their IP addresses. They are elusive. Nearly invisible. It's like trying to capture smoke."

"Sounds dangerous."

"You have no idea. Right now, they have the capability to take out entire power grids and disrupt worldwide transportation networks. They could scramble the air traffic control system from coast to coast and easily shut down every airport in the country. They can disrupt an election by messing with voter rolls or crash the financial system. Our entire nuclear arsenal is likely vulnerable."

"And you're writing a piece on this?"

"I am. Why are you asking about Ivanov?"

"He apparently has some big, new plan in the works. I don't have the specifics, but I hear it's something very dangerous."

"How do you know this?"

"His wife told me."

"You're in contact with his wife?"

"Anya. She knows what he's doing is dangerous, and she wants me to stop him."

"Why would she turn against him? They've been married for twenty-five years."

"She wants to leave him, but he won't let her go."

"Can you get me an interview with her?"

"I don't know. I doubt it."

"Can you ask?"

"I can try. One more thing. There's another woman involved, but I'm not sure how. Her name is Tammy Torkelson."

"Does she work with Ivanov?"

"I don't know where she fits in, but she keeps popping up. There's something deeply suspicious about her. I need you to find out exactly who she is and why she's here."

"What's her last name again?"

"Torkelson. T-O-R-K-E-L-S-O-N. She claims to be a neonatal nurse from Minnesota who is on vacation in London."

"I'll see what I can do. In the meantime, watch yourself with Ivanov. He is not someone to mess around with."

"Duly noted."

A pause. "You're not sleeping with his wife, are you?"

"I haven't yet."

"Are you planning to?"

"I'll do whatever I have to."

A chuckle. "I'm sure you will."

"Thank you, Bettina. You've confirmed much of what Anya already told me. Call me if you find anything interesting on Miss Torkelson."

"Will do. Later, James."

Flynn clicked off his call. He turned to see someone sitting next to him on the bench.

Tammy Torkelson.

He nearly jumped out of his skin.

"Sorry. I didn't mean to startle you."

"How long have you been sitting here?"

"Long enough to know you think I'm the enemy."

"Then let's not beat around the bush. Let's see who you are." Flynn pulled the large purse off her shoulder and began rummaging through it. She raised her hands as if to say, *be my guest*. Inside, he found a makeup bag, scrunchies, pens, a pack of tissues, a tiny London guidebook, a hairbrush, a wallet, and a US passport with her picture. Surname: Torkelson. Given name: Tammy June. Nationality: United States of America. Birthdate: 22 May 1985. Place of Birth: Minnesota, USA.

"I haven't lied to you about anything," Tammy said.

"Passports can be faked."

"Nothing I told you is untrue." She let go with an embarrassed sigh. "Though I haven't told you everything."

Flynn handed her back her purse. "Who do you work for?"

"I don't work for anybody."

"Then why are you here?"

She reached over and took Flynn's hand and locked her hazel eyes on him. "For you."

"Me?"

"I followed you here from the Langham. A classmate of mine works at City of Roses. She knows I'm a fan and feeds me information."

"A fan?"

"Well, more than a fan." She lifted Flynn's hand to her lips and kissed it.

"Tammy…" He tried to pull his hand away, but she wouldn't let go.

"All those women you seduce? They don't love you like I do. Not Caitlyn Valentine. Not that runaway bride at the Langham. Not that redheaded Russian hussy. They don't really care about you. They don't understand you. Not the real you."

"I'm flattered. I am. But if you really understood me, you'd also understand that I can't afford the luxury of falling in love. A relationship like that would be…a vulnerability."

"I know that's what you tell yourself, but it isn't true. You just haven't met the right woman. A woman who accepts you for who you are. All of you. Every part of you. The sane *and* the crazy. The beautiful *and* the ugly." Tears brimmed in Tammy's eyes. "*I see you.*"

"I see you too, and I appreciate your…admiration. It is deeply humbling. But I'm not sure I can give you what you want."

"I'm not here for a one-night fling. I'm here for the long haul. I'm here for forever. I left my husband and children for you."

"You what?"

"It wasn't fair to Warren for me to stay with him out of obligation. He deserves someone who loves him as much as I love you."

"I…I…I don't know what to say." Flynn tried to extricate his hand again, but Tammy squeezed harder.

"You don't have to say anything. I can see by the look in your eyes that we share the same deep, undying connection. We are soulmates. You are my destiny."

She put his hand to her heaving chest and leaned in to kiss him. A honking horn caught Flynn's attention. He turned his lips away just in time. The horn honked again. Through the wrought-iron fence, Flynn saw a black hackney parked at the curb. Anya waved to him from the backseat.

Flynn bolted to his feet and broke free of Tammy's grip. "Gotta go!"

"I'll go with you!"

Flynn didn't answer. He took off running like a man with his pants on fire. Tammy hurried after. Flynn leaped over a low hedge and vaulted over the wrought-iron fence. Anya threw open the door to the hackney. Flynn dove inside. He sat upright as the cab pulled away and looked back to see Tammy struggling to get over the fence, her skirt and purse tangled on top.

CHAPTER TWENTY-TWO

Belgian engineer Georges Nagelmackers launched the original Orient-Express on October 4th, 1883. The train traveled from Paris to Constantinople with forty passengers. The thirteen-day journey stopped in Munich, Vienna, and Varna. He was inspired by the American Pullman night trains he encountered on his trip to the U.S. He wanted European travel to be just as luxurious as what he experienced in America. With its oriental rugs, velvet draperies, mahogany paneling, deep leather armchairs, and fine cuisine, the Orient-Express attracted the elite of European society. The glamor also caught the imagination of writers like Graham Greene, Agatha Christie, and Ian Fleming, who helped make the Orient-Express world-famous.

Flynn sat back, relieved to be on the move and away from Tammy Torkelson. Strawberry-watermelon vapor infused the air. Anya took a drag on her vape as she studied Flynn. Big, designer sunglasses covered half her face. "Who were you talking to? Was it that annoying American tourist lady?"

"Tammy."

"She seemed so upset with me, and I have no idea why. Is it me or does she seem a little wacky?"

"It's not you."

Anya took off her sunglasses to reveal a painful-looking shiner.

Flynn unconsciously clenched his fists. "Oleg?"

"He thinks I'm sleeping with you."

"What did you tell him?"

"I told him I wanted to, but that you wouldn't have me. I don't think he believed me."

Flynn nodded. "I talked to a journalist friend of mine and what you told me about him…all checks out."

"Of course it does, but there's more. I'm pretty sure Oleg sent that hitman last night. To kill you in front of me and steal back the money you won from him. To show me the consequences of crossing him."

"So, Oleg's a sore loser?"

"He is indeed." She rapped on the Plexiglas partition. "Driver? Take us to St. Pancras International."

"Are we going somewhere?"

"The South of France. I'd stop at your hotel for your luggage, but I don't think it's safe. I'll have someone collect it and send it on."

"What's in the South of France?"

"Oleg's superyacht. The *Fancy*. He keeps it in Monaco."

"At the Royal Yacht Club?"

She nodded. "He bought it from the estate of another oligarch who met a mysterious end. He got it for a bargain back in 2015. It only cost him three-hundred million pounds."

"Must be a big one."

"It has a helipad on one end and an infinity pool on the other. There's a gym, a cinema, a wine cellar, a cocktail lounge, a bowling alley, a ballroom, and luxury cabins for thirty-two guests."

"Impressive."

"Oleg thinks so. He thinks it makes up for his tiny little penis."

"And why are we visiting the *Fancy*?"

"Because that's where Oleg is. He's meeting with his co-conspirators to work out the details of their plot."

Flynn searched her beautiful, inscrutable eyes. "Why aren't you with him?"

"Because he doesn't trust me. He wants nothing to do with me. He took your former lady friend and left me behind under lock and key."

"But you managed to escape?"

"The men on my protection detail are large, but not very smart."

"And you want to crash his party?"

"Yes, and while I distract him, you will sneak onboard to find out what he's up to."

Flynn nodded. "And stop him?"

"Or kill him." She put her hand on Flynn's knee. "Before he kills you."

"You think he still wants me dead?"

"I know he does. I apologize for putting you in this position, but you're in his crosshairs now. I'm afraid your only way out is to take *him* out."

Flynn smirked. "At which point, you will inherit everything he owns."

Anya nodded, a tiny smile curling her lips. "Yes, which is why Oleg needs to die before he decides to disinherit me."

"I'll investigate and expose his plot, but I won't murder him."

"Self-defense is hardly murder."

●　●　●

The Eurostar train arrived in Paris two hours and twenty minutes after departing King's Cross. The high-speed bullet train rocketed through the tunnel beneath the English Channel at speeds of up to three hundred kilometers per hour. To Flynn, it felt more like a jet than a train as the world outside zipped by in a blur.

Rather than continue the journey by bullet train, Anya booked them a luxurious suite on the Venice-Simplon Orient Express. The vintage 1930s carriages, all restored to their original elegance, were updated with a few modern touches. Flynn marveled at the size of their grand suite. Dubbed *Istanbul,* it consisted of a large sleeping compartment with a queen-sized bed, an elegant sitting room with a sofa, and a marble en-suite bathroom. The polished inlaid wood paneling, rich upholstery, and brass lamps and fittings were a throwback to a more gracious period in history. Provided one was a member of the upper crust and not the hoi polloi.

A bottle of Bollinger champagne chilled in an ice bucket next to a basket filled with fresh fruit and another filled with croissants, tiny silver tubs of butter, and preserves.

Anya scooted up behind him and put her hands on his hips. "Do you approve?"

"If you must travel, you might as well do it in style."

"My philosophy exactly."

"I suppose we could have flown."

"Yes, but where's the fun in that? We'll be in Monaco in the morning and my husband's guests aren't arriving until tomorrow afternoon."

Flynn removed the foil and the *muselet* before popping the cork. "Champagne?"

She picked up a crystal flute. "Please."

Flynn filled her glass and then poured some for himself. They clinked and Anya smiled. "*Santé.*"

"*Sláinte!*" Flynn replied.

They both took a healthy sip and then sat on the sofa. Anya scooted closer. "What *will* we do to while away the time?"

"Mrs. Ivanov, are you trying to seduce me?"

Anya laughed.

∎   ∎   ∎

Flynn always enjoyed traveling by train. It seemed the most civilized of all the modes of transportation, even more elegant than a luxury ocean liner. The rhythmic sway of the train as they trundled down the tracks lulled Flynn into a splendidly serene state. He watched the glorious panorama of the French countryside move by as the sun sank in the western sky. The gently rolling hills, the vineyards of Chablis, the towering mountains to the east.

Water splashed in the opulent art deco shower stall as Anya bathed. She wanted Flynn to join her, and he nearly acquiesced, but in the end, declined the offer. He wasn't sure how much longer he could put her off without putting her off.

Anya was a woman used to getting what she wanted, but despite his reputation, Flynn wasn't so easily swayed by the charms of a beautiful woman. Even one as beautiful as Anya. Other *femme fatales* had set their sights on him. Some wanted to seduce him. Some wanted to kill him. Some wanted to do both. But he usually flipped the script, capturing their affection, and turning them against their masters. In this case, he and Anya had the same enemy, but different agendas. Rescuing Caitlyn was paramount, but so was derailing Ivanov's evil plan.

He knew Anya couldn't be trusted, and it occurred to him that Ivanov might have frightened her into doing his bidding and luring Flynn to his doom. *Is that what she's doing? Is this all an elaborate ruse? Does Anya really want Ivanov dead?* Or was Flynn the one in danger?

■　■　■

At 8 p.m., they headed for the dining car. Flynn wore a vintage tux and Anya wore a midnight blue evening gown and a dazzling sapphire necklace that reflected the aquamarine of her eyes. As they moved through the cocktail car, every man she passed turned to stare for the briefest of seconds, clearly irritating the females who accompanied them.

Flynn could tell Anya enjoyed the attention.

Of course, a few females also made eyes at Flynn. Some young ones. Some slightly older ones. Even a stout woman wearing a long, navy-blue abaya and niqab that covered everything but her eyes ogled him.

The dining car was as luxurious as the rest of the vintage train. The maître d' seated them at an elegantly appointed table. A waiter wearing a white jacket and black slacks handed them menus. *"Accueillir! Je m'appel, Paul et je serai votre serveur ce soir."*

Flynn nodded as he took the menu. *"Merci, Paul. Je suis James et voici Anya."*

"Un plaisir de vous rencontrer tous les deux. Puis-ke vouse apporter un verre? Un verre de champagne? Un cocktail?"

Flynn smiled at Anya. "Would you like a cocktail or a glass of champagne?"

Anya grinned. "A vodka gimlet. Straight up."

Flynn looked back at their server. *"La dame aura une vrille de vodka. Directement. Et je prendrai une vodka martini. Secoué. Pas agité."*

"Tres bien, monsieur."

As their waiter went off to fetch their drinks, Anya smiled at Flynn with surprise. "You speak French?"

"Un petit."

"Did you take it in school?"

"My mother was Swiss, from Canton de Vaud. Though I lost both her and my father in a climbing accident in the Aiguilles Rouges when I was eleven."

Anya looked momentarily confused. "But I thought your parents were…ah…I see. Of course."

"Of course?"

"This is the history you've created for yourself."

"Aren't we all the architects of our own history?"

"I'd say so. We all make ourselves into who we want to be. I was born in the slums of Kapotnya, in the shadow of an oil refinery. My mother died of cancer and my father drank himself to death soon after. I lived in the streets for a time, and ran with the wild dogs that roamed in packs."

"So, you're an orphan too."

"Eventually, I moved in with my aunt and uncle. But they too lived in poverty, and I was determined not to die in poverty. I worked hard in school to better myself. To get a degree. To become a doctor. But I blossomed at age fourteen and met Oleg one year later. Three years after that, we wed. At the time, he was still in the military."

"So, you've been with him from the start."

"And from the start, he's been a bastard."

The waiter returned with their cocktails. "*Avez-vous décide dé dîner?*"

"Have you decided on dinner?" Flynn asked.

"The salmon," Anya said.

"*Nous aurons le caviar de beluga pour commencer et une Bouteille de Dom Pérignon. En plat principal, la dame aura le pave de saumon sauce cresson et le carpaccio de truffes. Je prendrai le carre d'agneau roti.*"

"*Tres bien, monsieur.*"

As the waiter went off with their order, Flynn caught Anya smiling at him with surprise. "You've lived in the US for such a long time. How is it you speak French with such fluency?"

"I use the Pimsleur method." He took a sip of martini. "Anything else you'd like to ask me?"

"Why won't you sleep with me?"

"I'm not that easy. I need to be wooed. Pursued. Romanced."

"Isn't that what I'm doing? Wooing?"

"Yes, but there's no need to rush into anything. Half the pleasure is the anticipation. It's not the destination, it's the journey."

"Yeah, but it's kind of disappointing if you never get to where you're going."

Their waiter returned with their caviar, blinis, and the bottle of bubbly. As they enjoyed their appetizer, Flynn pressed her for more details. "So, how do you plan to get us aboard Oleg's yacht?"

"If he's not in the harbor, if he's out at sea, I'll rent us a speedboat. You'll hide below and when night falls, you'll sneak aboard."

"Just like that?"

"Why not?"

"I'll need some equipment. Scuba gear. Weapons. A waterproof camera."

"I'll get you whatever you need."

The waiter returned with their main courses. Anya asked Flynn if he'd like to order another bottle of champagne.

"I better not."

Anya reached across the table and took Flynn's hand. "Are you afraid I'll take advantage of you?"

"I just think we need to stay sharp."

"From everything I've read about you, I thought you'd be more fun."

"Don't believe everything you read."

Flynn tried to pull his hand away, but Anya held on tight. "Who knows what might happen tomorrow. Life can be very unpredictable. I believe we should enjoy as much as we can while we can."

"I don't disagree."

"Yet you still play hard to get."

Flynn finally extricated his hand and used it to pick up his fork and start eating. "There's nothing wrong with the occasional, meaningless fling. For a long time, that was all I needed. But now…now I'm not sure that's enough for me."

"You want an emotional connection?"

"Something like that."

"You want to fall in love?"

"I'm not sure I'd use those words."

"But that's what you want?"

"It's what I believe I need."

"That's what I thought I needed too." Anya's eyes grew shiny. "But now, I'm not sure what I believe." She drained her glass of champagne and held it out for Flynn to fill again.

■　■　■

With dinner done, a slightly drunk Flynn and Anya returned to their suite. The narrow corridors in each carriage exhibited the same elegance as every other part of the Venice-Simplon Orient Express. They moved from carriage to carriage, past polished woodwork restored to its original posh perfection and large windows that framed the constantly changing countryside, turning sideways to let other passengers squeeze by: a rotund, older gentleman with a florid face, a thirty-something hipster couple, two painfully slender, seventy-something aristocrats.

"I'll sleep on the sofa," Flynn offered. "You can take the bed."

"Don't make me sleep alone."

"I'll be steps away in the other room."

"You don't have to make love to me. I'd just like you to sleep with me."

"That's a very slippery slope."

"Don't be such a baby. Can't you just lay beside me, wrap your arms around me, and hold me tight without popping a boner?"

Anya opened the door between the cars and entered the carriage that housed their Grand Suite. The portly lady in the navy-blue abaya and niqab waddled towards them from the opposite direction. She stopped and waited silently while Anya unlocked the ornate door that led to their sitting room. As Anya entered their suite, the stout Muslim lady eased herself past Flynn. He caught sight of the stun gun a half a second before she jammed it into the side of his neck. 50,000 volts took Flynn to his knees. He had no control of his body as he fell. Every nerve ending exploded in agony. She pushed the stun gun against his neck, jolting him again and again until Flynn's vision faded around the edges. He flopped around on the floor like a fish out of water as the lady in the abaya disappeared into the Grand Suite. Anya screamed a second before the door slammed shut.

Flynn couldn't tell how much time passed before he pushed himself to his knees. His muscles no longer twitched, but every nerve in his body burned. He pulled himself to his feet and tried the door latch. The lady in blue had locked it.

Grunting and screaming, shouting and crashing echoed from the other side. Flynn kicked at the door. He put his shoulder to it, but the damn thing wouldn't budge. He finally put his back against the opposite wall of the corridor and kicked the wood by the latch as hard as he could. Something gave. He kicked it again, and again, and again. Focusing all his frustration and anger, he raised his knee high and slammed his foot into the wood with everything he had. The door crashed open with a splintering crack. The large picture window inside the suite was shattered. The lady in blue struggled to push Anya through it.

Flynn grabbed the woman around the neck and wrenched her sideways. Anya fell to the floor and tried to crawl away as the lady in blue jammed the stun gun into Flynn's groin. He jumped back before she could zap him. She came at him again and he reared back to punch her, hitting his elbow on a brass fixture. His arm went dead as his funny bone vibrated with agony. The stun gun connected with his chest and down he went, every muscle in his body locked up.

The lady in blue grabbed Anya by the legs and dragged her back towards the window. Flynn, operating entirely on rage, sprang up and tackled the woman. She crashed backwards into the broken window but spread her arms wide to keep herself from falling out. She slammed her knee into Flynn's groin and tried to use the stun gun again. Flynn kicked her in the chest. She stumbled back towards the open window. Her feet flew up as she flipped over the edge. Flynn lunged to grab whatever he could to prevent her from falling. He had hold of her niqab, but it unraveled as she tipped backwards, revealing her face a split second before she fell.

Tammy.

Gone.

Out the window.

Flynn poked his head past the broken glass into the wind, but he couldn't see her. It was night and the world was pitch black.

"Was that the crazy American lady?" Anya was on her feet.

"Tammy."

"She must have caught a cab and followed us to St. Pancras." Anya sat on the edge of the bed and licked her bloody lip. "I think she has a thing for you."

"Apparently so."

"So much so that she wants to murder me."

Flynn looked back out the window. They were moving at a decent clip, but not so quickly that a fall would necessarily be fatal. "I hope she's all right."

"I don't."

Flynn's phone buzzed. A glance at the caller ID displayed Alyssa, Sancho's wife. "Alyssa?"

"Flynn? Is Sancho with you?"

"With me? No. He flew back home this morning."

"He never arrived. He wasn't on the plane. I tried his phone, but he won't pick up. I called the hotel, but they said he checked out."

"Last I saw him, he was on his way to the airport."

"Where are you now?"

"On my way to the South of France. I'll call Miranda Jacks at the FBI. She'll contact the *legat* in London and they'll coordinate with the local police."

"Oh, my god."

"Not to worry. I'm sure he's fine. He probably just missed his flight. He's likely stuck at Heathrow with no phone service."

"Maybe I should call the airport and see if they can page him."

"Good idea. I'm sure that's where you'll find him."

"Thanks, James. Sorry to bother you so late. I was just worried."

"No need to apologize. Perhaps you should get to bed now. You need to get your sleep. You have a little one to take care of."

"Okay, I will. Thank you. Good night."

"Good night, love."

Flynn poked his head back out the broken window and stared off into the darkness.

Anya picked a piece of glass out of her hair. "This is not at all how I thought this evening would go."

CHAPTER TWENTY-THREE

There are 12,261 millionaires per square mile in Monaco. That's one out of every three residents. The poverty rate is zero. But most people who work in Monaco don't actually live there. 30,000 French and 5,800 Italians commute to Monaco every day. Monaco also has more police per capita than any other place on Earth. One police officer for every seventy-three residents. The principality itself is smaller than Central Park in New York City. Of the 38,000 residents, 3,500 live in Monte Carlo. Government rules ban citizens from gambling or even working at the casino. But they do live longer than residents of most other countries. It has the world's highest average life expectancy at 87 years of age, beating out Japan, Hong Kong, and Liechtenstein.

When they checked into the Hôtel de Paris Monte-Carlo, Flynn had a vague memory of being there before. The magnificent and palatial Belle Èpoque structure stood right next to the Casino de Monte-Carlo. Lavish columns, arches, and spires embellished the bright white façade. Statuettes of naked nymphs adorned arched doorways and fountains. Flynn remembered the bronze statue of Louis the XIV on horseback in the cathedral-like lobby with its marble floors and cream white walls, glass-domed ceiling, and massive crystal chandelier.

Their Diamond Suite was no less opulent, if a little more modern. Anya stood on the balcony overlooking the Mediterranean and Port Hercules. She beckoned Flynn over. As he joined her, he remembered standing on a similar balcony with a dark-haired beauty with a dangerous smile and madness in her eyes. He had raced her on a mountain road, braving hairpin turns as she flashed that seductive smile and sped ahead, nearly forcing him off the edge of a cliff. He had faced her across the baccarat table at the Casino De Monte-Carlo and won. Later, when she seduced him, she bit his lip, drawing blood. For her, sex and violence were one and the same, and more than one man had lost his life between her thighs.

"James, where are you?"

Flynn shook off the old memories to focus on the present. "Here. With you. Taking in this magnificent view."

"Are you still worried about that crazy American lady?"

"I'm more worried about what your husband is planning."

"I don't see the *Fancy* in the harbor, so I'm thinking he's already at sea."

"Then there's no time to lose."

"I agree. Oleg often takes day trips to *Plage les Fossettes* at *Cap Ferrat*. There's good snorkeling, a beautiful coastline, and a private beach."

Flynn nodded and looked over the edge of the terrace. Two large, pale, naked people bobbed around a black bottom infinity pool on the terrace below, one with red hair, one with a bald head. "We'll need a boat of our own."

"I already arranged for a Sunseeker Superhawk with the equipment you requested. It's berthed down below in Port Hercules."

"When do we leave?"

Anya smiled. "Unless you have to pee, I was thinking maybe now."

■   ■   ■

Since neither Flynn nor Anya had a license to drive a motorized pleasure craft, their chartered Sunseeker Superhawk came with its own skipper and first mate. Captain Hugo Compeau was unusually handsome, like a ship captain out of central casting. Tall and broad shouldered, he had a dark beard with streaks of silver and eyes the color of the Mediterranean. His first mate, Lola Beaufoy, had a pierced nose, pierced lips, pierced eyebrows, and tats covering both her arms. Flynn thought they made an incongruous pair, but they seemed to know what they were doing. The Sunseeker Superhawk looked as sleek as its moniker. At seventeen meters long, it was probably more yacht than they needed. Its twin engines pushed the Superhawk to a top speed of thirty-eight knots. More than fast enough to keep up with the *Fancy*. The aft cockpit contained a large wet bar. Flynn mixed mojitos for Anya and himself. As the sun in the blue, cloudless sky already warmed his skin, a tropical drink seemed apropos.

With drinks in hand, Anya led Flynn down to the master cabin where he found the equipment he requested. A wet suit and scuba gear, a GoPro Hero9 waterproof camera, a Tanto knife with a Kydex sheathe, an HK Mark 23 with a suppressor, a nylon shoulder holster, and four additional magazines were laid out on the floor. Lastly, he pulled what looked like a dark brown caterpillar from a baggy and secured it to his lip with a tiny bottle of spirit gum. The theatrical-grade human hair mustache looked surprisingly authentic and matched his hair color perfectly. Flynn had given her a wish list and did not expect to receive anything close to what he requested. "I must say, I'm impressed. You found me everything I asked for."

"You forget who my husband is. I know lots of shady people too."

"International arms dealers?"

"More than a few. In fact, two live here in Monaco, and one has a bit of a crush on me."

"Did he ask why you wanted these things?"

"No, but he did ask me if I'd like to meet him for a drink tonight."

"What did you say?"

Anya smiled. "I said I was busy, but maybe another time."

"You do like to keep men guessing."

"It's not difficult. How did the American comedian Robin Williams put it? God gave men a brain and a penis, but only enough blood to run one at a time." Flynn checked the equipment as Anya looked on. "I had lunch brought on as well. They're setting it up on deck."

"You do think of everything."

"I try to. I wouldn't want to attempt this on an empty stomach."

"Perish the thought."

"Are you ready to do this?"

Flynn nodded. "It's what I do."

"Once we commit, there's no turning back. With Oleg, you can't take half-measures. He will come at you with everything he has."

"I would expect nothing less."

"Don't let your scruples get in the way of your survival. He will not hesitate to kill you. He's a modern-day Blackbeard. Why do you think he named his yacht the *Fancy*? He lives to plunder, steal, murder, and pillage, and God help you if you get in the way."

"I'm not an assassin."

"But you do have a license to kill."

"I did, but no longer. Besides, I don't just want Oleg; I want everyone involved. If this plot is as dangerous as you say it is, stopping it must be our first priority."

"Along with saving your lady love," Anya said with a smirk. "By the way, I like the pornstache. I think they're coming back."

■   ■   ■

Flynn and Anya sat in the rear seats as the Sunseeker cut a swath through the light swell, skipping over the scattered whitecaps, leaving a rooster tail of a wake. Captain Compeau and first mate

Lola manned the helm with its wheel, throttle, high-tech digital screens, and readouts for power and navigation.

Flynn enjoyed the sea breeze and tasted the salt spray on his lips. He glanced at Anya, her cascading red curls barely held in place with a scarf and a scrunchie. As he looked back at Monte-Carlo receding in the distance, rousing music played in his head, the kind that always accompanied him when the thrill of adventure lifted his heart. The deep, dark electric guitar. The pounding beat. The relentless rhythm that promised danger and excitement.

They cruised west along the coast of the Côte d'Azur towards Saint-Jean-Cap-Ferrat, past rising cliffs and tiny, picturesque towns like Cap d'Ail. Passing coves and capes and anchored yachts with drunken middle-aged men and scantily clad younger women waving at them with both arms. They edged south, farther out to sea, leaving the coast and the other pleasure boats behind.

Captain Hugo Compeau piloted them to the location Anya provided and there, on the horizon, far in the distance, Flynn caught sight of the *Fancy*.

"He is so predictable." Anya looked at Flynn. "You better get ready."

Flynn went below to put on his wetsuit and scuba gear. His gun hung in a shoulder holster inside his wetsuit, his knife in a sheath attached to his leg. Wearing neoprene dive boots, Flynn carried his flippers up the stairs. His camera dangled from a clip on his BCD vest. The mega yacht loomed closer now and Flynn hurried to the hydraulic platform and dive ladder in the stern.

Someone on the *Fancy* shouted through a bullhorn. "Unknown vessel! Keep your distance! Identify yourself or we will take defensive actions!"

Anya lifted her own bullhorn. "This is Anya Ivanov! And I demand to come aboard!"

"Who?" shouted the voice through the bullhorn.

"Anya Ivanov, you stupid *svoloch!* The wife of your glorious leader! That ship is as much mine as his! So stop threatening me and drop a goddamn ladder!"

Flynn poked his head up a little higher as they drew closer and spotted two men with assault rifles flanking the man with the bullhorn. "Please do not come closer!"

"Or what? You'll shoot me? Really? *Dolbo yeb*!"

Flynn watched the bullhorn man nervously confer with the man on his left. Finally, he brought the bullhorn back to his mouth. "Stay where you are! I will find your husband!"

"Where the hell am I going to go, idiot?"

Flynn put on his mask and flippers and slipped into the sea. He held onto the edge of the platform and kept his head just above water.

Finally, the irritated voice of Oleg Ivanov boomed through the bullhorn. "Anya? Is that you?"

"What? You don't recognize me? You forgot what I looked like?"

"What the hell are you doing here?"

"I thought I might enjoy some time with my husband on our beautiful yacht!"

Flynn lifted his head higher. Oleg wore board shorts and a tank top. Caitlyn stood next to him in a tiny white bikini. The argument continued in their Russian-accented British English.

"I told you I didn't want you here!" Oleg shouted.

"Since when have I ever cared what *you* wanted?"

"When you were younger, you did."

"No, I just pretended to. Just like you pretended to be faithful."

"You can't be here!"

"But your new young girlfriend can?"

"She is not my girlfriend! She is my bodyguard!"

Anya scoffed. "I don't see a gun! But then where would you hide one in that itty-bitty bikini?"

"I'm sunning myself and I told her to join me. Don't be such a prude!"

"You must think I'm an idiot!"

"This is business. I have clients coming."

"Who can charm your clients better than I?"

"Anya, please!"

"No, I'm not going anywhere!"

"Do not make me do something ugly."

Anya laughed. "What? Are you going to sink my little boat?"

"Put your captain on the bullhorn!"

"He works for me, and he has *nothing* to say to you!"

"Well, I have something to say to *him*! Turn your boat around and take my wife back to wherever she came from! Do it now or I will send my men down to make you. And they will not be gentle! Do you understand me, Captain?"

Captain Compeau pleaded with Anya. "Mrs. Ivanov, please. Let me just take you back to Monaco."

She replied to him through the bullhorn. "My husband did not pay for this charter."

"And I do not want any trouble."

"If you take me back to Port Hercules, I will not pay you the rest of your fee. Do you understand *me?*"

"I'll pay it!" Oleg shouted through the bullhorn. "I'll pay you ten times what she's paying you! Just get her the hell out of here!"

"I'm sorry, Mrs. Ivanov." Captain Hugo began backing the Sunseeker up and turning it around.

"Goddamn it!" she shouted through the bullhorn. "You work for me! Not him!"

Flynn ducked under the water and dove deep, muffling the voices above. All he heard was the rumble of boat engines and the bubbles burbling out of his regulator. He kicked hard and made his way towards the *Fancy.*

CHAPTER TWENTY-FOUR

Flynn hadn't donned scuba gear in quite some time. Not since that insanity with Sergei Belenki and that unfortunate incident at Cape Canaveral a few years previously. Flynn itched with anxiety. Sweat burned his eyes inside the foggy mask, and he couldn't quite catch his breath. Diving used to be second nature to him. He loved exploring coral reefs and the sea creatures of the deep. Now, panic paralyzed him. Throttled him. Suffocated him. He swam for the surface and ripped the regulator out of his mouth, sputtering and gulping for oxygen. Grateful to be above water, he inflated his buoyancy compensator with air from his scuba tank to stay afloat. He stayed close to the Fancy's hull and slowly swam around the mega yacht's endless circumference.

The Sunseeker cruised far off into the distance. Anya told Flynn if Oleg wanted her to leave, she would argue with him and distract him and his crew to give Flynn time to sneak aboard. She described a side hatch he could access right near the surface of the water. It led to a tender bay with a hydraulic lift. Apparently, they used the tender to reach isolated beaches and private coves. She said the side hatch should be open, and she was right. Flynn climbed up the ladder that led to the tender bay. There were two other smaller inflatable tenders and a variety of recreational equipment, but no crewmen.

Flynn pulled off his wet suit to reveal shorts and a t-shirt both soaked with sweat. His heart pounded as he pulled out a map Anya had sketched for him. A map now damp and smeary with perspiration. Apparently, the crew quarters were close by. Flynn made his way down a narrow corridor, hoping that most of the crew was topside. He passed through a small kitchen and lounge area before finding the communal locker room. Every locker was locked, but Flynn did discover a large laundry area with a number of uniforms and coveralls piled into two rolling baskets. He picked through them and found a pair of black slacks and a white short-sleeve shirt with epaulets. He also found a pair of black Sperry sneakers in his size and a dark gray Flexfit Delta cap with the *Fancy* logo. A black windbreaker rounded out his ensemble and concealed the nylon shoulder holster and the HK Mark 23.

Flynn pulled the brim of his hat down to obscure his face from the security cameras and made his way topside. His fake mustache itched, but he didn't want to scratch it and risk tilting it crooked. Flynn had used disguises to change his appearance before, but not always to great effect. There was the clown suit, the gorilla costume, and the time he shaved his eyebrows, tinted his skin, and wore a kimono to masquerade as a Japanese man. A mustache was a little less obvious and a little more believable. And with a crew of eighty, he hoped most crew members would assume he was a new hire.

Ivanov's yacht was massive. One of the largest in the world at 170 meters long. Between the gym, the cinema, the wine cellar, the bowling alley, and the ballroom, there were more than enough places for Flynn to hide until Ivanov's guests arrived. Because the yacht was so mega and Anya's map was so smeary, it took him a while to figure out the geography. He found the wine cellar and hid far in the back behind some wooden crates. The place was dead quiet and totally deserted. Flynn figured he'd be safe there. At least until dinner. He took advantage of the privacy to place a call to Bettina O'Toole-Applebaum by tapping into the ship's satellite Wi-Fi.

Bettina picked up on the second ring. "James?"

"Bettina, do you have a moment?"

"For you? Always. Are you still in England?"

"No, I'm in the South of France. The Côte de Azur. Floating off the coast on Oleg Ivanov's mega yacht. *The Fancy*."

"Are you a guest?"

"An uninvited one. He's meeting with someone here and I wanted to find out who."

"Does it have to do with that dangerous plan you mentioned?"

"It does. I'll try to get photos of everyone involved and text them to you. I'm hoping you'll be able to identify them."

"I'll do my best," Bettina said.

"Thank you."

"By the way, I found some info on that name you gave me. Tammy Torkelson. Apparently, she really *is* a neonatal nurse from Minnesota. She lives in Mendota Heights and works at Regions Hospital in St. Paul. She's married to a dentist, Warren Torkelson, and has two kids. Tom, fourteen, and Kaley, seventeen."

Flynn didn't know how to react to that and didn't say anything for a good five seconds.

"James, are you still there?"

"Do you think it might be a cover?"

"If it is, it's a very sophisticated one. I found pictures and social media posts going back fifteen years."

"So, you think she might actually be a civilian?"

"I do. What about her piqued your interest?"

"I met her in Pasadena, and then I met her again in London. And then I pushed her out a window."

"*You what?*"

"She attacked Anya. I thought she was an assassin."

"Why'd she attack Anya?"

"It's a long story."

"Is she all right?"

"Anya's fine."

"No, not Anya. Tammy Torkelson."

"I don't know. Probably not. The train wasn't moving all that quickly, but..."

"Train? You pushed her off a train."

"Well, I didn't know it was her until—" Flynn heard footsteps heading toward the wine cellar. He lowered his voice to a whisper. "Someone's here. I better sign off."

Flynn hung up, grateful to end that uncomfortable conversation. He peeked around the corner. A man in a chef's uniform pulled out a bottle of wine. He lumbered back up the stairs and, when he opened the door to the galley, Flynn caught the faint sound of a helicopter landing.

Flynn didn't want to follow the chef into the galley, so he headed down a utility corridor, past two huge walk-in freezers, and found another ladder/staircase that led to the next level up. He passed the Plexiglas walls of a spacious gym. No one was working out, but the floor to ceiling windows offered a magnificent view of the ocean. He squeezed by a maid in the corridor and nodded, tipping his head down so the brim of his hat obscured his face.

He peered into the two-lane bowling alley and the small cinema. Both were deserted. The corridor split into three shorter passages that led to three VIP staterooms. Each stateroom door had a keyless entry lock with an electronic keypad. Flynn wondered if one of them belonged to Caitlyn.

Using Anya's smeary map, he found a staircase that led to the next level up. High ceilings and huge windows filled a ballroom with light. He also located the salon, the cocktail lounge, and a dining room that connected directly to the sprawling stainless-steel kitchen and galley.

But no Caitlyn.

Flynn climbed up one more level to an outdoor patio deck. The thwump of the helicopter grew louder now, nearly thunderous. The large wet bar, lounge chairs, pool, and patio were populated exclusively by young women in tiny thongs and bikinis. None of them paid any attention to Flynn as they were clearly there to welcome the arriving guests. All eyes focused on the bird landing on the helipad on the bow. The black Eurocopter EC155 had the logo of the *Fancy* painted on the side. The fifteen-seat twin-engine helicopter was a favorite of the billionaire class.

Flynn lifted his GoPro Hero9 and used the touch zoom to zero in on Ivanov's arriving guests. Three men all in their thirties. They didn't look military. They looked nerdy. One tall and thin, one small and balding, one large and heavy. All three dressed casually for a cruise in shorts and t-shirts.

Ivanov's crew unloaded the chopper and carried the visitors' bags. The bikini-clad women watched them with great interest and talked to each other in Russian, laughing and pointing and ignoring Flynn completely. He would have been insulted, but he was too busy capturing the faces of the new arrivals. As Ivanov greeted them, Caitlyn stood right next to him. She no longer wore her tiny white bikini, but a khaki-colored outfit that accommodated a shoulder holster.

Flynn quietly captured some narration as he watched. "I am recording this on the deck of Oleg Ivanov's mega yacht, the *Fancy*. The timestamp will authenticate the date and time. He is greeting three guests who just arrived by helicopter."

Flynn shut up when Ivanov motioned in his general direction. Flynn lowered the camera and ducked behind a pillar. When he poked his head out, Ivanov and the others headed his way. Retreating down the stairs, Flynn made his way back to his hiding place in the wine cellar. He grabbed HD stills of the video and zoomed in even further on the faces. Then he connected the GoPro to an app on his phone and texted the stills to Bettina.

"Hold on," she texted back.

Flynn waited five minutes. And then texted Bettina in return. "Any luck?"

Another text from Bettina. "Hold your horses."

Flynn waited five more minutes, though it felt more like hours. Just as he was about to text her again, his phone vibrated.

Flynn answered. "You find something?"

"I recognized them as soon as I saw them, but I had to make sure."

"Who's he meeting with?"

"The tall skinny one is Nosferatu. AKA Dmitri Nikolayev."

"Who?"

"The leader of the Fang Dynasty."

"You lost me."

"One of the FBI's most wanted cyber terrorists. The fat one is Laughing Man. AKA Leonid Stepanovich, leader of Ghost in the Shell. And the short one is 0nyx, AKA Yevgeniy Kuznetsov, leader of Nightshade. They are the leaders of three of the most dangerous and destructive ransomware gangs out there."

"How do you even know what they look like?"

"I told you, they're on the FBI's most wanted list for cybercrimes. I've been researching these gangs for over a year."

"Do they often work together?"

"Never. They don't want to share the spoils."

"So why this summit? What's going on then?"

"It has to be huge. A ransomware attack on a scale never before seen. Bigger than *WannaCry*."

"Wanna what?"

"Cry. As in tears. It attacked computers worldwide. 300,000 servers across 150 countries were held hostage. The damage estimates were in the billions. It affected companies and governments globally. Among them the National Health Service hospitals in England and Scotland, Nissan and Honda factories worldwide, Spain's Telefonica, and Deutsche Bank."

"And you think this might be worse?"

"Much worse. Hackers are more sophisticated now and everything is far more accessible and vulnerable, including vital infrastructure. Governments and companies still aren't investing enough in cybersecurity."

"So, what would be the worst-case scenario?"

"Let's say they attacked the US. They could shut down electrical grids all across the country, crash the stock market, freeze supply chains, freeze the banks and oil pipelines, take down air traffic control, and bring mass transit to a standstill. Hospitals would go dark. Nuclear reactors would melt down. Law enforcement and the military would be crippled. People would starve. People would die. It would be a multi-trillion-dollar disaster."

"So, they wouldn't just be holding companies for ransom, but the entire US government?"

"Once the shit hit the fan, they could demand whatever they wanted, and they would get it."

"Could Putin be behind this?"

"I don't think he'd be opposed to it. Especially if it brings down the NATO alliance."

"I better contact Miranda Jacks."

"At the FBI? And tell her what?"

"Where she can find three of the world's most wanted cyber terrorists."

"The FBI has no jurisdiction outside of the US. She can contact the FBI legat in Paris and they can contact the Directorate-General for External Security in France, but if that yacht is in international waters, they won't have jurisdiction either. I'm guessing that's why Ivanov wanted to have this meeting at sea. By the time everyone involved figures out who has the authority to make an arrest, our three hackers will be long gone."

"Then I guess it's up to me to find out what they're up to."

"Okay, but please stay safe. In the meantime, I'll contact Miranda and give her a heads up on what's happening. Even if she can't swoop in and arrest them, she can track them and start an investigation."

"I'll be in touch."

"You be careful."

"Always."

Bettina snorted. "Yeah, right."

Flynn clicked off and put away his phone. He picked up a crate of wine, wended his way out of the wine cellar, and made his way topside. Oleg and the hackers from the helicopter sat drinking and talking with the women in bikinis. Caitlyn stood near Oleg's side, looking uncomfortable. As she turned in his direction, Flynn lifted the crate of wine high enough to hide his face. He crossed the outdoor area and set the crate down behind the bar. The blender blended and the girls in bikinis babbled and the hackers awkwardly flirted while Oleg talked to someone on his phone.

All of it in Russian.

Because Flynn didn't understand a word of what was being said, he recorded the conversation with his GoPro. He hid it in a large potted plant by the bar and then picked up a big empty cardboard box, holding it in front of his face as he headed for the stairs.

Thunk. He bumped into someone. "Sorry," he mumbled and continued on his way, cracking his shin on a low table and clipping the edge of a chaise before finally finding the stairs and nearly taking a header.

Flynn tromped down one level and dropped the empty box in a storage room near the galley. Then he made his way to the luxurious black marble men's room next to the cocktail lounge. He hid in a toilet stall with gold-plated fittings, and pulled up the video and sound from the GoPro on his iPhone. He still didn't understand a word, but at least he could send it to the cloud.

The door to the men's room opened. Flynn fumbled to mute his phone as someone entered, their footsteps nearly silent. Flynn gingerly and quietly locked the toilet stall and listened.

And waited.

The door rattled as someone tried to open it. Seconds later, two small hands grabbed the top of the stall and a face rose up over the edge. A face with two angry eyes.

Caitlyn Valentine's eyes.

CHAPTER TWENTY-FIVE

The Fancy *was one of the Golden Age of Piracy's most feared ships. The cannons on the 46-gun galleon launched explosive balls, iron bars, chain shots, and grapeshot to maim men and rip apart rigging. They would capture enemy vessels with grapple hooks and lob stink pots to cause panic and confusion as they boarded with cutlasses, blunderbusses, pistols, and daggers. Henry Avery and his crew took on much larger ships with much greater firepower by outmaneuvering and outsmarting them. His most notable capture was the Ganj-i-Sawai, a 62-gun treasure ship belonging to India's Grand Mogul. The fate of the* Fancy *is unknown, though it is rumored that Avery gave her to the governor of Nassau as a bribe to escape capture.*

Caitlyn knew as soon as she heard the word *sorry*. Ivanov's entire crew was Russian. Some of them spoke English, but the idiot who bumped into her clearly wasn't part of Ivanov's crew. He put on a fake Russian accent over his phony British accent and when she recognized the voice her heart just about skidded to a stop.

Flynn.

What the hell?

He nearly took a header down the stairs with that stupid box. She glanced at Oleg, but he was busy with his guests. Caitlyn hurried after Flynn and followed him down the stairs and through the galley, into the cocktail lounge, and then the men's room.

When she opened the door, she heard conversation from the upper deck playing on a smartphone. Somehow Flynn had planted a bug. He muted the sound, but not before Caitlyn figured out what stall he was hiding in. She tried the door. It was locked. So, she grabbed the top, pulled herself up, and peeked over.

Flynn smiled up at her sheepishly. "Fancy meeting you here."

She wanted to scream, but she kept her voice low. "What the *hell* is wrong with you?"

"You do realize this is the men's room?"

"Open the door."

"Caitlyn…"

Quietly furious. "*Open the goddamn door.*"

Flynn opened the toilet stall and tried to step out, but Caitlyn shoved him back in. He stumbled into the toilet as she closed and latched the door behind herself. "I thought I told you to stay away from me."

"I was worried."

"I told you I was fine."

"Oleg is using you. Manipulating you."

"Do you really think I'd let that happen? That I'm that weak? That I'm *that* stupid?"

"He sent someone to kill me."

"Who?"

"They had a mask, so I don't know *exactly* who, but—"

"Jesus Christ! Do you have any idea how many enemies you have? Because I don't! I've lost count of how many people you've pissed off. And how the hell did you get on this yacht? *Oh, shit.* It was Anya, wasn't it? That whole big scene was just a distraction to get you on board."

"Oleg's plotting something."

"Of course, he's plotting something."

"And she wants me to stop him from doing whatever it is…he's doing."

"What he's *doing* is none of your goddamn business," Caitlyn hissed.

"How is it not my business when someone I care about gets their mind twisted and turned against everything they ever believed in?"

"What are you talking about?"

"You! I'm talking about you. Do you know who those men are who just arrived by helicopter?"

"Yes."

"Do you know what they're planning?"

"No."

"Don't you want to know?"

"*Yes!*" Caitlyn fought to get her anger under control and lower her voice. "That's why I'm here, you idiot!"

Flynn looked confused. "But you said you left the CIA. You said—"

"I lied to you."

"Why?"

"To get rid of you."

"Why?"

"*So you wouldn't blow my fucking cover!*" she shout-whispered.

Flynn looked wounded. "You seem upset."

"No shit."

"So, you're…?"

"*Undercover.*"

Flynn nodded, but he still seemed befuddled. "Oh."

"Oh?" Caitlyn wanted to slap him. "*Oh!*"

"I thought—"

"I know."

"I only wanted to—"

"*I know.*"

Flynn sat down on the toilet seat. He looked defeated. "So, you're not sleeping with him?"

She closed her eyes tight and balled her hands into fists. "*No!* He wants to sleep with me. He keeps trying to. But I keep putting him off even while I string him along. It's a tricky balancing act. He needs to believe he has a chance. That I'm just playing hard to get. Men like him are used to easy conquests. I'm a challenge to him and I think he likes that."

The door to the men's room opened and Caitlyn sat herself on Flynn's lap. She lifted her feet as someone wandered in. A zipper was unzipped and the man at the urinal sighed with relief, then farted. It started on a high note and descended down the scale, staccato like a machine-gun until it finally petered out. Caitlyn looked at Flynn and nearly burst out laughing. He clamped her hand over her mouth and grimaced to stifle his own snicker. That only made her want to laugh harder. Both their shoulders shook as they struggled to keep their laughter from escaping.

The man washed his hands while whistling tunelessly. He let go with another squeaker that nearly set Flynn and Caitlyn off again.

And then he left the men's room.

Caitlyn pulled Flynn's hand off her mouth and whispered, "This isn't funny."

"It's a little funny."

"Listen to me. You need to lay low. Find somewhere to hide."

"There's a place in the wine cellar."

"Good. Get yourself out of view and stay put until we get back to shore. I'll sneak you out once we get there and make sure no one sees you."

Flynn started to say something, but then thought better of it. "Fine."

"Don't look at me like that."

"Like what?"

"Like a sad, little puppy."

"I just think—"

"Stop. Enough with the thinking. Your thinker isn't working. Please. Just do what I'm asking."

Flynn sighed. "Fine."

"Stay put and I'll make sure the coast is clear." Caitlyn left the stall and opened the men's room door. The cocktail lounge was deserted. "Okay. Come on."

Flynn followed her outside. She glanced back and noticed his fake mustache tilted off-kilter. She quickly straightened it and sent him on his way. He looked back once. She pointed forward to indicate he needed to keep moving. A deflated Flynn made his way to a staircase that led to the lower levels.

She returned topside to the party patio with the wet bar. The hackers continued to drink and get high on edibles and awkwardly flirt. As if those working girls were seduced by charm and not cold hard cash. One of the young Russian models sat in Oleg's lap and he unceremoniously pushed her off when Caitlyn returned.

Oleg's cheeks were flushed, and his eyes were bloodshot from one too many tropical cocktails. "Where were you?"

"I had to visit the ladies' room."

"You left me alone here, totally unguarded."

Caitlyn motioned to the two burly security guards in black slacks and Polo shirts, each wearing a bullpup submachine gun on a sling. "Hardly alone."

"But they don't look nearly as good as you do in a bikini."

"Depends on your point of view."

Oleg smirked. "I think you need a drink."

"You know I don't drink on duty."

"Consider yourself off-duty." Oleg shouted to the attractive female bartender. "Katya! Make Caitlyn a Zombie."

"No, thank you, Katya!"

"You want something else? A Singapore Sling? A Slow Comfortable Screw?" Oleg bounced his eyebrows.

"I'd rather have a Margarita. On the rocks. No salt."

"You heard the lady!" Oleg smiled. "We need to loosen you up."

"I'm as loose as I need to be."

Oleg motioned to the working girls giggling and flirting with the hackers. "Not as loose as these young ladies."

"I'm not in the same business."

"I pay you for your services, don't I?"

"Not *those* services."

Oleg stepped closer. Caitlyn stood her ground. She wanted to hold him off, but not put him off. He tried to look contrite. "I don't mean to offend," Oleg said.

"You could have fooled me."

"I just want to get to know you better."

"Clearly."

The bartender handed Caitlyn her Margarita. She took a sip and glanced at the stairway leading down below, hoping against hope that Flynn wouldn't show his stupid face again.

CHAPTER TWENTY-SIX

Caitlyn marveled at the extravagant spread in the dining room: seared foie gras, Dungeness crab, Wagyu filets, Muscovy duck breast with smoked duck sausage, Dom Perignon. Oleg clearly wanted to impress these nerds. He insisted Caitlyn sit beside him and kept plying her with champagne. But she stopped after two glasses and dribbled the rest on the floor when no one was looking.

She hoped they might discuss his mysterious plan, but no one talked business. The hackers were all paired with hookers, and Oleg kept his hand on Caitlyn's knee. She wanted to break his fingers, but also wanted to keep him talking.

Not screaming.

"What time's the meeting tomorrow?" she asked as casually as she could.

"10 a.m. But enough with the questions. Tonight's not about work. It's about fun. And you are off duty. So do me a favor and have some goddamn fun!"

He filled her empty glass with champagne and waited for her to drink it. Finally, she complied. He grinned and topped off her glass again.

Then he raised his and made a toast. "Everyone! Raise your glasses!" He looked around and waited until everyone had lifted their glass. "To us! To the future. To the new masters of the universe! Soon the leaders of the world will kneel before us!"

After dessert, the hackers and their lady friends retired to their cabins.

Oleg squeezed Caitlyn's leg. "I'm a little hammered."

"I noticed."

"Would you escort me back to my cabin?"

"Really?"

"Just to the door. I'll be a perfect gentleman. I promise." Both burly bodyguards rolled their eyes as Oleg stood and nearly toppled over. He lurched forward and grabbed Caitlyn's arm to steady himself. She escorted him out of the dining room and down a corridor to the master cabin. The owner's cabin. The largest one on the ship.

He fumbled with his keycard and dropped it on the floor. She picked it up and swiped it. Oleg pushed open the door. He stumbled in, dragging her after him. "Have a drink with me."

"I think you've had enough."

Large windows lined both sides of the cabin, revealing a dark moonlit sea. Oleg flicked a wall switch, lighting up the room and turning the windows into mirrors. The room had to be ten times the size of her cabin. The opulent décor combined modern touches like recessed lighting with art deco antiques and impressionist paintings. Oleg half-fell, half-sat on the edge of a sprawling king-sized bed.

"Help me with my shoes," he slurred.

"What are you? Five?"

"Don't be like that." He lifted his foot.

Caitlyn sighed and grabbed the Dolce and Gabbana loafer and pulled. First one. Then the other.

"Thank you." He reached for her hand. "Now pull me up."

Caitlyn grabbed him by the wrist and pulled him to his feet. He smiled and staggered to a small wet bar. "You ever try Yamakazi 25-year-old Single Malt? It's twenty thousand pounds a bottle."

"Pricey."

"The best always costs more. It's supply and demand. How else do you determine worth?" He poured two whiskeys, sloshing some. He handed one to Caitlyn.

She licked the side of the glass to stop it from dripping.

"So?"

"It's okay."

"Do you think it's worth twenty thousand a bottle?"

"Not to me."

"That's because you don't understand capitalism. It is worth whatever people will pay for it. That's how worth is determined. That's the genius of the free enterprise system. It's human nature to want what you don't have. To have more. To have better. It is why communism failed. A noble experiment, but people are not noble. They are selfish and capitalism understands that." Oleg leaned closer and whispered in Caitlyn's ear. "And so do I."

"Don't you have an important meeting in the morning?"

"I do indeed. Very important."

"Are you going to tell me what it's about?"

"Capitalism." Oleg grinned.

"So, your business partners are capitalists too?"

"Of course."

"Not outlaws?"

"Outlaws are the purest capitalists. Outlaws run every major multinational corporation in the world. They take what they want. They crush their competition. And they only stop when someone stops them. Andrew Carnegie, John D. Rockefeller, Bill Gates, Jeff Bezos – all robber barons. All outlaws."

"So, what are you and your outlaw friends up to?"

"I would tell you, but I'm not sure I can trust you."

Caitlyn grinned. "You already trust me with your life." Caitlyn finished the rest of her drink and set down the glass.

Oleg drained his as well and set his glass next to Caitlyn's. "Trusting you with my life is one thing. Trusting you with my money?" He took her hand in his. "I don't know you well enough."

"You think your money is more valuable than your life?"

"Without it I have no life." Oleg gently pulled Caitlyn over to the bed. She didn't resist. Not yet. He sat and she sat next to him. "Look how beautiful you are."

"I'm not bad, but I'm hardly beautiful. I'm not even the most beautiful woman on this yacht."

"Yes, they are beautiful, but not the way you are. I read about you last year. Saw you on the news. Watched you interviewed on TV. So strong. So confident. So brilliant. So tough. The things you've done. What you did to survive? You are a badass."

She smiled at that. "Does this line of bullshit usually work for you?"

"The CIA fucked you over and Putin wants to fuck me. He'll murder me and take everything I have…like so many others. But with your knowledge of the CIA and my knowledge of the FSB and the GRU, we will be unstoppable. We will make ourselves untouchable. Richer than anyone on Earth. And with money comes power."

"What about your wife? How does she fit into all this?"

"My wife and I were so young when we married. Such a beauty. So innocent. So naïve. Twenty-five years we've been together."

"Good for you."

"Good for me? Hardly. It's been a fucking nightmare."

"Divorce her then."

"No. She is bound to me, and I cannot stand the idea of her being with another man."

"You don't seem to have a problem being with other women."

"I admit it's a bit of a double standard, but so what? You said it yourself. I'm an outlaw. A pirate. I live by my own rules."

"Maybe that's why she resents you."

"Of course, that's why she resents me. She doesn't understand me. Doesn't *want* to understand me. Wants nothing to do with me. Sometimes I think she hates me."

"Maybe you just don't spend enough time together."

"You don't think twenty-five fucking years is enough time?"

"You know what I mean."

"You see me for who I am. You understand men like me and the life I lead. How ruthless I need to be. You are not spoiled or pampered or weak. You are strong. You are ruthless. And together we would make an unbeatable team."

Caitlyn smirked. "Are you asking me to marry you?"

Oleg laughed. "No. One unhappy wife is more than enough. I'm asking you to be my partner. My protector. My adviser. My inamorata. My wife used to be those things for me…but no longer."

"Your wife already resents me."

"For no good reason. Let's give her one."

"I just think this might complicate things."

"You want me to trust you? To bring you in? Make you a part of everything? Then you need to show me I can trust you."

"By spending the night with you?"

"By opening yourself up to me."

"I don't want to make an enemy of your wife."

"She's already your enemy, and if we are together and she continues to be an issue, I give you my permission to do what you need to."

"What are you saying?"

"You know what I'm saying." Oleg reached over to the nightstand, picked up a small remote control and pushed a button. The curtains on all the windows closed. He pushed another button and the lights dimmed. A third button and a blazing fire appeared in the fireplace. A fourth button brought the music. Duran Duran singing Bob Dylan's *Lay Lady Lay*.

Oleg leaned closer and kissed her. Caitlyn wanted to pull away, but she didn't. "You're drunk."

"What if I am?"

"I'd rather not do this when you're drunk."

"I understand your hesitation. You're a woman who doesn't like giving up her power. But this is not you surrendering." He embraced her, his cheek next to hers, his chin on her shoulder. "This is us coming together. This is—*What the hell?*"

Caitlyn turned to see what caught Oleg's attention.

A face peered in the window between a tiny gap in the curtains.

Flynn.

"*Svoloch!*" Oleg shouted and leaped to his feet. He snatched up the remote control and hit a fifth button. An alarm screamed. The door burst open. The two burly bodyguards rushed inside. Oleg pointed at the window, but Flynn's face was no longer there. "*Flynn!* He's on the ship! Find him!" As the burly guards hurried out, Oleg glared at Caitlyn. "Did you know?"

"What?"

"That he was *here*!"

"Of course not!"

"How is it possible? How could he—Oh, shit. *Shit!*"

"What?"

"Anya! It was *Anya!*"

"I'll find him!"

"Find him and kill him!" Oleg pointed at the door. "Go! *Go!*"

CHAPTER TWENTY-SEVEN

Nick Woodman initially funded GoPro by selling beaded belts from the back of his VW bus. He dubbed the bus The Biscuit. *It was stolen after he made his first deal in 2004. He designed the GoPro to capture surfers and surfing, which is why the housing has always been waterproof. Whenever an extreme athlete takes a death-defying risk, a GoPro often goes along for the ride. From base jumping to heli-skiing to ice climbing to cave diving to wing walking. A skydiver's GoPro once survived a 12,500-foot drop after falling off a helmet.*

Flynn fully intended to stay hidden in the hold, but the GoPro worried him. *What if someone found it?* Flynn's voice was at the start of the recording, documenting the time and the place. They may not rewind that far, but what if they did and recognized his distinctive accent? It wouldn't just expose him, but Caitlyn as well. Better safe than sorry, he decided.

Still in disguise, he crept from the hold and made his way to the patio deck on the stern. Not many crewmen were about. Most had retired for the night. He assumed that the majority of Ivanov's security were stationed on the bridge and top deck. The GoPro was where he left it, hidden in that potted plant.

He headed back the way he came but heard someone coming up the stairs from below. Flynn quickly turned on his heel and decided to do a lap around the upper deck before finding his way back down. He walked crisply, with confidence. Just another crew member on patrol.

Light leaked through curtains covering cabin windows. He couldn't help but glance into each cabin as he passed. Most of the curtains didn't close completely, so there was always a gap. He saw one hacker's large hairy belly as his date for the night struggled to pull off his shirt. Another hacker lay naked and face down on the bed. His rented girlfriend, still in her lingerie, sat astride his butt and massaged his back.

Flynn came upon a larger set of windows and glanced through a wider gap and saw something that brought him to a complete halt.

Caitlyn sat on a huge bed next to Oleg Ivanov. Both their backs were to Flynn, but he could see his hand on her knee. He held back her hair and whispered some sweet nothing into her ear. Caitlyn nodded and smiled. He lifted her chin…and kissed her.

Flynn pressed his face into the glass, stunned that Caitlyn would give herself over so easily, so willingly. Was she enticing Ivanov? Seducing him the same way Flynn had seduced so many beautiful female enemy agents in his time? Or was Flynn the one she was lying to? Setting him up. Betraying *him*?

Ivanov put his arms around Caitlyn and pulled her close, his cheek against hers, his chin on her shoulder, his eyes facing Flynn. Shock replaced bliss as he let Caitlyn go and pointed at the window.

Bloody hell!

Ivanov lunged for something on the nightstand. An alarm screamed. An earsplitting klaxon. Flynn raced back to the stairs. The ship's PA system came alive with a boatswain's whistle and then someone shouted orders in Russian. Only one word wasn't incomprehensible.

Flynn.

He drew his HK Mark 23 with the suppressor, rounded a corner and slammed into two sentries. One grabbed Flynn's right arm and twisted the weapon out of his hand. It clattered to the deck. Flynn head-butted him, staggering him back. The other raised his P90. Flynn executed a perfect crescent kick, slapping the submachine gun into the temple of the guard he head-butted. That guard went down as the gun fired, sending ricochets everywhere. One nicked Flynn's ear. Another pierced the boot of the man wielding the weapon.

As the sentry fell, the other guard, the one on the ground, raised his own weapon and aimed it at Flynn. Just as he fired, Flynn vaulted over the railing, dropping twenty feet to the main deck below. Flynn landed hard, falling on his shoulder, but was too full of adrenaline to register the pain.

With the klaxon still screaming, Flynn found his way to the stairway and hurried to the lower deck. Crew members spilled out of their quarters and raced for the stairs. Since Flynn was dressed like one of them, no one seemed to notice him. He finally reached the lower deck and from there, made his way to where he entered the ship.

The tender bay.

The *Fancy* had three tenders and three Jet Skis. The tender currently on the hydraulic lift was the largest. A ten-meter-long Delphia. It had the same art deco décor as the *Fancy* and room for eight passengers.

To escape, Flynn needed to open the exterior door and lower the craft with the hydraulic lift. He scurried around, looking for some kind of console or control panel. The klaxon continued to scream.

"*Behind you on the wall!*" Caitlyn shouted and hurried past him and punched some buttons on a panel. Machinery groaned, the hydraulic hatch opened, and cool evening air filled the tender bay. Flynn could tell she was irritated with him. Her angry tone confirmed it as she shouted over the klaxon. "*What the hell did I say to you?*"

"I'm sorry. I was worried about the GoPro."

"*What?*"

Flynn patted his jacket. "Don't worry. I got it."

"Forget the goddamn GoPro! If they find you, they will kill you!"

"I saw you."

"Saw me what?"

"Kiss him." Outraged. "You *kissed* him."

"He kissed *me*."

"Why were you sitting on his bed?"

"Why aren't you in the tender? Get in the goddamn tender!"

The klaxon suddenly stopped screaming, though his ears continued to ring. Flynn found the sudden quiet unsettling. Caitlyn grabbed him by the arm. "*Would you please get in the goddamn tender!*"

"So, you *did* know he was here," Ivanov shouted. Flynn spun around. Oleg and two burly guards stood in the tender bay. Ivanov aimed an accusatory finger at Caitlyn. "And now you're helping him escape!"

"He is mentally ill," Caitlyn cried. "He doesn't know what he's doing!"

"*Stop*." Oleg shook his head. "*Stop lying to me.*"

"Yes, I *knew* he was onboard. Your wife helped sneak him on. But he is not in his right mind. He is very easily manipulated, especially by a beautiful woman pretending to be a damsel in distress. This was Anya's doing! Not mine!"

Caitlyn was apparently trying to salvage the situation by falling back on Flynn's mental patient cover story. She likely hoped to keep him alive and maintain her cover. But Flynn wasn't sure it was possible at this point.

Oleg did not look convinced. "What are you asking me to do? Let him go?"

"I promise he isn't a threat to you."

"Really? Because I believe my wife sent him here to kill me."

"If I wanted to kill you, you would be dead," Flynn said.

"James, I'm begging you," Caitlyn pleaded. "Let me handle this."

Flynn motioned as if to say *fine, go ahead*. She took a step towards Ivanov. "He is obsessed with me, but he is no danger to you. I will put him on a plane back to L.A. and you will never see him again."

Ivanov smiled sadly. "You know, I didn't completely trust you, but I was beginning to *begin* to. I meant what I said to you, about partnering with you." Ivanov put his hand on the massive shoulder of the larger of the two guards flanking him. A nasty scar cut across the edge of his mouth and bisected his cheek. His gray eyes were empty of anything but fury. "Kalishnik here was sent to assassinate me. Luckily, Putin is a cheap bastard and I'm a far more generous employer. I put Kalishnik on my payroll. He used to be my right hand. But when I hired you, I demoted him and he resented that. Resented you. Maybe resented me. But he likes what I pay him, so, he stayed. Isn't that right, Kalishnik?"

Kalishnik nodded with no expression.

"I think he hoped I would eventually tire of you and restore him to his former position. After all, he's a very capable man. He boxed in the Olympics and trained with Spetsnaz, becoming an elite killer for GRU unit 29155. Look at him. He is hard as nails. But even harder on the eyes. Which is why I hired you. Prove to me you're more than a pretty face, Miss Valentine. Put Mr. Flynn out of his misery."

Caitlyn's voice went up an octave. "You want me to shoot him?"

"Please. Show me I can trust you. Kill Mr. Flynn and I'll know that everything you told me is true. End his suffering. It would be a kindness."

Caitlyn didn't move. She stood there, frozen.

"Or don't shoot him and Kalishnik will shoot you both. Up to you."

Caitlyn drew her SIG Sauer P228. She looked at Flynn and pointed it at his chest. Center mass. Flynn watched a dozen different emotions flicker across her eyes. *Is she actually considering it? Is she stalling for time?* The smart thing would be to shoot him and prove her trustworthiness.

Flynn had foolishly blown her cover. Of course, he thought she was in danger, but in his attempt to save her, he had put her in much worse jeopardy. To save herself, she'd have to shoot him. Flynn could see no other course of action. There would be very little pain. One shot in the brain. He closed his eyes and braced himself for the end.

The Sig barked twice. Flynn heard a grunt. A shout. Yet still he stood. He opened his eyes. One guard lay on the ground and the one called Kalishnik pushed Ivanov behind cover. Caitlyn fired at them again. "Flynn! *Get in the fucking tender!*"

Flynn scrambled into the tender as Caitlyn sprinted for the control panel. She hit some buttons. Machinery groaned as the mechanism lowered into the water.

Flynn motioned for her to join him. "Come on!"

Caitlyn hurried for the tender, but a gun boomed. Pain widened her eyes. She grabbed her leg, limped for two steps, and fell.

Flynn's tender splashed in the water and automatically detached. He couldn't see Caitlyn, but Oleg and Kalishnik appeared in the open hatch, both holding P90s. They opened fire. Flynn hit the deck. Bullets splintered wood and plastic, and ricocheted off metal as he crawled to the center console, reached up, and pushed the throttle. The twin engines roared, creating a giant rooster tail as the bow rose out of the water. The tender took off and Flynn kept low as bullets continued to pepper the boat.

The *Fancy* turned to chase him. Oleg clearly intended to run the tender down and splinter it into a thousand burning pieces of wreckage. It would take time for the mega yacht to make the turn, but once it did Flynn knew he couldn't outrun it. And then he saw something shooting across the sky with a trail of smoke. The RPG hit the water and exploded, splashing a spray of saltwater into the air. Another RPG came rushing right at him. That one landed just behind the tender. The muffled boom created a bowl-shaped spray of water. As yet another one shot across the sky, Flynn turned the wheel, steering in a serpentine fashion, hoping to make himself a harder target.

An RPG exploded into the sea to his left. The huge splash soaked him with saltwater. Glancing back, three jet skis dashed after him in pursuit, each with a driver and a machine gunner in the back. The cack-cack-cack of three P90s filled the air. They roared forward, skipping over the swell like rocks skipping across a pond. That made firing with any accuracy a problem. But soon they'd be close enough to shoot him point blank.

And Flynn had no weapon.

Bloody hell!

Caitlyn was wounded, but probably alive, and now their prisoner. Ivanov would torture her. Likely for days. Flynn couldn't just leave her. He had to do something.

He had to try.

Flynn turned the wheel hard. The tender tilted to an alarming degree. He eased up, making a wider turn. If he wasn't careful, he could flip it. That maneuver surprised the attackers on the Jet Skis. Especially the one closest, who tried to steer out of the way before crashing into the side of the tender. The driver flew ass-over-teakettle and slammed into Flynn. The one with the P90 landed in the drink.

The driver pulled a sidearm. Flynn grabbed his wrist and wrestled for it. With his hand off the wheel and the tender bouncing on the swell, neither one could stay on their feet. They fell to the deck and the driver lost his weapon. He kicked Flynn in the face and crawled for his gun. Getting his hands on it, he stood up to shoot. Flynn head-butted him in the gut, knocking him right off the boat.

Bullets pinged and hit the tender as Flynn took control of the wheel and throttle. He accelerated back towards the *Fancy*, and the last two Jet Skis followed.

A rocket-propelled grenade arched across the sky, heading right for him. Flynn ducked as it whooshed over his head, just about parting his hair. It hit one of the pursuing Jet Skis and it exploded in a ball of fire.

The roar of the last Jet Ski screamed through the lingering smoke of the explosion. The machine gunner fired. Flynn fell to his knees. Bullets tore up the tender. He rooted through an equipment box for something to fight back with and closed his fingers around what he was looking for.

A flare gun.

He loaded it and popped up to see the Jet Ski right beside the tender. The machine gunner grinned until Flynn fired the flare gun. The red-hot flare hit the machine gunner square in the chest. He flipped off backwards as the Jet Ski crashed into the tender, nearly sending the driver into the sea.

But he held on.

Another RPG exploded just off the tender's bow. The *Fancy* loomed closer and Ivanov's men, lined up on the prow, fired assault weapons. Flynn flattened himself on the deck. Bullets tore up the console and punctured the spare gas tanks, setting the craft aflame.

The Jet Ski ran parallel with the tender. Flynn sprang to his feet and jumped, tackling the driver as the tender burst into flames. The Jet Ski came to a bobbing stop, but the tender kept going.

Flynn struggled in the sea with the driver as both tried to climb aboard the tiny watercraft. A well-placed elbow in the face knocked the driver back into the drink. Flynn climbed aboard.

He twisted the throttle handle and chased after the now-flaming husk of the tender as it roared towards the *Fancy* at high speed.

Whoever piloted the mega yacht tried to maneuver out of the path of the burning tender. But a ship that size can't turn on a dime. Ivanov's men fired AKs and P90s and RPGs in a desperate attempt to blow the flaming craft out of the water.

But it just kept coming.

The crew scrambled every which way as the tender slammed into the *Fancy* in the worst place possible. The fuel storage tanks. A massive explosion rocked the mega yacht, and the water surrounding it burned with leaking diesel fuel.

As the fire had yet to reach the swim platform on the stern, Flynn tied the Jet Ski to a ladder and made his way up. The stench of melted plastic, fuel, and other toxic chemicals assaulted Flynn as he climbed aboard. He hurried up to the main deck and found pandemonium. The crew ran this way and that. People jumped off the main deck and splashed into the sea. They swam for crowded tenders and inflatable life rafts. No one paid any attention to Flynn.

"Caitlyn!" he screamed. "*Caitlyn!*"

He fought his way forward past fleeing crew and security, and pushed and struggled to reach the upper deck. Fires blazed everywhere and small explosions rocked the sinking mega yacht. As Flynn climbed higher, he heard the beating blades of a helicopter. He followed the sound to the helipad. Ivanov and his thugs helped the hackers into the Eurocopter. Kalishnik had Caitlyn. She fought as he dragged her on board.

A mob of frightened crew members clamored to climb on the copter, but Ivanov's security men beat them back with their boots and the butts of their guns. Even the three beautiful blondes weren't allowed on. They begged and screamed in Russian, and one tried to climb aboard, but Kalishnik kicked her off. She tumbled backwards and hit the deck hard, flat on her keister.

As the helicopter lifted off, it generated a mini windstorm. Flynn struggled to shove his way forward, his hair whipped by the wind. Ivanov's private chef held on to one of the skids. He continued to hang on as the helicopter climbed.

The Eurocopter turned and headed over the sea. The downwash created all kinds of chop and nearly capsized one of the inflatable life rafts. The chef lost his grip and fell. He plunged at least forty feet before hitting the choppy water. Luckily, someone on a lifeboat threw him a line.

Flynn stood on the burning deck and watched the helicopter soar away. Soon, the three Russian blondes joined him, still in their scanty lingerie, their faces messy with melted mascara and frightened tears.

CHAPTER TWENTY-EIGHT

Clayton Jacobson II grew up in Southern California and attended Manual Arts High School and L.A. City College. Though he studied physics and engineering, he spent most of his time street racing and working as a car mechanic. His strong interest in aviation led him to the Marine Corps reserve, where he learned drafting and jet engine technology. He raced motorcycles in the Mojave desert. One day, after totaling a bike, he took a break for a beer and lamented that there wasn't a way to experience the exhilaration and excitement of a motorcycle without the danger of wiping out at high speed. That same night, he sketched his "motorcycle for the water." By the mid-60s, Jacobson quit his job in finance to develop his concept full time. He finished the prototype in 1965. The first model, the Sea-Doo, was produced from 1968 to 1970. In 1986, he consulted with the Yamaha Motor Company to collaborate on the Yamaha Super Jet. Today they're so popular, the companies can't keep up with the demand. Dealers regularly sell out every year.

Two people could fit comfortably on a Yamaha FZR Jet Ski. Three made for a tight fit. Four made it wobbly and easier to capsize. Luckily, the three Russian blondes were very petite. One held tight to Flynn. The others held tight to each other, all scooched together, bosoms to back, as Flynn twisted the throttle.

Flynn headed due north away from the burning *Fancy*. At least, what he thought was north. But after an hour of bouncing, spine-shaking, teeth-rattling travel, Flynn wondered if he was heading in the right direction. The lady squished against Flynn tapped him on the shoulder and pointed out that the digital gas gauge hovered just above empty. Ten seconds after that the Jet Ski coughed, sputtered, and died.

Flynn couldn't see anything but water in every direction. The ladies started whining and complaining and castigating him in Russian. Flynn had no answer for them. Without forward momentum, any large wave could upend them. They'd all be in the drink and Flynn was pretty sure that the implants the ladies sported wouldn't work very long as flotation devices. He'd been in tight spots before, but nothing quite like this.

One of the ladies spotted a fin flashing in the water and shrieked. They all joined in, pointing and screaming.

"Bozhe moy! Akula!"

"My sobirayemsya umeret!"

"Nyet! Nyet! Nyet! Jaws!"

A shark surfaced and Flynn locked eyes with it. He knew that sharks, like dogs, reacted to assertiveness. Apex predators expected their prey to panic and run or swim away. Flynn stared back and showed no fear. The shark looked away and then turned away, diving back down into the depths.

Flynn caught sight of something on the horizon. He squinted into the sun. *Is that a boat?* The blondes saw it as well. They all started screaming and waving their arms, nearly flipping the Jet Ski.

"Zdes'! Zdes'!"

"Pomoshch'!"

"Pomogi nam!"

"Ladies! Please! Please keep your arm movements to a minimum! We don't want to capsize."

As the watercraft drew closer, Flynn worried that if they sped by without stopping, their wake would surely topple them. But then Flynn recognized a familiar figure on the bow. She wore white capris and a red off-the-shoulder crop top that left nothing to the imagination. Anya's red hair was tied back and she greeted Flynn with a delighted smile.

"James! I see you found some new friends."

Flynn tossed the line to First Mate Lola, and she tied the Ski Jet to a cleat. Lola then helped the sunburned blondes onto the deck of the Sunseeker Superhawk.

Anya took Flynn's hand and pulled him aboard. "The *Fancy* is all over the news."

"Really?"

"The navy is out there rescuing the crew and, so far, they haven't found my husband. He wouldn't happen to be dead, would he?"

"The last time I saw him he was very much alive."

Disappointment turned Anya's smile upside down. "Then he will be very irritated with you for blowing up his boat."

"Technically, he blew up his own boat."

"Did he escape on a tender?"

"He flew off in a helicopter, along with a handful of lackeys, a number of guests, and Caitlyn."

"Caitlyn went with him?"

"Against her will after one of them shot her in the leg."

"Why'd they do *that*?"

"She was trying to protect me."

Lola handed Flynn a towel and a bottle of water. "Thank you, Lola. I'm glad to see you and the captain are still in Mrs. Ivanov's employ."

Anya shrugged. "How could I blame them for taking Oleg's bribe? Besides, I knew the *mudak* would never let me on board. The idea was for *you* to get on. Not me."

"So, how did you find us?"

"When the navy told me they had yet to locate you, I figured you were either dead or heading in the wrong direction."

"Well, I'm clearly not dead."

"Exactly."

"Though I am a bit dehydrated."

The three blondes sat shivering with towels around their shoulders and bottles of water in their hands.

Flynn twisted open his water and took a long, deep swig. He sat on a bench next to Anya and chugged down the rest of his bottle, the plastic crackling from the suction.

Anya handed him another bottle. "Did you find out what Oleg is up to?"

"I have a vague idea, but no specifics. Do you have any idea where he might be?"

Anya ignited her vape and took a puff. "London would be my guess. Why? Are you going to try to kill him before he kills you?"

"I told you. I don't kill willy-nilly."

"There's nothing willy-nilly about defending yourself. You blew up his favorite boat. He will send men to kill you until you are dead. He also will send men to kill me."

"You?"

"He will know that I am the one who snuck you aboard."

"So, I also put *you* in danger?"

"Me *and* your lady love."

"She is *not* my lady love."

"Well, whoever she is to you…there's only one way to save her."

Flynn held Anya's unflinching gaze. Finally, he nodded. "London it is then."

■　■　■

Sancho sat locked in a closet. Ohana didn't bother tying him up because where would he go? They waited for Flynn's return and kept him as a hostage. A bargaining chip. Once Flynn arrived, Sancho knew Ohana would kill them both.

The closet door opened and the outside light blinded him. Avi stood poised with a pen and handed him a room service menu. "What do you want for lunch?"

Sancho perused the menu. "Well...I had the black truffle pizza yesterday and the lobster roll the day before."

"How was the pizza?

"Not bad."

"The grilled sea bass is pretty good," Avi opined.

Sancho handed him back the menu. "Can I just get a burger?"

"They have a cheeseburger with somerset brie, truffle mayonnaise, and yuzu pickles."

"What's a yuzu pickle?

"Fuck if I know."

"Fine. Get me that. But hold the yuzu pickles."

Avi nodded and closed the door, plunging Sancho back into darkness.

■　■　■

Flynn stood naked in the shower as six powerful water jets pummeled his aching body. The violent events of the last few days left him covered in bruises and painful muscle strains. The large rainfall showerhead above didn't just dribble hot water on his head, but cascaded down like a tropical downpour. Hot water hit him from all directions as billowing steam filled the stall. Every muscle in his body relaxed, and he let go with an audible, "Ohhhhh."

Flynn couldn't remember the last time he felt this relaxed. He heard the door to the marble bathroom open. A fuzzy silhouette appeared in the steamy glass. *Anya making another play?* The thought of fending her off again exhausted him. "I'm flattered, darling, but completely knackered. Perhaps we shouldn't complicate our relationship."

Flynn used his hand to wipe away the condensation and saw the barrel of a gun with a silencer on the end leveled at his head. He dropped to his knees as the shooter shot, shattering the tempered safety glass into a million pieces.

Flynn launched himself forward, driving his head into his assailant's solar plexus. The man *oofed* as Flynn clamped onto his wrist. More shots shattered marble and glass, yet Flynn remained unscathed.

As his attacker tried to push back, Flynn drove his knee into the man's nether regions. He crumpled. Flynn then caught his gun hand, twisted, and disarmed the attacker. The weapon clattered across the marble floor.

The killer pulled a butterfly knife as Flynn grabbed a squeeze bottle of body wash and squirted it into his assailant's eyes. The hitman slashed at Flynn blindly. Flynn evaded, blocking his arm, squirting the body wash into the man's mouth. Blind and spitting, he slashed again, missing and hitting his hand on the frame of the shower door.

Flynn hit his attacker with an uppercut, and he stumbled back, slipping on the soapy water. He danced in place like a cartoon cat before falling back and smacking his head on the marble sink. Bleeding profusely, the man pulled himself to his feet and searched for his knife. He found it stuck between his own ribs. As he struggled to pull it out, he slipped on the soapy floor once more, and fell straight back, cracking his head on the side of the toilet. This time he didn't get up.

Flynn found the man's gun as a terrified scream carried into the shower. He followed the sound through the suite and found Kalishnik and a smaller man subduing Anya. She cursed at them in Russian until the smaller man zapped her with a stun gun. She collapsed to the floor. Kalishnik picked her up as if she weighed nothing and threw her over his shoulder.

And then they saw Flynn.

Dripping wet and totally naked, he pointed a gun at them. "Put her down and step away. Hands in the air." They did none of those things. Instead, they simply stood there and stared. "Just because I no longer have a license to kill doesn't mean I won't shoot you if I have to."

Kalishnik and his comrade traded a smirk.

An expandible baton smacked the gun out of Flynn's hand. He neglected to notice the other evildoer in the room. Kalishnik's smaller comrade now aimed a pistol at him.

Anya, still slung over Kalishnik's shoulder, kicked the comrade in the hand, knocking the shot wide.

"Run, James! *Run!*"

"*Ubey etoga idiota!*" Kalishnik shouted.

Flynn ran out onto the terrace, staying just ahead of the silenced gunfire. Clay pots exploded. Bullets whizzed by. With nowhere else to go, he vaulted over the balustrade and disappeared over the edge. He plummeted twenty-five feet and plunged into the infinity pool below. Chlorinated water splashed the bald, sixty-something man floating on an inflatable pool chair. He looked surprised, but not alarmed.

"Bonjour!" said the man. He lifted a cocktail from a cup holder and held it in the air. "Would you care for a Piña Colada?"

CHAPTER TWENTY-NINE

Kalishnik rushed to the edge and peered over the balustrade. An old, bald man in a floating pool chair looked up at him while sipping a cocktail.

No Flynn.

Police sirens wailed. Hotel security would arrive soon. This was the second time Kalishnik failed to end that lunatic's life. First in London, when that American tourist lady stabbed him in the head with a tiny fork. His shoulder still hurt from landing on that car. Now here.

Again.

He wouldn't fail a third time. He'd find him and end him, but that would have to wait. They needed to be gone before the authorities arrived.

Anya kicked and wriggled. Kalishnik shocked her with the stun gun. She stiffened and all the fight went out of her. He carried her out the door, smacking her head on the jamb as they hurried through. They went down the same way they came up—on the service elevator. Their rental van sat parked outside. Kalishnik slid into the backseat as another one of Ivanov's men drove. Anya awakened with a start on the way to the airport.

Once she assessed the situation, she didn't bother struggling. "Did you bring my belongings?"

"Nyet."

"You didn't bring my vape?"

"Nyet."

"What about my phone?"

"Nyet."

"Arsehole."

Kalishnik ignored her.

"What about Flynn? What happened to him?"

"Don't worry about him."

"I'm not. I'm worried about me. And you should worry about you. Oleg is trying to screw over Putin, and that will not end well for him. Or you. You know what happens when people don't pay what they owe. However, if we tell our dear leader what Oleg is up to, he will be very grateful. And if you eliminate Oleg, he will be even *more* grateful. I can assume Oleg's role and you can be my partner." She put her hand on Kalishnik's knee. "In everything."

Kalishnik hit her in the neck with the stun gun. She vibrated, stiffened, and went silent.

Kalishnik enjoyed the quiet.

■　■　■

Sancho banged on the closet door until one of Ohana's men finally opened it.

"What? *What?*"

"I have to pee."

"Again? *Ben zona!* All you do is pee!"

Sancho shielded his eyes as he stepped out of the closet, squinting into the light. Ohana's two men watched the flat screen TV while Ohana paced like a caged tiger. Flynn's fancy Connaught hotel suite looked like a frat house after a kegger. Empty bottles and cans covered every surface. They hadn't let the maid in for days.

Ohana caught Sancho staring, crossed the room in five steps and angrily slapped him in the face. "Where is he?"

"I don't know."

"Why's he paying for a room he's not even using?"

"Maybe because he's *crazy*."

"How come he hasn't contacted you?"

"Because he thinks I'm back in L.A."

"Try calling him again."

"The calls just go to voice mail."

"Try again."

"Can I pee first?"

"No." Ohana handed him his phone and Sancho called Flynn. He put it on speaker. After two rings and a pickup, they heard, "Your call has been forwarded to an automated voice messaging system. James Flynn is not available. The mailbox is full and cannot accept any messages at this time. Goodbye."

"Maybe his phone's dead," Sancho said. "Maybe he lost it."

"Maybe *he's* dead," Ohana said.

"Maybe." The possibility filled Sancho with worry. Flynn had a lot of enemies. *A lot.*

"I thought I'd be able to use you to lure him in. But if he's not even bothering to call, why do I even need you alive?"

"Dude, I am no threat to you."

"How can I let you go?"

"I will *not* call Interpol. I will *not* call the FBI. I don't need this shit. I got a kid. A wife. I just want to live my life."

"Put him back in the closet."

Sancho sighed. "I still need to pee." Ohana motioned to the bathroom and Sancho relieved himself. They then marched him back to the closet, but Sancho held onto the edge of the doorframe when they tried to push him back inside. "Come on, bro, I can't breathe in there. I get claustrophobic."

"You'd rather stay out here?"

"If you don't mind."

"Fine." Ohana turned to one of his men. "Tape him to a chair."

A wave of hopelessness swept over Sancho as Avi taped him to the chair and tore off one last piece of duct tape to put over Sancho's mouth.

"Come on, man. Don't. I got no reason to—"

Avi taped Sancho's mouth, shutting him up.

■ ■ ■

Flynn borrowed a white Hôtel de Paris bathrobe from the man whose infinity pool he landed in. His name was Dave, and he was visiting from Schenectedy. Flynn declined the offer of a Piña Colada.

Instead, he hurried back up to his own diamond suite to find it empty. Even the man in the marble bathroom was gone. Kalishnik and his men had cleaned up the blood and left no trace of themselves. Or Anya. Oleg didn't want her dead or she would be. Flynn was another matter. Oleg clearly wanted his head.

Hotel security arrived soon after. Apparently, a guest had complained about the noise. Flynn apologized for all the commotion and claimed he simply slipped in the shower. He could tell the head of hotel security didn't believe him, but the Hôtel de Paris, like the Connaught, avoided adverse publicity and prized discretion.

Flynn packed his things and took a cab to the airport. The British Airways flight from Nice to London took a little over two hours. An hour after that, he found himself in the elegant lobby of the Connaught.

A familiar voice called out. "James!"

Tammy Torkelson stood by the front desk and waved him over. Except for the halo neck brace, the black eye, the cast on her left leg, and the crutches, she seemed no worse for the wear.

Flynn crossed to Tammy, relieved to see she survived her mishap. "I was worried about you."

Tammy blushed. "Me? Really?"

"You fell off a moving train."

"Yeah, thanks for trying to pull me back in."

"Unsuccessfully."

"Sorry I had to use that stun gun on you, but that Russian, pardon my French, bitch, had you totally snookered."

"Excuse me?"

"That guy who attacked you at the hotel? I think she had something to do with that. You know who her husband is, don't you?"

"Did you follow us to the train?"

"Of course, I did. I sat next to a very nice Muslim lady who traded me one of her outfits for a bunch of traveler's checks."

"So, you were trying to *save me*?"

"Someone had to. I apologize if I overstepped, but I just thought, you know, better safe than sorry."

"Are you checking out?"

"Yup, I'm heading back home. This has been a marvelous adventure, but I have some serious decisions to make."

"What kinds of decisions?"

"Life decisions. I'm just not sure about the whole marriage thing. Warren and I have been together forever, and we don't have much in common anymore."

"I'm sure he loves you very much."

"Maybe. If he does, he sure doesn't show it much. But I'm no perfect wife either. You get busy with work, kids. It's tough to keep that fire alive."

"Did you know I was married once?"

Tammy shook her head. "I didn't."

"She was everything to me, and my enemies used my love for her against me. They killed her because I loved her. I can never let that happen again."

"I read everything there is to read about you, but I never saw anything about that."

"Because it's private. My private pain. Something I alone must live with."

"That's so sad."

"It's the life I've chosen. Recently, I considered leaving the service for the love of a good woman. She lives the same life I do. Takes the same risks and understands the danger."

"Why didn't you?"

"The woman in question wouldn't have me."

Tammy toddled closer and cradled his face. "Maybe you just haven't met the right good woman."

Flynn took her hand in his and held it to his chest. "Tammy, I am deeply flattered, but don't throw away what you have for something that can never be. You have a family back in Minnesota. A husband who loves you. Children who adore you."

"My kids are teenagers. They just find me embarrassing."

"I doubt that's true. I'm sure they miss you. And I'm sure your husband does too."

Tammy let Flynn go and sighed. "I don't know. After twenty years, you start to lose the spark."

"Reignite it then. Take Warren on an adventure. Go somewhere you've never been. Take chances. Get in trouble. Find some fun. I'm guessing Warren needs excitement too."

"Maybe."

"This was good for you, Tammy. This adventure woke you up. You know what Henry David Thoreau said about that, don't you?"

"Who?"

"The mass of men live lives of quiet desperation and go to the grave with the song still in them."

"They do?"

"Sing your song, Tammy. Help Warren to find his song and sing it too."

She nodded, her eyes resolute. "Maybe I will."

"Do." Flynn kissed her on the cheek. "Safe travels, Tammy."

"You too."

She kissed him goodbye. On the mouth. Hard. Her hand behind Flynn's head as she pulled him close, her tongue on the attack. Flynn gently, yet firmly, extricated his tongue as he backed away. Tammy teetered forward, nearly falling off her crutches. Flynn steadied her and left her breathless as he started for the elevators.

"Mr. Flynn?" The desk clerk beckoned him. "I have several messages for you. They came in while you were gone."

Flynn approached and the clerk handed him a stack of handwritten messages. He quickly glanced through them. All were from Alyssa. Sancho never arrived and she wanted Flynn to call her.

"Is everything all right?" asked the clerk.

"My friend Sancho checked out, correct?"

"He did indeed, but then he returned that same day and told us he was staying in your room while you were out of town."

"When did he do that?"

"A few days ago."

"Have you seen him since?"

"No, sir. He hasn't even let the maid in to service the room. But he has been ordering a lot of room service."

"Can I see the bill?"

The clerk printed up a list of running room service charges. Every charge contained four separate food and drink orders with silverware and place settings requested for each.

CHAPTER THIRTY

Sancho stared into the barrel of Ohana's gun. He pled his case and begged for his life, but the duct tape covering his mouth made that difficult. From the look on Ohana's face, he could tell his argument was unintelligible. Still, Sancho read reluctance in the former Mossad agent's gaze.

Ohana sighed and lowered his weapon. "What am I doing?" He closed his eyes and shook his head. "Look what Flynn has turned me into. I can't do this. This isn't your fault. You're as much a victim of him as I am."

Sancho thanked him loudly and profusely, but the duct tape made his *thank you* as unintelligible as his begging.

"Stop! Enough! *Sheket*!" Ohana holstered his pistol. "I'm not going to shoot you, but I'm not untying you either. The next time the maid comes, she'll find you. By that time we'll be—"

The swipe of a key card unlatching the door to the suite stopped Ohana mid-sentence. The door opened only as far as the security chain would allow. Ohana called from the living room where he and his men had Sancho tied up. "We don't need maid service today!" When no one answered back, Ohana called out again. "Hello?"

Nothing.

Ohana and his men all drew their guns and took positions, facing the doorway. Sancho quietly panicked. *Tied to a chair in the middle of a gunfight? Not the best place to be.* Sancho flinched as someone kicked the door open and broke the chain. He tried to scoot away, rocking the chair to make it move, and crashed over onto the floor, facing away from the door. Shouts from men entering the suite ricocheted off the walls. *"Police! Guns on the Ground! Get Down!"*

Two officers in black body armor rappelled onto the terrace. They were SFOs—Specialist Firearms Officers. The same guys who scared him and Flynn away from MI6 headquarters. They carried submachine guns and burst through the terrace door, surprising Ohana and his men from behind. *"Drop your guns! On your knees!"*

Ohana's men dropped their weapons and fell to their knees, but not Ohana. He raced into the bedroom. Glass broke. More shouting. Sancho glimpsed Ohana running across the terrace behind the SFOs. He snapped a carabiner attached to a rope on the wrought iron balustrade and jumped over the edge.

. . .

Ohana swung through the air and crashed through a window one floor down, startling a middle-aged lady lying in bed, talking on the phone. He raced through the room, out the door, and down the hall. He found the entrance to the service stairs and made his way down to the fourth floor and then the third floor. The crackle of a radio alerted him that the tactical police waited below. Ohana exited the service stairs on the second floor and hurried down a corridor until he reached the grand circular staircase that led to the Connaught's elegant lobby.

He caught the eyes of two startled tactical officers as he barreled past them. He didn't draw his weapon as he didn't want to shoot at law enforcement or cause any collateral damage. And then he glimpsed Flynn out of the corner of his eye, racing to tackle him. Ohana stopped short. Flynn leapt right past him, crashing into an SFO reaching for his weapon. As they both went down, Ohana took out another surprised officer by sweeping his feet out from under him.

The double front doors lay straight ahead. With no obstacles left in his way, Ohana pushed through them and outside. All of Mayfair stretched before him. *Freedom at last.* He darted down the stairs, tripped on something unseen, and went down hard, smashing his nose on the pavement. He tried to rise, but something whacked him across the head. He rolled over to fend off his attacker. A stout blonde lady loomed over him, wielding what looked like a crutch as she smacked him in the face with it, knocking him senseless.

. . .

One of the SFO officers escorted Sancho down to the lobby. An EMT administered first aid to Flynn. Someone tapped Sancho on the shoulder, and he turned to see Tammy with a big grin on her face. "I got him."

"Who?"

"Ohana. I was outside, about to get into a cab, when he came barreling out."

A smiling female tactical officer patted her on the shoulder as she passed. "Tripped him with her crutch, she did. Broke his bloody nose. She is one tough nut."

"Did they already take him away?"

"Yup. And I gotta go too. Gotta flight to catch."

Flynn walked up and gave Tammy a big hug. "Did she tell you what a hero she is?"

Sancho grinned. "She did."

Tammy hugged Flynn back, grabbing his ass in the process. "Guess I better go before I miss my darn flight." She kissed Flynn on the cheek and hobbled away.

Flynn clapped Sancho on the shoulder. "Glad to see you survived unscathed."

"I'm a little scathed. I haven't had a shower in three damn days."

"First things first. Call your wife. She's worried sick. She left ten messages for me at the front desk."

"Oh, shit."

"That's how I knew Ohana was holding you prisoner. Well, that and the room service orders for four."

"And the police believed you?"

"They believed the local FBI legal attaché, and he believed Special Agent in Charge Miranda Jacks back in L.A."

He nodded. "I better call Alyssa." Sancho used one of the archaic wooden phone booths off the lobby.

Alyssa answered on the third ring. "Hello?"

"Hey, babe."

"Sancho? Oh, my God."

"Sorry if I woke you."

"Where *are* you?"

"I'm still in London."

"What happened?"

"It's a long story, but I'm okay. And I'm coming home soon." Sancho heard a sob. "Tomorrow?"

"Probably the day after."

"Is Flynn okay?"

"He's fine."

Angry now. "What the heck happened to you? Why didn't you call me? I was worried sick!"

"I would have if I could have, but I'm okay. I promise I'll call you later and tell you everything."

"I miss you."

"I miss you too. Both of you. And I'll call you soon. I promise. I love you."

"I love you too."

Sancho hung up and returned to Flynn.

"Come!" Flynn took Sancho by the arm and led him to the Connaught Bar. They commandeered one of the comfortably upholstered banquettes and ordered drinks. A double Pappy Van Winkle for Flynn. A beer for Sancho.

Sancho took a sip and made a face. "What do Brits have against cold beer?"

"Ice cold beer doesn't have much flavor. To really appreciate a good ale, beer, or stout it needs be served at room temperature."

Sancho put down his pint, sat back and sighed.

Flynn watched him with concern. "You okay?"

"I thought that was *it* for me."

"Where'd he grab you?"

"In the driveway at 9 Elms. Never even got my passport."

"Well, you'll have it by tomorrow and be in L.A. the following day."

"Should I book a ticket for you too?"

Flynn shook his head. "I'm not going anywhere. Caitlyn and Anya are in grave danger. All because of me."

"What did you do?"

"I blew up Ivanov's boat and I blew Caitlyn's cover."

"Did you talk to Miranda Jacks about this?"

"I did, and she contacted the CIA, but they still won't admit that Caitlyn's working for them. And since MI6 won't claim me as an agent, the Chief of Station at the American Embassy thinks I'm crazy."

"Even after handing Ohana over to the FBI?"

"The CIA has a rivalry with the Bureau. They often don't see eye to eye."

"What about Scotland Yard?"

"They would need a warrant to raid Ivanov's home, and for that they need hard evidence that someone there is in danger."

"Jesus."

"So once again, it's up to me."

"What does that mean?"

"You know what it means."

"Jesus."

"Don't worry, my friend. I can handle this on my own. You need to pick up your passport, get on a plane, and return to your wife and child."

"I understand you feel responsible, but you can't do this by yourself, amigo."

"What choice do I have?"

Sancho made a face as he drank the rest of his room temperature beer. "I'm not leaving until tomorrow." Sancho belched. "So, let's go knock on Ivanov's door."

CHAPTER THIRTY-ONE

The city of London is home to sixty-six billionaires. Few cities in the world have more high-net-worth individuals. And many of those individuals have purchased homes in Belgravia. Inside Belgravia is Eaton Square, nicknamed Red Square *for the many Russian oligarchs who now call it home. A garden district, originally constructed in the early 1800s by the Grosvenor family, Eaton Square is known for its neoclassical architecture and celebrity homeowners. Sean Connery, Roger Moore, Elton John, and Andrew Lloyd Webber have all lived there. Lloyds of London named it the most expensive street in the UK. The average property currently lists at just over 16 million pounds.*

As day turned to night, Flynn and Sancho sat on a bench in Eaton Square Garden and watched the front entrance to Oleg Ivanov's eleven thousand square-foot flat. The formal lawn was still perfectly manicured, and the Yew hedges stood just as tall as the last time they sat there. The spring blooms had faded, but the clematis vines that covered the pergola looked even bushier than before and kept them well hidden.

"This didn't go real great the last time we tried this," Sancho said.

"We'll do it a little differently this time. You knock on the front door and when they answer you ask to speak to Ivanov. If they refuse, you insist. The point is to keep them occupied while I find another way in."

"Are you sure about this?"

"I'm sure she's still alive if that's what you're asking me. But *only* because Ivanov needs to know what she knows. He'll torture her for days. As long as it takes. And as tough as she is, it could take a long time, but not forever. Eventually, he'll kill her. Whether she cracks or not."

"Fine. *Fine*."

"Just keep them at the door and I'll do the rest."

Sancho threw up his hands. "Fine. I'll keep 'em at the door as long as I can, but please, man, be careful."

"When am I not?"

Before Sancho could answer that, Flynn stood, winked, and disappeared into the shadows and shrubbery. Sancho made his way out of the gardens and across the street to 70 Eaton Square. As before, no one stood guard outside. Sancho approached the grand front door and stared at the large brass knocker with a lion's face.

He reached for the knocker just as the door opened partway and an enormous man poked his nose out through the gap. Sancho recognized his giant bald head from before.

"*You?*" The hulk spoke English with a thick Russian accent.

"Hi, can I—"

"Go! Get out of here!"

Sancho wanted to run, but he steeled himself and stood his ground. "Not until I talk to Mr. Ivanov's bodyguard."

The bald man raised an eyebrow. "You mean, Kalishnik?"

"Who?"

"I just told you who."

"Is he here?"

"Kalishnik?"

"Mr. Ivanov."

The bald man shook his nose. "Nyet."

"Where is he?"

"With Kalishnik."

"What about Caitlyn Valentine?"

"What about her?"

"Is she with him?" Sancho asked.

"Kalishnik?"

"No, Ivanov."

"I just told you," the bald man barked.

"Told me what?"

"Ivanov's with Kalishnik."

Sancho sighed. "Are we really going to do this again?" The man started to close the door, but Sancho put his foot in the way. "If *Ivanov's* not here, why are *you* here?"

"What do you care?"

"I care because I'd like to talk to him."

"About what?"

Sancho didn't expect that response. "Um…stuff. Things. You know."

"I don't know."

"Do you know *anything*?"

"I know if you don't go, I will beat you dead."

Sancho tried to peek inside. "I just don't understand why you're here if he isn't—"

The door slammed on Sancho's shoe. "Ow! Shit!" He quickly pulled his foot out of the way and the big man slammed it in his face, the brass knocker knocking him in the nose.

■　　■　　■

Flynn crept around the periphery of the property. The building stood five stories tall with grand terraces, pristine white walls, and countless wooden sash windows covered by curtains. A few lights glowed on the first level, but the upper-level windows remained dark. Or perhaps the curtains were so thick they let out very little light.

Every house in Eaton Square had the same Georgian architecture, the same white stucco facades, black railings, and

Corinthian columns. Though, Flynn suspected Ivanov had created multiple levels below the street. Basement levels with safe rooms and interrogation rooms and rooms with vaults packed with gold, illegal weapons, and secrets of all sorts. He imagined a security command post filled with monitors connected to dozens of cameras watching the perimeter. A man with as many enemies as Ivanov would have a state-of-the-art alarm system with door and window sensors and motion detectors inside. He would think the place impregnable. But Ivanov's belief in the building's inviolable security might also be its greatest vulnerability. The guards would believe that no one could surprise them and breach the building's defenses without alerting them.

They would be wrong.

Flynn climbed the construction scaffolding on the building next door until he reached the roof. From there, he took a running start and leaped from one building to the next. He misjudged the distance, and barely caught the edge. He struggled to muscle himself up and over.

He smelled cigarette smoke and caught sight of a large man in a black suit, lounging on a chaise, leaning back and smoking a fag while scrolling through his phone. Flynn suspected that the help couldn't smoke on the premises, so this is where the security men took their breaks.

Flynn dropped right on top of him, straddling his middle. The guard opened his mouth in surprise and the lit fag fell right inside. He gagged and choked and Flynn took advantage of his panic to pick up an ashtray on a nearby table and smack him in the head, knocking him cold. Flynn flipped him over and bound his hands behind him with his own belt. He then took off the man's pants and used them to tie his legs together. Flynn searched for a weapon, but he didn't have one. *Perhaps the man left it inside.* He probably never thought he'd need a loaded weapon on the roof. With his enemy secure, Flynn entered the opened French doors.

The house was quiet, but Flynn noticed the occasional security camera with a blinking red light. If someone had seen him, they would have raised the alarm by now. Clearly, no one was monitoring the monitors.

Flynn marveled at the ornate, over-the-top gilt and marble décor in the wood-paneled corridors. He passed a giant sitting room with original paintings and sculptures by Renaissance masters and French impressionists. Marble fountains, crystal chandeliers, Victorian antiques, and vintage Persian rugs lined every inch of the townhouse. Every room had a massive fireplace, though none were lit. He could hardly believe anyone actually lived there as it resembled a museum more than a human habitation.

Flynn heard no voices and saw no people. No servants. No security. Not a soul.

The next floor down was taken up entirely by a sprawling bedroom suite with an enormous four-poster bed, and a large seating area illuminated by a giant crystal chandelier. The electric bill alone had to cost a fortune.

The gold and marble bathroom was larger than most apartments, and it connected to an even larger dressing area with endless closet space. Flynn glanced inside: dresses and gowns and every other kind of clothing a woman might possibly wear. A giant makeup table took up almost an entire wall. *Is this all for Anya?* If so, where was she?

One floor down, Flynn found a huge, ornate, empty office and a private cinema with twenty leather recliner chairs and an eighty-inch flat screen TV. Security cameras blinked at him, but no human beings.

Flynn found an antique wooden elevator with a metal gate that needed to be pulled shut. It took him into the bowels of the house, and a corridor with slightly more modern décor. He passed a huge gym filled with all kinds of equipment (and no one using any of it). Flynn continued on and heard splashing. Double doors led to an indoor pool area with gold leaf tiles and a gold-paneled ceiling.

A naked woman swam laps in the pool. Tall and slender, she swam with power and confidence. She reached the far end of the pool, did a graceful kick turn and swam back in Flynn's direction. But not for long. She saw him and stopped with a start and swam to the side, ripping off her goggles and pulling out her earplugs.

"Who the fuck are you?" Her husky voice had a tinge of fear and an American accent.

"I might ask you the same question," Flynn answered.

"How the hell did you get in here?"

"Where is she?"

"Who?"

"Caitlyn Valentine."

"*Who?*"

"The man who owns this place took her prisoner and kidnapped his own wife. Perhaps you're his mistress. Or perhaps you're just a high-priced prostitute."

"*Excuse me?*"

"I'm not judging you. What you do is your own business, but the man who invited you here is not who you think he is. He is a predator. A monster." Flynn could see he was scaring her. "Please don't be afraid. I'm not here to hurt you. I'm here to help."

Eyes wide, she stared at something behind him. He quickly turned. A short woman in a maid's outfit slapped him across the face with a pool noodle. He staggered back. She slapped him again before kicking him in the groin with her tiny sneakered foot. Flynn bent at the waist from the pain. He reached out to grab her, but she shoved him away. He tumbled backwards over a patio chair and smacked his head on the concrete floor.

The naked woman climbed from the pool, picked up her phone, and hit some buttons. An alarm screamed, the sound deafening as it reverberated around the indoor pool area. She put on a robe and ran. The tiny woman in the maid's outfit ran after her. They closed and locked the doors to the pool area just as Flynn reached them. He banged on the tempered glass. It wouldn't budge. He smacked the glass with a rattan chair, but it just bounced off. Soon help arrived in the form of four uniformed police officers.

CHAPTER THIRTY-TWO

In the year 1247, during the reign of Henry III, Bethlem Royal Hospital began as the Priory of the New Order of our Lady of Bethlehem. Those sent to Bethlem suffered from complaints such as "chronic mania" or "acute melancholy," as well as those convicted of crimes like infanticide and homicide. Treatment consisted of isolation and experimentation. One treatment of the time was called "rotating therapy". A patient sat in a chair suspended from the ceiling and spun at one hundred rotations a minute. The purpose? Induce vomiting. The idea being that illness existed in the body and not the mind and could only be exorcised through rigorous physical activity.

Sancho sat in the park, in the dark, across from Ivanov's incredible mansion. He waited for Flynn. *Did he make it inside? Did he find Caitlyn? Did Ivanov find him? Should he knock on the door again? Should he call the police?* As that last thought occurred to him, four Metropolitan Police vehicles came screeching up, their sing-song sirens screaming. They didn't pull up in front of Ivanov's mansion but parked in front of the palace next door. A tiny maid opened the door and the police rushed inside. More police arrived. Ten minutes later, Flynn emerged in handcuffs. *What the hell?*

They loaded him into a police SUV and took off. Sancho stood and watched until all the police vehicles and their flashing blue lights were gone.

Shit.

■　■　■

Sancho called FBI Special Agent in Charge, Miranda Jacks, in Los Angeles and she contacted the FBI legal attaché at the American Embassy at Nine Elms. The legal attaché contacted MI5, who phoned the Metropolitan police.

The Crown Prosecution Service charged Flynn with trespass, assault occasioning actual bodily harm, violent disorder, and voyeurism. He was sectioned under the Mental Health Act as unfit to stand trial and sent to Bethlem Royal Hospital for a psych evaluation.

Forty-eight hours later, Sancho found himself at the infamous hospital, sitting at a long table in a large treatment room with dull yellow walls. The FBI legal attaché, Special Agent Fuentes, sat across from him with an open briefcase and pored over paperwork. They shared the space in silence.

Sancho first met Fuentes at the embassy, and he was just as much of an asshole there. The gruff, wiry, bantam-weight Texan seemed to have it in for Flynn. When Sancho first entered the room, Fuentes looked at him and nodded before returning to his paperwork. That was the beginning and end of any acknowledgement.

Sancho sat there silently for five minutes. He hesitated to break the quiet by asking a question. But five minutes after that, his anger grew. *Is Fuentes purposely trying to piss me off?*

"Agent Fuentes?"

Fuentes raised his gaze, not happy to be interrupted.

"Do you want to tell me why I've been invited here?"

"You're here on behalf of Flynn."

"Have they told you what they want to do with him?"

He shook his head. "No."

"What's the embassy's position?"

"There is no official position."

"Well, what do *you* think?"

"I think Flynn's a psychopath who is a danger to himself and others."

"He's not dangerous."

"Tell that to Ophelia Beaubois."

"Who?"

"The supermodel whose house he broke into. The one who was swimming naked in her pool."

"An honest mistake."

"Was it an honest mistake for Flynn to beat her famous actor boyfriend senseless? To tie him up on the roof?"

"He believes that Caitlyn Valentine is in danger. That Oleg Ivanov is holding her prisoner."

"He also believes he's a double 0 agent with His Majesty's Secret Service."

"I'm not saying he's not crazy, but what if he's *not* wrong? What if Caitlyn's cover has been blown?"

"The Chief of Station was quite clear about that. Valentine is no longer an employee of the CIA."

"But what if they're lying about that? You know, that whole 'we'll disavow you if you get caught' thing?"

"Then they will handle it. That's what they do. That's what they're trained to do. Flynn isn't trained to do shit. He's a fucking mental patient. And you're his psychiatric nurse. So, you do *your* job and I'll do mine and—"

The door opened and a beefy orderly escorted Flynn into the room. He sat him down at the table and stood directly behind him. Flynn's hands were cuffed, and he wore baggy green hospital scrubs. Pupils dilated, eyes unfocused, mouth slack, his chin slick with drool. Sancho glared at the orderly. "What did you do to him?"

The orderly didn't bother answering.

The door opened and a silver-haired woman entered with a tall, slender man in his late forties and a smaller, well-dressed man of African descent. They all sat at the table across from Flynn and Sancho.

The woman offered everyone a wintry smile. "I'm Dr. Tina McClusky and I'm the forensic psychiatrist assigned to Mr. Flynn's case."

The tall man raised his hand. He had thinning red hair and a much warmer smile than Dr. McClusky's. "And I'm Detective Chief Inspector Reynolds with the Metropolitan Police."

Finally, the smaller man piped up. "And I'm a prosecutor with the CPS. My name is Mr. Davis." He glanced at Sancho. "Are you representing Mr. Flynn?"

"I'm a psychiatric nurse, but I'm also a friend. Sancho Perez."

"And I'm SA Fuentes. The FBI's special attaché in London. We spoke earlier."

Mr. Davis nodded and aimed his gaze at Sancho. "All right then. Dr. McClusky evaluated Mr. Flynn and diagnosed him as indeed mentally ill. I talked with DCI Reynolds and Special Agent Fuentes and between us we came to an accommodation."

DCI Reynolds picked it up from there. "The complainant will drop all charges against Mr. Flynn, if Mr. Flynn agrees to immediately leave London, return to the U.S., and check himself into the City of Roses Psychiatric Facility for care and observation."

Sancho sighed. That was better than he could have hoped. "So, he just has to leave town?"

"And return to City of Roses."

Agent Fuentes handed Sancho two plane tickets. "We booked you both a flight that leaves in approximately six hours. I will personally escort you to the airport and wait there until you take off."

Sancho glanced at Flynn to see if he was catching any of this, but he was totally out of it. Heavily sedated. "Fine," Sancho said. "I already packed up Flynn. I've been packed since yesterday. We are good to go." Sancho reached out and grabbed one of Flynn's handcuffed hands. "What do you say, pal? You ready to go home?"

Flynn had no answer.

CHAPTER THIRTY-THREE

Sancho sat next to a dozing Flynn as they rode to Heathrow in a black U.S. Embassy limo. Special Agent Fuentes sat up front, next to the driver. When the sedatives finally wore off, Flynn would be furious. Sancho worried about Caitlyn too, but he had to believe the CIA wouldn't just hang her out to dry. They had the resources to find her and save her if she needed saving. The powers that be were never going to tell him or Flynn what they were up to. He had to trust they would do the right thing.

Special Agent Fuentes checked them in at the airline and handed them their boarding passes. He escorted them through security and to the gate where he waited with them to board their flight. Before they left Bethlem, Sancho helped Flynn change out of his hospital scrubs into one of his more casual outfits. Gray denim jeans, a navy-blue cable knit sweater, and chukka boots. As sedated and floppy as Flynn was, dressing him was like dressing a two-hundred-pound toddler. No different than dressing little Miguel. He struggled to get his legs in his pants, his arms through the armholes, and his head through the head hole.

The plastic chairs in the Gate 17 waiting area weren't meant for someone with no muscular control. Flynn sat slumped and kept sliding down the seat. Sancho sat next to him and worked to keep him upright. Fuentes sat across from them both, irritated and bored.

Something buzzed in Flynn's pocket. Sancho felt around and found his phone, rousing Flynn into semi-consciousness. A text appeared on the screen. *Culzean Castle.* The person texting clearly wasn't in Flynn's contact list as there was only a UK phone number and no name.

Sancho showed the screen to Flynn. "Do you know what this means?" Flynn's eyes remained unfocused. Drool dangled from his chin. *What the hell did they dose him with?* Their flight was due to board in ten minutes. "James? You want to hit the can?"

"Huh?" Flynn mumbled.

"Pee? Before we board the plane?" Flynn slowly nodded, shaking the string of drool hanging off his chin. Sancho helped him up and called over to Fuentes. "Bathroom!"

Fuentes rose and helped Sancho get Flynn to the men's room. Flynn shrugged Sancho off when they reached the door, his voice thick and slurred. "Don't need you to hold my bloody willy, do I?"

Sancho backed away. "Fine. I'll be right out here."

Fuentes stood outside the door with Sancho.

■　■　■

Whatever they injected into Flynn hit him like a cricket bat across the forehead. It left him staggered, dazed, and stupefied. But as the sedation wore off and Flynn grew sharper, he continued to play the fool and drool and stumble and nod off. He wanted Fuentes to think he was helpless. He needed to find a way to escape. He needed to save Caitlyn. But he had no idea where Ivanov was holding her.

Until that mysterious text arrived.

Flynn sat in a toilet stall and called Bettina O'Toole-Applebaum. She answered on the third ring.

"Flynn?" She sounded surprised to hear from him.

"I don't have much time. Culzean Castle. Can you find out where it is and who owns it?"

"I can try. What's this about?"

"Find out as soon as you can. When you get the answer, let me know immediately."

"Where are you? Are you still in London?"

Sancho shouted into the restroom, his voice echoing off the tile walls. "Flynn? You okay?"

Flynn replied with a drunken slur. "How 'bout a little bloody privacy?"

"They're boarding the plane."

"All right! *All right!*"

"Boarding what plane?" Bettina asked.

Flynn lowered his voice to a whisper. "Gotta go, Bettina. Get cracking on that answer."

Flynn stepped from the men's room and acted befuddled. Sancho took him by the elbow and led him to the gate. The gate agent scanned their boarding passes and they headed into the air bridge. Flynn glanced back. Fuentes watched as they boarded.

"James, come on, man." Sancho tugged Flynn along. They waited in line and finally found their seats in the rear of the cabin, not far from the restrooms in the back. Flynn plopped himself in the aisle seat.

Sancho let go with an exasperated sigh. "Dude, that's my seat."

"Hmm?"

"My seat! I have the aisle seat."

Flynn's chin rested on his chest, and he began to snore. Sancho shook him, but his noggin just bounced around like a bobble head. "I hate sitting in the middle, man." Flynn didn't reply, so Sancho sighed and climbed over him to get into the middle seat. "God dammit."

Flynn maintained the fiction that he was drugged to near unconsciousness, but kept one eye on the aisle. The last stragglers put their belongings in the overhead bins before taking their seats. With no more passengers left to board, the flight crew closed the cabin doors.

Sancho tilted his head back and closed his eyes as an attractive older female flight attendant made an announcement. "Ladies and gentlemen, welcome aboard. We ask that you please fasten your seatbelts at this time, and secure all baggage underneath your seat or in the overhead compartments. We also ask that your seats and table trays are in the upright position for take-off. Please turn off all personal electronic devices, including laptops and cellphones. Smoking is prohibited for the duration of the flight. Thank you for choosing British Airways."

Flynn pretended to be inert so he wouldn't have to turn off his phone or put it in flight mode. Bettina might text or call at any moment. What if she had an answer for him? *And what if she didn't?* Once they were in the air, it would be too late. They would be thirty-five thousand feet over the Atlantic. Flynn had a decision to make. And he had to make it quickly. The last few days had taken their toll on his young friend. The light snoring on his left indicated Sancho was fast asleep.

Good.

While the flight attendants were busy with other passengers, Flynn unbuckled his belt, slipped from his seat, and crept to the back of the cabin. Years before, he snuck aboard billionaire Sergei Belenki's private 747 to save the world from economic collapse. He entered through the luggage hold and made his way to the main cabin.

Flynn did exactly the reverse this time.

He found the narrow stairs to the lower galley and the trapdoor that led to the luggage hold. From there, he moved through another door into the forward storage hold and crouched down a tight corridor packed with wiring and insulation, avionics equipment and other electronics. Finally, he located the maintenance door near the front of the plane. That led to a ladder and the pavement below.

Flynn dropped to the tarmac. Fuel smoke filled his nostrils. The rumble of jet engines shook the air. He hitched a ride on the back of a departing baggage trolley. When they pulled up close to the terminal, Flynn jumped off and headed inside. He joined up with a stream of arriving domestic passengers, made his way through baggage claim, and out the hydraulic doors to the arrivals curb. He called Bettina. She picked up on the first ring. "Any luck?"

"As a matter of fact, I was just about to call you. Culzean Castle is in Scotland. Fifty miles south of Glasgow. Right on the Firth of Clyde. Leased by a shell corporation owned by a shell corporation owned by another shell corporation owned by Oleg Ivanov."

"He leases it?"

"From the National Trust of Scotland. He must be paying them a pretty penny because they don't just lease it to anybody. Are you going to tell me what this is about now?"

"He has Caitlyn and Anya, and he's holding them both against their will. I believe Anya sent me this clue."

"Ivanov's wife, Anya?"

"Yes, but of course, she has her own agenda."

"Are you going to tell the authorities?"

"I doubt they'd believe me, being I'm currently a fugitive from justice who they think is crackers."

"What about Miranda Jacks?"

"After what happened in Belgravia, I don't think they'd believe her either."

"I hope you're not planning to do something stupid."

"Hope does spring eternal." Flynn clicked off.

■　■　■

Sancho awakened with a start, the loud buzzing hum of the engines drowning out almost every other sound. A few scattered voices floated around his head. A lady laughed. A baby cried. He must have slept with his mouth open, because his tongue felt thick and tasted weird. A dozen rows up, a flight attendant handed out drinks from a cart. They had to be in the air. He must have slept through take off.

Flynn's seat was empty. He must have hit the can. According to the digital map on the screen on the seatback in front of him, they were flying over Greenland. When Flynn didn't return in five minutes, Sancho kept his cool. Ten minutes later he lost it. After fifteen minutes, he was on his feet and on his way to the back of the plane. All three toilets were occupied.

Sancho knocked on one. "Flynn?"

"Give me a goddamn minute," an angry old lady said behind the door.

"Sorry." Sancho rapped on another.

"*Occupata!*" a younger man said.

"Sorry." Sancho went to knock on the third door, but it opened before he could. A frazzled thirty-something woman with mussed hair and wild eyes walked out with a toddler.

Shit.

Sancho checked all the other bathrooms on the plane. In business class. First class.

No Flynn.

What the fuck?

The attractive older flight attendant approached Sancho with concern. "Sir, I'm going to have to ask you to return to your section."

"I can't find my friend."

"He's probably in one of the lavatories."

"I checked every single one. I can't find him anywhere."

She smiled at that. "Well, he's here somewhere, sir. Maybe he sat in someone else's seat by mistake."

"I looked up and down the plane. He's not here."

"What's his name?"

"James Flynn."

She went to the PA system microphone and made an announcement. "Mr. James Flynn, please return to your seat."

Flynn didn't return, and when they couldn't find him anywhere else, Sancho convinced one of the flight attendants to check the downstairs galley and luggage compartment. They reluctantly went down to search for him and returned empty-handed.

"There's no one down there, sir."

"How is that possible?"

"Are you sure he boarded the plane?"

"*Yes, I'm sure!*" Sancho snapped. He saw someone filming him with their phone. "Sorry. I don't mean to be one of those crazy passenger people who go ballistic…I just…I just need to find my friend."

"Sir, we're forty thousand feet over the Atlantic. No one has opened an emergency door. No one has left the plane. If he boarded the plane at Heathrow, he has to be here."

"Does he?"

"He does. Now have a seat. I'm sure we'll find him soon."

Sancho screamed at the top of his lungs. "FLYNN! *FLYNN!*"

Some of the other passengers looked scared. A few glared. Some continued to film him. One large man sitting on the aisle beckoned Sancho over with a smile.

Sancho approached him. "Have you seen my friend?"

"No, I haven't. But you really need to sit your ass down before a few of us concerned passengers beat you down and tie you up."

.   .   .

Flynn returned to the terminal and bought a one-way ticket to Glasgow on British Airways. Four hours later, he arrived at Glasgow International. Soon after he touched down, he placed a call to someone he hadn't talked to in quite some time. Francisco Goolardo. Five years previously, Flynn foiled his plan to make himself the richest man in the world. Back then, Goolardo wanted Flynn dead. But later they worked together to save humanity, and eventually became brothers-in-arms. As the former head of the Goolardo Drug Cartel, he was wanted by law enforcement all over the world. So, he changed his name to Afonso Espinola and bought a mansion by the sea in Oerias on the Portuguese Riviera.

"James Flynn! It's a pleasure to hear from you!" The deep voice resonated across the line, the accent Brazilian.

"Francisco!"

"Afonso now. Please."

"Of course."

"It's good to hear from you, amigo."

"It's good to hear your voice as well." Flynn sat at the Beardmore airport pub and enjoyed a ten-year-old Talisker.

"How can I be of service, *camarada*?"

"I need to storm a castle."

"Of course, you do. Are you rescuing a fair damsel?"

"I am indeed."

Goolardo laughed. "I would have expected nothing less. What can I do to help?"

"Do you have any contacts in Glasgow who might be able to supply the proper equipment?"

"Scotland? Let me think. Actually…yes. There is someone there who owes me a favor. Keithen MacGregor."

"Who might he be?"

"The head of the MacGregor crime family. We did some business back in the day. I'll make some calls. Put you in touch. He'll supply you with whatever you need."

"I owe you one, amigo."

"No, you do not. I am always here for you. So never hesitate to call me. Our world has fewer and fewer men like you. Men of action. Men of valor. I consider it an honor just to know you. There are those who think you are crazy, but that is because they are cowards. They don't have your courage. They don't have your cojones."

"I'm just a humble civil servant."

"You are much more than that, my friend."

"Thank you…Afonso."

"*Tchau, amigo.*"

CHAPTER THIRTY-FOUR

Legend has it that Glasgow was founded in the sixth century by Christian missionary Saint Mungo, the patron saint of salmon, though there have been settlements on the River Clyde since prehistoric times. Glasgow Cathedral was built over St. Mungo's original church, and contains his remains in the lower crypt. He was the bastard son of the Princess of Lothian who was impregnated as a result of an illicit love affair. Thus dishonored, the princess was thrown off a cliff, but unexpectedly survived the fall. She was then cast off in a coracle and came ashore near Culross Fife, where she was taken in by Celtic monks and soon after gave birth to baby Mungo.

The Drum and Monkey Pub used to be a bank. At least that's what it said on the website when Flynn looked it up. A bank built in 1924 in Glasgow's City Centre. That was where Keithen MacGregor wanted to meet.

Flynn walked past many well-preserved Victorian buildings en route to his rendezvous. He had expected MacGregor to pick a dark dive in a rundown part of town. A place that hoodlums and gangsters might frequent. There was nothing dingy or dark about the Drum and Monkey. Spacious and full of light, it had high ornate ceilings, black marble columns, and a long mahogany bar with a brass foot rail. A fire blazed in a Victorian-style fireplace, and there were many cubbies and booths and little hideaways. There were also quite a few tourists. But perhaps that was MacGregor's strategy. Hide in plain sight.

A big barrel-chested man in his fifties with a shaved head waved to Flynn from across the room and beckoned him over. Two huge associates with menacing eyes stood nearby, surveying the crowd.

"Flynn, is it? Ah recognized ye fra th' tellybox."

Flynn figured it was MacGregor even though he didn't understand the last half of the man's sentence. "Mr. MacGregor, I presume?"

McGregor motioned to his menacing men. One looked to be in his late fifties. The other in his early thirties. "Mah lads. Faither and son. The faither worked for my Da. Young MacDonald 'n Old MacDonald." He pointed to the bench on the opposite side of the booth. "Tak' a load aff."

"Hmm?"

"Sit!"

Flynn sat. "Thanks for meeting me."

"Nae bother, pal. Whit kind o' accent is thon?"

"Excuse me?"

"Where ye from?"

"Right here. Though I was raised elsewhere."

"Ye dinnae sound Scots."

"Hmm?"

"That accent. It's naff. You an American?"

"Well, I have lived in the states for quite some time."

"You puttin' me on?"

"I'm sorry."

"Whit urr sorry aboot?"

"Say again?"

"Is yer heid in a fankle?"

"A what?"

MacGregor sighed in frustration. "Want a wee bevvy?"

When Flynn had no answer to that, MacGregor pointed to his cocktail and then pointed at Flynn.

"A drink? Yes…um…perhaps a vodka martini."

MacGregor shouted to Old MacDonald. "Vodka martini fur Mr. Flynn."

"Shaken, not stirred," Flynn shouted after him.

"A got whit ye asked fur."

"Come again?"

"I got yer shite!"

"Here?"

"Naw, nae 'ere! We hae tae gang get it!"

"Go get it?"

"Aye."

"Ah, right, got it."

They sat there in silence, both afraid to communicate. Old MacDonald returned with the vodka martini and Flynn took a long pull.

MacGregor drank half his pint in one go. "Howfur lang hae ye kent Goolardo?"

Flynn had no idea what MacGregor just asked him but did catch Goolardo's name and tried to make sense of it from there. "Goolardo? Yeah. Good man."

"He made me a lot 'o dosh."

Flynn nodded sagely. "Indeed."

"Dae ye ken me?"

"Hmm?"

MacGregor looked irritated as he drained his pint. "Ye ready tae gang?"

"Ready to what?"

"Gang! It's nae far. It'll be a skoosh."

When Flynn didn't answer, MacGregor sighed and climbed from the booth. Flynn assumed that meant they were leaving. He drained the rest of his martini, stood, and followed MacGregor and the MacDonalds through the crowded pub and out a side door into an alley. MacGregor mumbled an aside to Old MacDonald. "A wee bit of a numpty bawbag, aye?"

Old MacDonald smirked and looked back at Flynn.

Were they talking about me?

Flynn sat in the back with Old McDonald. Young McDonald drove. MacGregor rode shotgun. No one said a word as they traversed the city and ended up in some kind of warehouse district near the docks. They pulled up in front of a corrugated steel warehouse that had seen better days. Two large goons stood guarding the door.

As they climbed from the car, vicious guard dogs growled and barked at them from behind a chain-link fence. MacGregor talked to them in a happy sing-song voice. "There's mah guid wee jimmies!" He looked at Flynn. "Pure radge bastards, they ur. Swatch at them th' wrang way an they'll tak' yer arm aff at the' elbow."

They snarled at Flynn until he followed MacGregor into the warehouse. It was well-lit with hanging banks of fluorescent lights suspended from the ceiling. Flynn spotted a panel truck with a long table set up in front of it. A greasy-looking blanket covered whatever was on top. An old Ford Transit Courier Van sat parked a short distance away.

An unsmiling man even bigger than Old MacDonald stepped from the panel truck and stood behind the table. MacGregor greeted him. "How ye daein?"

"Nae bad, hou's yersel?"

"Nae bad."

"Who's the galoot?"

"Flynn. Goolardo's mate." MacGregor motioned to the big man behind the table. "Meet Abernathy."

Flynn nodded. "Good to meet you."

Abernathy grunted and pulled the greasy blanket off a panoply of weaponry: an Ingram MAC-10, a SIG Sauer P226, suppressors, holsters, and ammunition for both and additional magazines. There was also a combat knife, night-vision goggles, a tactical flashlight, three flashbang grenades, three smoke grenades, asbestos gloves, five thermite breach pens, wrap-around safety glasses with darkened lenses, a set of lock picking tools, a nylon climbing harness and climbing rope with carabiners, two bricks of military-grade C-4 and two-timed detonators with keypads.

Everything he had asked for.

MacGregor slapped Flynn on the shoulder. "Guid tae gang?"

Flynn didn't bother answering since he didn't know what MacGregor just asked him. Instead, he pointed to the Courier Van parked a short distance away. "Is that for me?"

"Aye."

"Appreciate the help."

"Remember now, we ne'er mit."

"Hmm?"

"Ye and me. We dinnae know each other."

"I'm not sure I—"

MacGregor raised his hand to shut Flynn up. "Enough awready! Time tae gang!"

"Go?"

"Aye."

The MacDonald's and Abernathy helped Flynn load up. Five minutes later MacGregor sent him on his way with a bit of incomprehensible Scottish wisdom. "Lang may yer lum reek!"

■   ■   ■

Driving like a Brit no longer came naturally to Flynn, and it took a preternatural amount of focus to stay on the left side of the road. He headed south over Kingston Bridge and eventually merged onto M77 south. Because of the tremendous amount of concentration it took to drive, he almost didn't answer his phone when it buzzed. Curiosity finally got the better of him. He fished out his phone to discover Sancho had tried to call him five times.

Flynn answered. "Sancho?"

"What the hell, man!"

"I trust you arrived safely?"

"What the hell happened to you?"

"Sorry to leave without saying goodbye, but you were sleeping so peacefully I didn't have the heart to wake you."

"They closed the cabin door. How the hell did you get out?"

"Do you remember that time we snuck onboard Sergei Belenki's private jet?"

"Oh, shit. Are you shitting me?"

"Did you alert the British authorities that I flew the coop?"

"Of course not. You're already in enough trouble as it is."

"What about the FBI?"

"I haven't told anybody, and I won't if you promise to get your ass back here."

"I will," Flynn promised. "As soon as I rescue Anya."

"What about Caitlyn?"

"Caitlyn doesn't want to be rescued. At least not by me. But if she wants to leave with Anya and I, she is more than welcome."

"Dude, you don't even know where they are."

"Actually, I believe I do. Remember that text I received? Culzean Castle? Guess who owns it?"

"Ivanov?"

"Bingo."

"You think that text came from Anya?"

"Who else?"

"Where the hell are you?"

"Scotland."

"*Scotland*?"

"Thanks to Bettina O'Toole-Applebaum."

"What does she have to do with *any* of this?"

"She used her skills as an investigative reporter to discover the true owner. She also sent me copies of the original architectural drawings, as well as detailed plans and diagrams on the castle and all the buildings surrounding it."

"What are you planning to do?"

"I'm mounting a rescue. Obviously. And time is of the essence."

"He probably has an army guarding the place. It's a goddamn castle, for Christ's sake."

"And I know exactly how to get in."

"Are you renting a battering ram? Or are you just going to catapult your ass over the wall?"

"The catapult's not a bad idea, but Bettina found an easier way. The castle has a vast complex of caves beneath it."

"Seriously?"

"Smugglers used them in the 17th century. Five years ago, spelunkers unearthed ancient walls and a doorway into the castle that date back to medieval times."

"So, you're gonna sneak around a maze of caves in the dark with all those rats and snakes and spiders and bats?"

"I'm not fond of bats."

"Nobody is, bro. That's why you can't do this on your own."

"What choice do I have?"

"Look, I know you're trying to do the right thing here, but I care about you and I don't want to see you get hurt. Let me call Miranda Jacks. She's on your side, man. She believes in you and she'll do whatever she can to help. I know she will. Just give me a little time before you do anything dumb."

"Time is the one thing we don't have."

CHAPTER THIRTY-FIVE

Culzean Castle (pronounced kul-AYN) stands on a cliff overlooking the Firth of Clyde on the west coast of Scotland. Originally built in the late 1500s, David Kennedy, the 10th Earl of Cassilis, had it renovated in 1777. The project took twelve years, and he transformed it from a dowdy fortress to a grand romantic fantasy castle, incorporating elements from Greek, Roman, Gothic, and Egyptian architecture. A massive drum tower with a circular saloon offers a panoramic view that overlooks the sea. There are drawing rooms, dining rooms, a library, and an elegant oval staircase supported by Corinthian columns. In 1945, the Kennedy family gave the castle and grounds to the National Trust of Scotland. As part of the gift, they stipulated that the apartment at the top of the castle be given to General Dwight D. Eisenhower in recognition of his role as Supreme Commander of the Allied forces in Europe. Eisenhower visited only four times. Once while President of the United States. A popular if pricey tourist destination for many years, the castle is said to be home to seven ghosts, including a bagpiper and a servant girl.

The three-room suite on the top floor of Culzean Castle presented an incredible view of the Firth of Clyde. Dark, windblown clouds filled the sky above a stormy sea. For Caitlyn, the spacious, ornate, and beautifully appointed suite suggested a Victorian-era whorehouse. Her mother would have loved it, but Caitlyn was more of a minimalist, and the room was a little much. Dramatic and romantic oil paintings of women standing on cliffs adorned the walls. Oak and mahogany antiques crowded the Persian carpets. There were delicate doilies, bronze sculptures, crystal figurines, medieval tapestries, and a massive fireplace with an intricately carved marble mantlepiece.

Even if Caitlyn wasn't a prisoner, she would have found the room suffocating. The windows wouldn't open. And if they did, there was nowhere to go but down. The bullet wound to her calf was minor. A flesh wound that creased the epidermis but didn't puncture the muscle. Painful, but not critical. One of Ivanov's maids doubled as a nurse, and she cleaned and dressed the wound soon after they arrived.

They flew to Glasgow on Ivanov's private jet, and he didn't say a word to her the whole way. She sat next to Kalishnik, who kept her wrists tightly bound. She assumed Ivanov planned to torture her, but watching Kalishnik eat lunch was torture enough. She had no appetite but forced down a little something to keep her strength up. She wasn't sure when she'd eat again. The ride to the castle took a little over an hour, and Ivanov rode in a separate car. His wife, Anya, rode with Caitlyn. Guess Ivanov didn't want to talk to her either. She had a black eye and fat lip, but she didn't look afraid. She looked angry as fuck.

Kalishnik was a little rough getting Caitlyn in the helicopter, but he hadn't smacked her around. Not yet anyway. Now she sat in a velvet-lined prison, in a Scottish castle, with a killer view.

Fucking Flynn.

Kalishnik told her how Flynn escaped from him in Monaco and later tried to break into the Ivanov residence in London. He forced his way into the wrong house and ended up in jail. The very next day, the British government deported his ass back to California. Kalishnik chuckled when he told her, but admitted he found Flynn's stupidity disappointing. He wanted one last crack at him. One more chance to end him.

Anya snored in the other room. That was the worst part of this whole screwed up mess. Ivanov decided to lock them up together.

Torture for both of them.

The woman was annoying as hell, and they hated each other from the get-go. Caitlyn had assumed Anya was jealous, but later learned she was mostly suspicious. That was partly why Oleg wasn't. He'd defy Anya just to be contrary, and Caitlyn used that to her advantage.

Ivanov had an ego that wouldn't quit, and she used that against him too. She convinced Oleg that the CIA had totally screwed her and, in truth, they had. She told Oleg she could never trust them again. That wasn't a lie. She also turned on the charm. Not something she often did. She knew some men found her attractive, and occasionally she'd use that to her benefit. But it irritated the hell out of her and eventually she couldn't hide her contempt. Strangely, some men found that even more attractive. They liked her disdain. Liked that she didn't seem to need them. Rich men especially seemed turned on by that. They never knew if women were interested in them or their money. If a woman didn't seem to be interested at all…that made them doubly attractive.

She knew if she ever slept with Ivanov, he would lose interest immediately. It was the chase he enjoyed. The challenge. So, she tap danced to stay just out of reach. She also knew she couldn't keep him running after her forever. Eventually, he'd lose patience. It was a tricky balancing act. She just had to keep him interested long enough to suss out his plan.

Fucking Flynn.

Caitlyn turned on the big flat screen TV in the sitting room. She flipped between *Celebrity Mastermind*, *The Great British Sewing Bee, and Snooker World Championship Highlights*. Finally, she settled on a show called *Escape to the Country*, a reality show that follows people who want to buy a fancy dream home somewhere in the UK countryside.

Anya wandered in from her bedroom, her hair mussed, her eyes sleepy and puffy. She wore yoga pants and a t-shirt and sat on a chair across from Caitlyn. Lighting up a cigarette, she pointed it at the TV. "What is this shit?"

"I have no idea. Would you please put out that cigarette?"

"Why don't you go suck a dick?"

Caitlyn gave her a murderous glare. She cultivated the glare as a patient at the most dangerous psychiatric hospital in California. Her fellow patients were serial killers and mass murderers and, somehow, she still scared the crap out of them. That was where she met Flynn, saving him from one of the most dangerous sicarios who ever lived.

Anya glared back and put her cigarette out on the polished mahogany armrest. "I don't understand why anyone would want to buy a house in the middle of fucking nowhere."

Caitlyn turned down the sound. "Can we not do this?"

"What?"

"Talk."

"I mean, I get why you'd want to live on the beach in Hawaii, or Bali, but it's dreary as hell here and there's nothing to fucking do. Cloudy. Cold. Damp. Rainy. I told Oleg I didn't want to live here, but did he care?"

"Oleg owns this place?"

"He leases it from the Scottish National Trust. After Covid, they were having trouble keeping the place going. The County stopped giving them money. They couldn't afford the upkeep. They finally shut it down and let half the staff go. Oleg came in and offered them a deal they couldn't refuse. They rented a national treasure to a Russian national. Pissed off a hell of a lot of people. I told him not to lease this place, but he wouldn't listen. He never listens. He wanted a castle. He wanted to be a king."

"So, he has delusions of grandeur."

"Like most men I know," Anya said.

Caitlyn nodded. "Like one man in particular."

Anya smirked. "Delusional, yes, but not unattractive."

"You used him."

"And Flynn used me."

The woman was infuriating. Bitchy, entitled, and stubborn as hell. "You manipulated him."

"He wanted to save you, and all I did was try to help," Anya said.

"You wanted him to kill your husband."

"My husband is a dangerous man."

"And Flynn's a sucker for a damsel in distress."

"I wasn't the damsel he was after."

"Are you saying you didn't sleep with him?"

"What do you care? You dumped him."

"I was *never* with him. We were never a thing. He wanted to be. He thought we were, but we weren't. How could we be?"

"You broke his heart."

"He's not in his right mind."

Anya shrugged. "Who is?"

"Look, I'm not saying I don't care about him. I do. But he's damaged. Broken. He's not capable of….of…"

"Falling in love?" Anya's smile had a lot of snark. "Admit it. You still have feelings for him."

"I told you I did." Caitlyn's cheeks flushed.

"But he's not really a one-woman man, is he? Most men aren't. And he has that crazy confidence that most women find very attractive. So, I can see why you decided to walk away. Dump him before he could dump you."

"You don't know anything about him."

Anya smiled at that. "I see why he likes you. You're very fiery. Very fierce. And I think we can use that if we work together."

"Excuse me?"

"Oleg locked us up in the same room because he thought we would drive each other crazy."

"He wasn't wrong."

"No, but I think we can use our differences to our advantage."

"You want to work together?"

"I'll do the seducing. You do the ass-kicking."

"But we don't want the same thing. I want to stop Oleg and you want him dead."

"Too-MAY-toe. Too-MAH-toe."

Caitlyn wanted to slap her, but maybe she was right. Maybe they could help each other. "What do you know about Oleg's plan?"

Anya pushed herself up off the chair and paced. "I'm no computer expert, so I don't know the details, but I do know what he told the generals at the GRU. He wants to extort trillions from the U.S. and Western Europe, and bring down the NATO alliance."

"He's doing this for the Russian government?"

"No. That's what he told the GRU. But I believe he's tired of playing Putin's game. Tired of giving him half of everything he makes. Which makes me think he's not just going after the NATO alliance, but Russia too."

"What about China?"

"Why not? Might as well go for the whole enchilada."

"Seriously? He told you this?"

"No, not in so many words, but I listen. I pay attention. I've been with the man for twenty-five years. I know how he thinks. Oleg is a fan of Ayn Rand. He's a big believer in radical capitalism. He wants to stop the motor of the world, and he has the ego to believe he can do it. Every country on the planet will pay him trillions to save themselves. They will all be at his mercy. And he will become the richest and most powerful man who ever lived."

"So why try to kill him? Why not sit at his side as the queen of the world?"

"Because if he pulls this off, every country in the world will come together to hunt him down. Doesn't matter how much money or power he thinks he has. He will have burned all his bridges. He will have nowhere to go and no one to protect him. No, *krysha*, as we say in Russia. They will find him and they will kill him. And if I'm at his side, I'm dead too."

Caitlyn nodded. "Okay, well, that actually makes…sense."

"We already have more money than we'll ever spend. But somehow that's not enough for him. He can't just enjoy life and do whatever he wants. He must have everything. All of it. And no one else can have anything. And *that* is an actual mental illness."

"Are you saying he's crazy?"

"Of course he is. Most men like him are. He has both a narcissistic and antisocial personality disorder. He is paranoid. He has zero empathy. He is an asshole."

"Okay then."

Anya smiled. She stopped pacing, grabbed the collar of her t-shirt and ripped it hard. It hung off her shoulder and revealed the top of her cleavage along with a little side boob. "Stand up."

"What?"

"Up."

Caitlyn stood and Anya stepped closer. "Now hit me."

"Excuse me?"

"Not hard enough to knock me out. But bleeding would be good."

"I can't do that."

Anya slapped Caitlyn hard across the face, staggering her back. Caitlyn retaliated with a hard left hook that knocked Anya on her ass. She crashed into a table, knocking a marble bust and a bunch of crystal figurines to the floor.

Anya wobbled as she righted herself and touched her lip to see blood on her finger. "Good." She smeared it on her face and cleavage and then went to the locked door to their suite and pounded on it loud and insistently.

Bang! Bang! Bang! Bang! Bang!

An agitated male voice came from the other side, English with a Russian accent. "What?"

"She's trying to kill me," Anya screamed.

Bang! Bang! Bang! Bang! Bang!

Someone unlocked the door and abruptly opened it.

"Help me!" Anya shrieked. *"She's trying to kill me!"*

Two of Oleg's thugs pushed their way in. Caitlyn grabbed Anya by the back of her shirt and dragged her away from the door. Anya slapped at her and Caitlyn put her in a headlock. One thug grabbed Caitlyn. One grabbed Anya. They fought to pull them apart and finally separated them.

Anya and Caitlyn squirmed and screamed and spit and clawed at each other like two battling cats.

"Prekrati eto! Prekrati eto!" shouted one of the men.

"Uspokoit'sya!" yelled the other.

Caitlyn headbutted the man holding her with the back of her cranium. Once. Twice. He finally let her go after the third smack. She caught him in the throat with an elbow and hit him in the balls with a back fist. As he stumbled back, grabbing his groin, she took him to the ground with a sidekick to the knee and knocked him out with a boot to the head.

The thug holding Anya released her to take on Caitlyn. Anya grabbed a bronze figurine and cracked him in the back of the head. He staggered forward. Caitlyn kneed him in the chin, back to Anya, who smacked him in the head again.

Down he went.

Anya pulled his iPhone from his pocket and Caitlyn snatched his pistol from his holster. She twisted the barrel into his temple and gave him her insane asylum stare. "What's your passcode?"

He told her the code and Caitlyn cracked him in the head with the butt of his gun, knocking him cold.

Anya unlocked the phone and reset the Face ID using her own face. "Let's go!"

They hurried out the door into the corridor, turned a corner and ran right into Kalishnik, a big grin on his face. Before Caitlyn could strike, two of his men grabbed her from behind, each taking an arm. She drove her heel into one of the men's insteps. He grunted in pain but held on. She wriggled and fought and tried to kick Kalishnik in the balls, but he blocked her, dropped his shoulder, and threw a left uppercut that caught her right in the solar plexus.

The punch paralyzed her diaphragm and knocked all the air out of her. She gasped like a fish out of water as the two men dragged her back into the room and dropped her face down on the floor. Out of the corner of her eye she saw Anya go flying and heard her crash into a table, tchotchkes falling, glass shattering.

Caitlyn tried to push herself up, but Kalishnik put his foot on the back of her neck and smashed her to the floor. The thugs she and Anya knocked out were carried from the room by Kalishnik's other men.

"If Oleg didn't want to interrogate you, I'd snap your neck right now," Kalishnik said. "But once he knows everything you know, I'll have my opportunity. I'm looking forward to some alone time with you."

"I knew you were nasty," Anya said. "But I had no idea how creepy."

"*Suka*," Kalishnik spat. He took his foot off Caitlyn's neck and left the room, locking the door.

Caitlyn sat up, rubbing her neck. "Well, that went well."

Anya pulled out the iPhone she stole from the unconscious thug, opened it with her face, and frowned. "No bars in here and the Wi-Fi sucks balls. There's a cell tower on the property, but this fucking castle has five-foot-thick walls."

"So, we need to get out of this room to use it."

"And fast. This thing's almost out of power. The battery's in the red."

CHAPTER THIRTY-SIX

The stars burned bright in the moonless sky. Flynn stood on the bluffs overlooking Maybole Shore. He wore black cargo pants, a black t-shirt, black combat boots, a black tactical softshell jacket, a military backpack, and a dark gray digital watch. The time flashed blue. 2:54 a.m. Low tide. That would allow him to traverse the beach to Culzean Castle and enter the caves without scuba gear. He attached his climbing rope to a thick shrub and pulled it tight to test it, then threaded the rope through his climbing belt and stepped backwards off the bluff to rappel down to the beach below.

The mind rebelled at stepping backwards off a cliff, but Flynn had to override that primitive animal instinct, that fear of falling, and step into the unknown. He leaned straight back and rappelled down the bluff. Soon the muscle memory took over and he heard the familiar music in his head. The thrilling thrum of the electric guitar. The throbbing beat. The excitement. The exhilaration.

Then the shrub gave way as Flynn's weight ripped it out of the ground. He fell straight back, twenty feet down, hitting the beach hard. Gasping, stunned, all the air knocked out of him. A smoke grenade came undone and when he grabbed it, he dislodged the pin. Billowing smoke obscured everything as he rolled over onto his knees and crawled out of the cloud. The saltiness of the sea air filled his nostrils. When his head stopped swimming, he worked his way to his feet. He watched as the smoke slowly dissipated and wondered if he had alerted anyone. But the only sound was the crashing of the waves on Maybole Shore.

Flynn put on his night-vision goggles and turned the world from dark and shadowy to bright green. He was a half-mile from Culzean Castle and didn't think Ivanov would send a patrol so far up the beach, but he kept to the cliffs just in case, and kept a sharp eye out. That was when he noticed the wooden staircase that led to the beach from the bluffs.

Bloody hell.

Flynn made his way carefully down the rocky beach, strewn with boulders covered with brown seaweed and moss. Soon the exterior and window lights on Culzean Castle came into view, shrouded in fog. On the beach, just below the castle grounds, angry voices rose. Some sounded young and Scottish, and some had Russian accents. Flynn noticed the unmistakable aroma of weed.

He stepped around the edge of the bluff. Two teenagers stood by a campfire, arguing with a trio of security men.

"It's trespassing!" barked a Russian baritone.

"But we've been comin' 'ere forever!" a Scottish teenager countered.

"I don't care! It's private property now!"

The other teen shouted. "Tis a public beach, ye bleedin' gowk!"

"Get up! Get out of here! Go!" demanded the Russian.

"Or whit?" said the second teen, his voice full of righteous indignation. "Ye gonna feckin' shoot us?"

Flynn heard a slap and a grunt as the teens struggled and protested.

"Ow! Awright!

"Git yer bloody hands aff me!"

"Let me go, ya roaster!"

"Yer hurting me!"

Flynn took advantage of the commotion to sneak past. The entrance to the cave was close, just below the castle bluffs. A dark entrance veiled in shadow and fog loomed ahead. The Russians were too busy hassling the teens to notice Flynn.

He entered and disappeared into the earthy darkness. The angry voices faded as he made his way down a tight passageway. Vermin scurried past his boots. With his night-vision, Flynn saw rats scampering into the shadows. The hairs went up on the back of his neck. He crouched to move forward and found multiple branching paths. The cold damp air carried hints of something dead. Something rotting.

Which way to go? How to know?

He figured any path that led upward might lead to somewhere inside the castle itself. But he kept running into dead ends. *And what the hell is that smell?* Some small woodland creature must have died in there. He didn't think there'd be wolves or bears living in the cave, but there could be bats and badgers to keep company with the rats.

Badgers were vicious and plentiful in Scotland. If he stumbled upon a den, he'd have to go toe-to-toe with who knows how many savage, blood-crazed badgers.

Flynn stopped short when he heard a sound behind him. *Was that a hiss? A growl?* He quickly turned, but didn't see anything. Sweat trickled down the middle of his back. He tried another passage, and another. He turned a corner and the flapping of wings startled him. Something smacked him in the face and squeaked and squealed. Furious flapping clapped at his ears. The frightened faces of blind, screeching bats filled his field of vision. Tiny mouths with pointy teeth and little claws caught in his hair. Flynn turned to run and the bats tried to get past him. Flying into him. Flying over him. Beating against him with their creepy, leathery wings. Flynn tripped and fell, and the bats flew over him. How many, he couldn't tell. But finally, they were gone, their panicked flapping receding as they disappeared into the musty gloom.

Flynn fought to compose himself. Every square inch of his skin crawled with disgust. He pushed himself to his knees, and then to his feet. He had to get a grip. Anya and Caitlyn were in danger, and he might be their only hope. He knew Caitlyn resented being treated like a damsel in distress, but he also felt responsible for blowing her cover and putting her in even greater peril. So even though she might take offense, he had no choice but to rescue her. (Not that he would ever admit to that.) Flynn steeled himself and shook off his heebie-jeebies before continuing on, determined to find that secret doorway into the castle.

His night-vision flickered off and on, and the green strobe effect only made the cave that much creepier. *Did one of the bats knock something loose? Bloody hell.* He smacked his goggles and the flickering stopped just as he stepped into a spider web.

He spun around in a panic and clawed the web off his face. Some got in his mouth. He spat and flailed like a lunatic. Flynn ran as he batted at his head, his night-vision flickering. He tripped on something and fell hard, his face kissing the dirt as a chorus of muffled squeaks caused him to leap right back up. With his night-vision dead, he flicked on his tactical flashlight. Rats scurried away. Flynn was sure he had smashed one flat, but then rats can flatten themselves like roadkill to get through the tightest of places. He aimed his flashlight on the one he landed on. It popped up abruptly, threw him a dirty look, and limped away.

Flynn pressed ahead, crouching lower and lower to keep moving forward as the passageway narrowed. His flashlight threw weird shadows. Soon he'd have to crawl on his hands and knees.

Is this another dead end?

He backed up just as something scuffled behind him. *What the hell was that?* He moved forward. *Faster!* Finally, falling to his hands and knees, he crawled quick as he could. The snarls behind him grew louder. Closer. Cold air hit him in the face and he realized he could stand and run. Whatever stalked him still pursued him. *Growling. Snarling. Hissing.* His flashlight beam went everywhere as Flynn ran, panting. Heart pounding. Gasping. Breathless.

A bright light blinded him a second before he crashed into someone coming from the other direction. Their heads cracked together. Flynn's flashlight hit the ground and rolled, illuminating the face of the monster pursuing him.

A raccoon stood up on its hind legs and raised its tiny hands to hide its glowing yellow eyes from the glare of the light. It bared its teeth and growled and hissed and scurried off the other way.

"Whit the hell, pal?"

Flynn recognized the voice as belonging to one of the Scottish teens from the beach. The shorter scrappier one. "Sorry, mate, I didn't see you."

"Because yer were running like a damn lunatic!" The kid picked up his flashlight and shined it in Flynn's face. "What the hell is that on yer head?"

"Night-vision goggles, but they seem to be on the blink." Flynn pulled them off and dropped them in the dirt.

"Why was that trash panda chasing you?"

"I have no idea."

"Those wee bastards are vicious buggers."

"I saw you boys on the beach. Why were those guards hassling you?"

"Because they think they own the world."

"Fookin' Rooskies," the taller one said from out of the darkness.

"They're buying up everything!" said the shorter one. "One of 'em bought Chelsea F.C. for fook's sake."

"Yeah, but the fooker just sold it, didn't he?"

"'Cause they fookin' made him sell it."

"Now another one goes n' buys Culzean Castle joost cause he can."

"We've been using this beach since we were weans. How is this private property?"

"It's the fookin' beach, for fook's sake!"

"We let those Rooskies think we left, but came in here to wait 'em out."

A match flared as the shorter teen lit up a joint. "You want some ganj?"

"I'm good," Flynn said. "Is that legal here?"

"You a copper?"

"Not exactly."

"Well, whit then? Whit's that outfit yer sportin'?"

"Yeah, what the fook ye doin' 'ere?" asked the taller one.

"I'm with His Majesty's Secret Service."

The teens laughed. When Flynn didn't, they both smirked.

"No fookin' way."

"You serious?"

Flynn nodded. "A CIA agent is being held prisoner in this castle and I'm here to extract her."

The two teens laughed again.

"Come on, pal?"

"What are you really here for?"

Flynn unzipped his jacket, revealing a shoulder holster on each side. One with the SIG Sauer and one holding the MAC-10.

"Those fookin' real?" asked the smaller one.

Flynn drew the submachine gun. "An Ingram MAC-10 with a Gemtech suppressor."

"That ain't fookin' real," the taller teen scoffed.

Flynn shot a suppressed burst into the dark. Sparks flew as bullets ricocheted off rocks. Both teens jumped.

"Holy bugger!"

"Whit th' hell!"

Flynn re-holstered the MAC-10 and zipped up his jacket. "I heard there was a secret doorway to the castle, but it's like a bloody maze down here."

"The old door?" The shorter teen lit up his face with his flashlight. "We kin show you the way."

"You know where it is?"

"Pal, we've been playin' in these caves since we were ten."

"But there's no way in," the taller teen warned. "That fookin' door's locked tighter than a nun's hoo-ha."

"You let me worry about that," Flynn said.

"You get in, you gonna shoot the assholes who hassled us?"

"If they shoot at me."

"Braw!"

"Tidy!"

"What's that accent then?" asked the shorter teen. "Is that American?"

"No, I'm from the UK originally," Flynn replied.

"The UK?" the smaller teen asked.

"No way," said the taller friend.

"I did spend a long time in the states."

"Well, it's a strange fookin' accent, isn't it?" the short one said.

"Pure weird is what it is," his friend agreed.

"I'm Rory by the way." The shorter teen reached out his hand. Flynn shook it.

"Ewan," said the other. Flynn shook his hand as well.

"James."

"All right, then, James" Rory took a big hit of *ganj*. "Let's fook some shite up!"

. . .

Flynn never would have found the door on his own, but even stoned out of their minds, the teens knew exactly where to go. Up one passageway and down another. Within ten minutes, all three had their flashlights aimed at a rusted, wrought iron door bolted into the stone. Two massive padlocks held it shut.

Ewan examined one of the locks. "These look pretty new."

"You ain't cutting that with a bolt cutter," Rory said.

Flynn nodded. "They're keyless combination locks made with hardened titanium steel. Pry proof and pick proof."

Flynn set down his backpack and pulled out one of the thermite breach pens. He unscrewed the bottom and retrieved the high temperature match. He then donned his asbestos gloves and his safety glasses with the darkened lenses.

"What's that?" Rory asked.

"Thermite. It burns at 4,000 degrees Fahrenheit."

"And that can cut through steel?"

"Hardened steel and titanium. Back up now and don't look directly into the light."

Flynn struck the match on the rough red surface at the bottom of the breaching pen. The match ignited like a sparkler, and he used it to ignite the thermite itself. It caught and burned as bright as a welding torch.

"Holy shite!" Rory exclaimed. Ewen laughed.

Flynn kept his distance as he used the thermite on the padlocks. It crackled and popped and threw off a shower of bright sparks. After twenty seconds, the hardened steel glowed red, softened, and melted. Flynn pulled the padlock free and let it fall before igniting another thermite pen, and melting the second lock. Glowing hot slag covered the ground.

Flynn pulled on the door. It didn't budge. Rory gave him a hand, but even together they couldn't move it.

"I think the fooker's rusted shut."

Flynn used the other two breach pens on the old hinges. The rusted wrought iron melted quicker than the titanium steel. The teens helped Flynn pull on the door. It finally came free and fell to the floor. They all jumped out of the way as it landed with a loud clang.

"Let's hope they didn't hear that upstairs," Rory said.

Flynn shined his flashlight through the door and illuminated an ancient corridor lined with stone and brick. "All right, boys, I appreciate the help, but from here on out I go alone."

"You got that right," Ewan said. "Those Rooskies are mean fookers."

"You sure you don't want a hit off this?" Rory offered Flynn the ganj again.

"I'm good." Flynn took off his safety glasses and headed into the tunnel.

Rory took a big hit. "See ya!"

"Laters!" Ewan added as Rory passed him the ganj.

CHAPTER THIRTY-SEVEN

In the summer of 1946, Larry Taylor, a graduate student in Civil Engineering at Stanford, bumped into Al Baxter buying hobnails at the campus shoe shop, giving him away as a rock climber. Together with Fritz Lippman, they founded the Stanford Alpine Club, one of the first rock climbing clubs at an American university. Woman climbers joined that very first year. In 1965, four women from the club made the first all-female climb of the North Face of Grand Teton. One of those women, Irene Beardsley, became the fourth woman to ever earn a Ph.D. in physics from Stanford. In 1978, Irene and a group of six female climbers were the first Americans to ascend Annapurna in Nepal.

While a student at Stanford, Caitlyn took up rock climbing to improve her upper body strength. She worked out every day on the university climbing wall and joined the Alpine Club. Yosemite National Park, a mecca for rock climbers, became her regular weekend getaway. She ascended Half Dome countless times and became one of the first women to solo free climb El Capitan.

So, the idea of climbing a castle wall five stories above a rocky bluff didn't bother her the way it would most people. Because of the overhang, she couldn't see a way down without a rope. But she could see a way up. It wouldn't be easy. There weren't obvious handholds, and the ocean mist made the rock slick. However, waiting for Kalishnik to show up and torture her didn't sound like a walk in the park either.

She shattered one of the windows and broke out the wooden panes.

"You're as crazy as Flynn," Anya said.

"When that guard wakes up, he's going to realize he doesn't have his phone. They will come looking for it, and when that happens, we are screwed."

"Are you climbing all the way down?"

"Not down. Up."

She raised an eyebrow. "Up?"

"If I can get to the roof, I might be able to get a cell signal."

"If."

"*If* is all we have right now."

"And you actually think this is doable?"

"Back at Stanford, we used to climb the buildings in the quad. Memorial Church. Hoover Tower."

"The school let you do this?"

"No, but we did it anyway. Usually at night. So, I have some experience."

Anya shook her head. "Well, I'm not staying in here alone."

"You ever do any rock climbing?"

"We have a climbing wall at my gym."

"It's not really the same thing."

"Then you're going to have to help me."

"You're safer staying here."

"If they open this door and *you're* gone, and *I* don't have the phone, that won't go well for me. I have a low pain threshold. If they tortured me, I'd have to tell them where you are. Besides, you need my face to unlock the phone."

"Not if you give me the new passcode."

"Screw that. Screw you. I'm coming with."

"Fine." Caitlyn knocked the last of the glass shards off the window frame and climbed out onto the exterior windowsill, using a sidepull to reach a higher handhold on the stone. She called to Anya inside. "I see a lot of handholds, but the stone's a little slippery, so make sure you have a solid foothold before you start climbing."

"Got it! Just go already."

■   ■   ■

The corridor from the cave led to an ancient stone staircase. At the top of the steps, Flynn found another door, not iron, but steel, with a keyed doorknob and a keyed deadbolt. Both were relatively easy for Flynn to handle with his lock picking tools. He eased the door open and poked his head inside to find a brick-walled corridor with a vaulted stone floor. Flynn moved past various storage areas and climbed another staircase to a heavy wooden door with another easy-to-pick lock. That door led to a much more up-to-date hallway with a concrete floor and fluorescent lights overhead. It was like stepping from the past into the present; from the middle-ages to modern day.

Muffled voices echoed down the corridor. Flynn crept forward past storage rooms and windowless offices with workers typing away at computers. The voices grew louder, the air cooler. He heard the hum of an air purification system and noticed vents high up on the wall. Security cameras watched him from the corners.

He passed a glass door. Inside, fluorescent lights illuminated a large data center. Computers in racks lined the walls, and cables snaked everywhere. A few techs in black cargo pants and anti-static lab jackets worked on the system. They were too absorbed in their duties to notice him, but even if they had, Flynn's all black attire fit right in.

Further down the corridor, Flynn found an elevator, but needed a key card to access it. He continued past a set of double-glass doors that revealed a large open office filled with dozens of cubicles. Two of the hackers from the yacht, Nosferatu, the founder of the Fang Dynasty, and 0nyx, leader of Night Shade, argued with a woman sitting at a workstation.

Is this the nerve center of the operation? The heart of the plot to blackmail the planet?

Over the years, Flynn confronted and foiled several evil masterminds who had tried to blackmail the world. One threatened to annihilate a major city with a nuclear bomb. Another threatened to vaporize an entire country with a space laser. But this might be the worst threat yet. If Bettina O'Toole-Applebaum was correct, Ivanov's plot would allow him to access nuclear missile silos and launch codes, shut down water systems and electrical grids, disrupt stock exchanges and financial networks. He could kill thousands if not millions and plunge the world economy into chaos. Somehow, Flynn had to stop him, but he didn't want to raise the alarm.

Not until Anya and Caitlyn were safe.

Where could he be holding them? Down here somewhere? Does Culzean Castle have a dungeon? Are they being interrogated? Tortured? Are they even alive?

Flynn had one more pressing concern as well.

He suddenly needed to pee.

There had to be a loo down here somewhere. What evil mastermind would build a secret underground lair without a place to piddle? Before he could save Caitlyn or the world, he needed to have a tinkle.

Flynn searched the corridors, passed what looked like a snack room, and bumped into someone coming around the corner. The man wore glasses and a short-sleeved checkered shirt with a plastic pocket protector. His eyes widened with alarm.

Flynn smiled apologetically. "Excuse me, but can you please point me to the loo?"

The guy seemed surprised by the question. Flynn decided that the man assumed that anyone politely asking for a toilet wasn't likely to be an intruder. He pointed past Flynn down the hallway. "Straight to the end, make a right, and then a left at the server room. You can't miss it."

"Thanks."

Flynn found it without a problem. A large men's room greeted him with a cement floor and six urinals. Flynn quickly unzipped, piddled, and sighed with relief. He heard a flush and the door to a toilet stall opened behind him. He glanced in the mirror over the sinks and caught the reflection of the man who emerged.

Nosferatu.

Flynn saw the look of recognition and surprise in Nosferatu's eyes. With no time to zip up or even stop peeing, Flynn turned to confront him. Nosferatu dashed for the door. Flynn lunged, tackling him. They wrestled on the cold tile, and Flynn locked him up in a classic Brazilian Jiu-Jitsu submission hold. The Triangle Choke. Using one's legs, the attacker traps the opponent's neck and head. The pressure of the thighs disrupts the blood flow to the brain, causing the target to either submit or pass out. Nosferatu went limp and Flynn released him, zipped up, and stood. He ripped the key card off Nosferatu's neck, and hurried into the hall to find Onyx with a hulking security guard standing just behind him.

Recognition dawned.

"Mr. Flynn?"

Flynn crossed his arms and reached under his jacket. He drew his SIG Sauer and MAC-10, one in each hand. Onyx turned to run and collided with the security man, knocking him to the floor.

The security man pulled his sidearm. Flynn kicked it out of his hand before taking off around a corner.

An alarm screamed.

Flynn rounded another corner to face another guard. The man unloaded on him. Bullets ricocheted everywhere. Flynn ducked back the other way and raced down another corridor. He caught sight of another security man reaching for his weapon. Flynn fired, forcing him back.

He headed for the elevators and turned a corner. Two more guards came from the other direction. Both raised their weapons. Flynn pushed through a set of double-glass doors to escape and found himself in the data center. He fired his weapons into the ceiling. Technicians scattered. Shredded acoustic tile floated down like snow. As he moved deeper into the center, the techs scrambled to escape.

Flynn hid behind one of the computer racks and checked his ammo as more enemies arrived. A familiar voice shouted orders.

"Do not fire or draw his fire! We do not want to damage these servers!"

"Mr. Ivanov," Flynn said. "We meet again."

"You're supposed to be in California, Mr. Flynn! What the hell are you doing here?"

Flynn stayed hidden behind a server rack. "Caitlyn Valentine! Where is she?"

"You're here for *her*? *Are you kidding me*?"

"And your wife as well. What have you done to them?"

"Nothing! I haven't done anything!"

"Then where are they?"

"Here. Upstairs! They're both fine!"

"Somehow, I doubt that!"

"Let me show you. But first, you need to put down your weapons."

"And make me your prisoner as well? No, I don't think so. Bring them down here. Bring them both to me now."

"And if I don't?"

"I will set off an explosive charge and blow this data center to smithereens!"

"Like you blew up my yacht?"

"That was an accident."

"*You* are an accident! A walking disaster, bringing catastrophe wherever you go."

"I'm not the one threatening to unleash chaos on the world," Flynn shouted.

"Chaos is already what we have! Chaos is what we've *always* had. Temperatures are rising, glaciers are melting, nuclear superpowers are fighting for supremacy. If the leaders of this world don't unleash nuclear Armageddon, they will kill us all by destroying the climate. Because no one is in charge. No one can agree. Millions fight for their little piece of the pie, and in the end we all will die."

"That's not a very optimistic view."

"I'm not a very optimistic person."

"So, what's *your* plan?"

"Simple. Someone needs to take charge."

"And that would be you?"

"Why not? This squabbling has to end, and I can end it. I can be the voice of reason."

Flynn chuckled. "World domination. The same old dream. Our asylums are full of people who think they're Napoleon. Or God."

"You would know."

"So, I suppose you want me to join you."

"Why would I want *that*?"

"Because every villain I've ever clashed with claims they could use a man like me. Someone with my particular skill set. They always expect me to abandon King and Country and join their mad cause."

"I don't."

"I think you do," Flynn replied.

"I'm telling you I don't."

"You're using reverse psychology, but it won't work on me."

"Reverse psychology?"

"Just admit it."

"Admit what?"

"You want me to join you."

"No. *I don't.*"

"Okay, then. What if I said yes?"

"Then I would say no," Ivanov retorted. "I don't want you."

"I think you do."

"What is your problem?"

"What is *your* problem?"

"*You're* my problem!" Ivanov shouted.

"Is that why you want me to join you?"

"Would someone please shoot him?" The guards standing behind Ivanov traded looks, wondering if their boss was serious. "*SHOOT HIM!*"

Flynn fired his MAC-10 at the fluorescent lights overhead. Ivanov and his men dove for cover. Flynn moved from aisle to aisle, shooting out every overhead light in the room, plunging the data center into darkness. The blinking computers offered the only illumination. Ivanov's men returned fire, but had no idea where Flynn was. Muzzle flashes and showers of sparks from shattered computers lit up the room.

"Stop shooting! Hold your fire!" Ivanov screamed.

Flynn shot out the glass doors a second before diving through them and somersaulting into the corridor. He turned to run and slammed into Kalishnik. He grabbed Flynn by both wrists and wrenched the weapons out of his hands. The brute kneed Flynn in the groin and then in the face when Flynn bent over at the waist.

Flynn hit the ground hard, landing on his arse. Dazed and bleeding, he scrambled to his feet, but Kalishnik blocked his path to the elevators. A tiny smile curled the corner of Kalishnik's mouth as he took a fighting stance. Flynn nodded in acknowledgement and took his own stance, left foot forward, knees slightly bent, arms up and elbows in to protect his ribs.

Ivanov and the other guards stepped into the corridor to watch the confrontation.

Flynn rolled his head to loosen his neck and raised his fists. "So, it's mano a mano then?"

Kalishnik growled.

Flynn simultaneously pulled a flashbang from one pouch and a smoke grenade from the other. He gripped both pins in his teeth and pulled, tossing them, and turning, closing his eyes as the flashbang exploded, blinding everyone in the room but Flynn. White smoke billowed everywhere.

Flynn bumped into someone and kneed them in what he assumed was their groin. He heard grunts, punches, shouts, scuffling, and then someone started shooting and bodies started dropping and Ivanov screamed, *"Nyet! Nyet! Derzhi svoy ogon!"*

CHAPTER THIRTY-EIGHT

Caitlyn found a straight-forward route to the battlements above. Even with the damp night air and the cold, crumbling, slippery rock, her climbing skills made the ascent a breeze. She edged, pinched, smeared, and crimped her way up and over onto the top of the tower. Caitlyn leaned over the ledge to check on Anya. The Russian struggled up the wall, making slow and shaky progress.

Caitlyn shout-whispered, "You okay?"

"No!"

"Put most of the weight on your legs."

Anya reached out with one arm. "Can you pull me up?" And nearly lost her balance. She scrabbled, finding a panicky handhold.

"Careful!"

"No shit. If I fall, you're totally screwed."

"More screwed than you?"

"Yeah, because you need my face to unlock the phone, so you better hope I can hang on."

"You're doing great. Just keep coming. Slow and steady. And don't look down."

"Why'd you say that? Now I *have* to look down."

"Don't. Just keep looking for that next handhold."

"You used to do this shit for *fun*?"

"Less talking. More climbing."

"Talking takes my mind off falling and dying." She climbed a little higher, lost her grip, slipped, and barely caught herself. "*Pizdets!*"

"Just a little farther."

"*Fuck you!*"

"You can do it." A light drizzle began to fall.

"Is it *fucking* raining?"

"Drizzling."

"*Goddammit!*"

"Keep climbing!" Caitlyn leaned through a crenel, braced herself on the battlement, and reached down. "Almost there!"

"All that yoga and pilates for what?" Anya bitched. "A lot of goddamn good it did me!"

"Keep coming!"

"Bite my ass!" She reached up and Caitlyn grabbed her by the wrist and pulled. Anya scrambled up and over. She collapsed on the flagstone and tried to catch her breath.

"You did it."

"*Fuck you.*"

Caitlyn held the phone in front of Anya's face and unlocked the screen. Only one bar. She moved across the ramparts, checking the phone. Two bars. She memorized the emergency extraction code right before she started her assignment. The number went directly to a burner carried by the CIA's Chief of Station in London. No one else at CIA or at the embassy in London knew she was undercover. The Chief of Station, a woman by the name of Haskell, picked up on the second ring. "Talk to me."

"This is Renegade."

"What's the code?"

"Tree, shoe, car, blue, fire, rock."

"Location?"

"Culzean Castle. Scotland."

A pause. "We have a team in Glasgow. I'll scramble them immediately."

"That might not be soon enough."

Haskell hung up. Caitlyn turned to see Anya with her hand out, reaching for the phone.

"My turn."

"Who are *you* calling?"

"Quick!" Anya snapped her fingers. "Before it runs out of juice."

Anya took the phone and stepped away. She punched in a number and started speaking in Russian. As Caitlyn spoke passable Russian, she stepped closer to eavesdrop, but the conversation, like her own, seemed to be in code.

■　■　■

Flynn made it out of the smoke still suffering from flash blindness. After bumping into a few walls, he found an open stairwell and bounded up the steps. He heard enemies behind him, their heavy boots pounding up the stairs. He pulled a flashbang, yanked the pin, and dropped it behind him, closing his eyes as he headed up the stairwell. He heard the *bang* and the high-pitched whine and chaos as his pursuers collided into walls and each other and shouted curses in Russian.

Flynn found himself on the first floor of the castle and called out for Caitlyn, but couldn't find her and raced up an elegant staircase. He dropped a smoke grenade behind him as he quickly searched room after room, calling Caitlyn's name. He continued to the top floor and moved down a corridor lined with huge oil paintings and beautiful antiques.

Every room was open, except for one.

He rattled the knob. He banged on the door. "Caitlyn! Anya!" He took a step back and tried to kick it open, but it wouldn't budge. Then he heard heavy footfalls behind him. Flynn turned and tried a jiujitsu move but Kalishnik easily countered it, pounded him in the solar plexus, and hit him with an uppercut that sent him into the air. Flynn landed with a thump. Two of his men held Flynn down while Kalishnik opened the locked door. His men dragged him inside and dropped him on the floor. From his position on the Persian rug, Flynn looked around the ornate suite and noticed that one of the large windows that overlooked the sea was shattered. Kalishnik shouted something in Russian. His men raced around, searching every other room in the suite. Kalishnik poked his head out the broken window, cursed in Russian, and shouted orders to his men. They all hurried into the corridor. Kalishnik, the last one out, locked the door behind himself, locking Flynn inside.

Could this be where they were holding Anya and Caitlyn? Is it possible they escaped? Flynn painfully rolled over onto his hands and knees and used an antique table to pull himself to his feet. *The broken window? A dead giveaway.* Flynn knew Caitlyn was an accomplished rock climber. Would she risk climbing down? Of course she would. She had no physical fear. In fact, she was the bravest person Flynn had ever met.

Flynn leaned through the broken window to see a wide overhang. Without a rope, there was no way down to the ground. But up was another story. The battlements were just a floor or two above. Flynn had no reason to wait for Kalishnik's return. In the end, they would torture and kill him. A five-story fall to his death would likely be less painful.

Flynn eased himself out the window and found a foothold and then a handhold. A cold wind blew from the sea, and the castle walls were damp and slippery. Still, this had to be the way Caitlyn and Anya escaped.

Unless they both fell to their deaths.

With shaky and weary arms and legs, Flynn made his way up the castle wall. His ribs ached and his head throbbed, but he concentrated on making one foothold and one handhold after another. Slow. Careful. He didn't dare look down. The vertigo would pull him off the wall and send him plummeting to the rocks below.

Look up. Straight up. Concentrate. Search for the next handhold. The next foothold. Focus.

Flynn was nearly to the top when he lost his grip and started to slip. He scrambled to find purchase and felt himself slide as someone grabbed his wrist. And then another someone grabbed his other wrist. Together they pulled. Flynn found a foothold and finally grabbed the battlements. Up and over and flat on his back on the cold stone. Winded. Trembling.

Caitlyn and Anya looked down at him with a combination of relief and consternation. They grabbed his arms and pulled him to his feet.

"Appreciate the help, ladies."

Caitlyn tenderly touched his bruised and bloody face. "What the hell happened?"

"You look like you were hit by a truck," Anya said.

"A truck named Kalishnik."

Flynn wavered. Caitlyn steadied him. "How did you even know we were here?"

"On the way from Glasgow, I borrowed the phone of the guard sitting next to me and unlocked it with his sleeping face." Anya said. "I only had time for two words before we hit a bump and he woke up."

Flynn offered Anya a wan smile. "Those were all the words I needed." Exhausted from his ordeal, Flynn sat his tired arse on the edge of the battlement.

Anya sat next to him. "You came here to rescue me?"

"That was the plan."

Caitlyn looked miffed. "You came here to save *her*?"

Flynn smiled at that. "Why would I rescue you? You can take care of yourself. You made that abundantly clear more than once. But if you want to tag along with Anya and I as we make our escape, you're more than welcome."

"MI5 is already on the way," Caitlyn said. "We were hoping we could hide here until they arrived, but since they put you in the room we were in, they must know—"

"—that you escaped." Ivanov finished Caitlyn's sentence as he stepped through a rooftop door. Kalishnik and five huge guys followed behind him. Everybody had a weapon and every single one pointed at Flynn, Caitlyn, and/or Anya. "Annoying as you are, I do admire your persistence." Kalishnik whispered something to Ivanov. "I don't see why not," Ivanov replied. He looked at Flynn. "Kalishnik would like to throw you off the roof."

"I might have something to say about that."

"Something to say, perhaps, but nothing you can do about it."

"*No?*" Flynn positioned himself in a fighting stance.

Kalishnik and the five thugs laughed.

Ivanov waggled his head. "You are as embarrassing as you are exhausting. It's time to put you down."

A faint buzz mingled with the sound of the wind. The buzz grew louder, like an angry bee. Flynn followed the sound to a distant light in the night's sky. Kalishnik followed Flynn's gaze as the angry buzz became a distant chuntering. Closer still. Flynn recognized the whip of blades beating the air. Soon, everyone turned to watch the approaching helicopter.

One of Kalishnik's men aimed his weapon at it, and an invisible hand slammed him to the ground. The crack of the sniper rifle arrived seconds later as another thug literally lost his head. Shock and awe widened Ivanov's eyes as the next high-powered bullet sent the thug to his left flying off the edge of the battlements.

Flynn tackled Anya and protected her body with his own as Kalishnik dragged Ivanov back into the building. The chopper hovered above, the roar deafening. Kalishnik's last two men fired on it to cover Ivanov's escape. Both were cut down almost instantly by what sounded like a minigun.

Ropes dropped down and a dozen commandoes rappelled to the rooftop. Dressed in black and wearing ballistic masks, half of them went after Ivanov. The other six pointed their assault rifles at Flynn, Caitlyn, and Anya.

"Lower your weapons!" Caitlyn shouted. "I'm the one who called this in!"

The commando leader shouted, "On your knees! Now!"

Flynn couldn't help but notice the Russian accent and the fact that they carried AK-12s, standard issue for Spetsnaz.

Stunned, Caitlyn raised her hands and dropped to her knees. "Who the hell are you? You aren't MI5."

"No, they are not," Anya said as she pushed Flynn off her and took command of the situation.

The squad leader asked Anya a question in Russian. She shook her head and translated for Flynn and Caitlyn. "They asked me if they should shoot you, and I said no. The enemy here is Ivanov. You two are free to go."

The commandoes ushered Anya through the rooftop doorway, leaving Flynn and Caitlyn alone on the battlements. Gunfire echoed below.

Flynn turned to Caitlyn to find her glaring at him. "What?"

"You shielded her with your body."

"Who?"

"Anya! You tackled and protected her. You were ready to take a bullet for her."

"Would you rather I tackled you?"

"No. Yes. Maybe. I don't know," Caitlyn sputtered.

"*Clearly.*"

"Are you in love with her?"

"Anya?"

Caitlyn searched Flynn's eyes. "If you are. Just tell me."

"I'm in love with *you*."

"Jesus Christ." Caitlyn blinked away tears.

"Perhaps this isn't the time or place to be talking about this."

"I think Anya works for the FSB."

"I agree."

"I think she's using them like she used you."

"Anya wasn't using me. I was using her. And we can't let the Russians get what's on those servers."

"What servers?"

"Ivanov has a huge data center down in the basement. I shot up some of it, but most of it's still intact."

Caitlyn took a shotgun from one of the fallen thugs. "That must be where Ivanov's headed."

Flynn grabbed a pistol from the holster of another thug and followed her into the building.

CHAPTER THIRTY-NINE

Ransomware gangs have preyed on companies, industries, and governments the world over. It is estimated that cybercrime costs the worldwide economy upwards of eight trillion dollars a year. In 2022, KP Snacks, the UK's second largest snack company, suffered such an attack. Systems were compromised and orders could no longer be processed or dispatched. Hackers wiped out their entire IT and communication system. Stores ran out of top selling snack brands like Skips, Wheat Crunchies, Hula Hoops, Space Raiders, Pom-Bears, Choc-Dips, and Nik Naks. The entire snack supply of the UK was compromised, and stores were bereft of crisps, popcorn, and nuts for months.

Continuous gunfire echoed up the stairwell as Flynn directed Caitlyn deeper into the castle, down one stairwell and then another, through the corridor and past the room where Caitlyn was held prisoner. Down another stairwell, closer to the fight. Shouts of anger. Screams of pain. The muffled reports and reverberation of shotguns, assault rifles, and machine guns. Once they reached the bottom of the castle's ornate spiral staircase, the gunfire echoed everywhere. A bullet whistled by Flynn's head and thudded into the wall behind him.

Rather than fire back and get bogged down in a fight, Flynn retreated down a hallway. Caitlyn stayed with him, and bullets followed, smashing antiques and *objets d' art*. Flynn rounded a corner to find more of Ivanov's men coming from the other direction.

"Flynn!" Caitlyn shouted. She pointed to a doorway before shouldering her way in. Flynn rushed in behind her. A vast array of 18th century armaments covered the walls, including flintlock rifles, sabers and claymores. The door burst open before Caitlyn could bolt it. A handful of Ivanov's men barreled inside. Flynn dove behind a settee. Caitlyn ducked behind a sideboard. A thug with a shotgun blew the settee to bits, and Flynn scrambled behind a marble pillar, firing on them until his weapon clicked empty.

As Ivanov's men bolted the door and took positions around the room, Flynn grabbed a fallen saber off the floor. He knew if they surrendered, they'd be executed on the spot. He glanced at Caitlyn, crouched behind the sideboard. They shared a last look. Her anger softened to affection and regret. She nodded to him. He knew she was determined to go down fighting. Flynn steeled himself for the battle ahead, but before he could make a move, Spetsnaz commandos breached the door, blowing it off its hinges. The heavy door flattened one of Ivanov's men. The other two threw up their hands in surrender. The commandos disarmed and zip-tied them, leaving them face down on the floor before rushing back out.

Flynn waved his saber, motioning for Caitlyn to follow. "Come on!"

Out in the corridor, the gunfire sounded more sporadic now. Flynn headed for the stairwell. They passed a number of bodies along the way. Most seemed to be Ivanov's men. The door to the stairwell hung open when they arrived and Flynn took the stairs two at a time, leading Caitlyn into the undercroft below the castle. Two hundred years previously it was likely a dungeon, but previous owners had modernized it and turned it into an underground office space.

Flynn found the corridor where he challenged Kalishnik. No bodies, but a lot of blood. Most of it probably his.

He led Caitlyn through the smashed glass doors into the data center. One of the techs hiding behind a computer rack jumped out with his hands up. *"Don't shoot! Don't shoot!"* He barreled past them and out the shattered doors.

Flynn found his backpack where he left it, along with the two blocks of C-4 and the two detonators. Caitlyn eyed the explosives. "Do you know what you're doing with that?"

"Of course, I do."

"Are you sure you don't want me to—"

"Watch the door. I got this."

Flynn set up the explosives, inserting the timed detonators before hiding each in a different server rack. Using the keypads, he set the timers and activated them. Flynn picked up his saber. "Go! Run! It's set to blow!"

Caitlyn darted out the broken glass doors. Flynn followed over the shattered glass and into the corridor, where he found Kalishnik holding Caitlyn with a gun to her head. Ivanov aimed his own weapon at Flynn. A Colt Anaconda .44 Magnum. The scared tech who ran out earlier stood between them, trembling.

"Finish gathering my hard drives, Mr. Popov," Ivanov demanded.

"The bomb's set to blow in three minutes," Caitlyn pointed out.

"Two minutes and forty-five seconds now," Flynn said.

"Mr. Flynn will disarm them, but in the meantime, you need to get those hard drives. Move, Mr. Popov! *Now!*"

Popov rushed past Flynn, through the shattered glass doors.

"You too, Mr. Flynn! Get moving! Disarm those bombs before I put an extra hole in this lovely lady's head."

"There is no defusing them," Flynn said. "If I try to disarm them, they will blow."

"I don't believe you."

"You don't have to. Because two minutes and thirty seconds from now we'll all be blown to kingdom come," Flynn replied.

"Your lady friend too? Didn't you come here to rescue her? Exactly how crazy are you?

"Pretty damn crazy," Caitlyn said.

Popov shouted from the data center. "I can't do this in time!"

"Do you want her to die?" Ivanov asked.

"Do *you* want to die?" Flynn replied.

"I don't want to die!" Popov screamed. He raced through the double-glass doors. Ivanov shot him in the foot. Caitlyn took advantage of the commotion to slam her heel into Kalishnik's instep and duck away. But not soon enough. The hair trigger clicked. The gun boomed. A spray of blood and Caitlyn collapsed.

Flynn roared and raised his saber. Ivanov blasted his blade clean in half. Flynn kept coming. He plunged the broken blade into Ivanov's upper arm. The oligarch dropped his weapon. Kalishnik aimed for Flynn's center mass. Flynn tore the broken blade from Ivanov and threw it at Kalishnik. He shot it out of the air. Flynn dove for cover as Kalishnik fired again. A bullet tore through Flynn's left leg. He took a step and fell.

"Pizdets!" Ivanov screamed. *"Be-zhat'!"*

Ivanov grabbed his gun and took off running. Kalishnik followed. The tech Ivanov shot pushed himself to his feet and limped after them.

Flynn rolled over onto his knees. The bullet in his leg missed bone, but cut deep into muscle. Caitlyn lay bleeding on the floor. Flynn crawled to her. When he pushed back her hair, all he saw was blood. He felt for a pulse. She was alive, but out cold. Flynn hadn't lied about the explosive charges. If they didn't move, they'd soon be dead.

He steeled himself and lifted Caitlyn off the floor. He stood straight and rested her on his shoulder. Staggering, grunting, his head swimming, he headed down the corridor for the door that led to the tunnels. He carried her through the ancient stone and brick passageway, and through the wrought iron door he breached. He started down the stone steps when the charges detonated.

The entire castle trembled as if rocked by an earthquake. Parts of the ceiling collapsed, and dust filled the air. Flynn fell down the stairs with Caitlyn in his arms. He landed in the dirt. Eyes and mouth caked with grit, he could barely breathe. He felt around until finally he found her motionless on the cave floor. Using all the strength he had left, he lifted and laid her over his shoulder, and hurried forward into the darkness. Rocks fell. Dust rose and choked the air and obscured the way forward. He tried to remember the way out. Tried to remember the layout of the labyrinth. Tripping. Stumbling. Holding her tight. Hoping that everything wouldn't come crashing down on them.

"Hold on," Flynn whispered. "Almost there."

She didn't answer. She couldn't. But he wasn't trying to reassure her as much as he was himself. *What if the path ahead was blocked? What if there was no way out?* They'd be trapped here forever, slowly bleeding out as they suffocated in the dark.

No.

This can't be the end. After finally finding her. After finally saving her. To die like this?

No.

Flynn tromped through the dark for what felt like forever. His back ached and the wound in his leg pulsated painfully. He wanted to stop. Wanted to give up. He couldn't take another step. And then he saw it.

A tiny glimmer of light.

Were his eyes playing tricks? The darkness suddenly seemed a little less dark, and the outlines of fallen rocks slowly grew more distinct. The air felt cooler, and Flynn breathed in the sea air. Waves crashed in the distance. He picked up his pace as the chance of surviving energized him. He finally emerged from out of the darkness and into the dimness. He took a bracing breath of ocean air and stared up at the foggy, starlit sky.

"Thank God." He sank to his knees and gently laid Caitlyn on the rough sand, still unconscious and probably concussed. "We need to get you to a hospital."

"She's not going to make it, and neither are you." Ivanov and Kalishnik emerged from the fog.

Acrid smoke wafted on the breeze. Flynn glanced up at the castle on the bluffs. Flames danced in the windows, the light of the fire penetrating the fog.

"You blew up my boat. You blew up my castle. You blew up my life."

Flynn stared into the barrel of the .44 Magnum. "It's nothing personal. I just do what they pay me to."

"No one pays you, Mr. Flynn. You don't work for *anybody*. You are a loose cannon! A lunatic!"

"I think you're projecting."

"I think we are done talking. Time to die, Mr. Flynn."

"Before you pull that trigger, can I ask you one question?"

"No."

"Are you working with M?"

"Who?"

"Are you his puppet master?"

"Excuse me?"

"Did you kidnap his family in Pasadena?"

"Whose family?"

"M's family. You probably know him as Dr. Michaels."

Ivanov sighed and thumbed back the hammer on his Colt Anaconda. "Goodbye, Mr. Flynn."

"Weapons down!" shouted a Russian-accented baritone. Four Spetsnaz commandos emerged from the fog, their weapons trained on Kalishnik and Ivanov. "On the ground!"

Frustration flashed across Ivanov's face as he tried to make the calculation: kill Flynn and die in a hail of gunfire or surrender and die in prison?

"Weapons on the ground!" growled the commando.

Kalishnik obeyed and let his weapon dangle before carefully setting it on the ground.

Ivanov hesitated, but self-preservation eventually took precedence over revenge. He dropped his gun in the sand. The Spetsnaz swooped in, patted them down, and zip-tied their wrists.

"This isn't over, Mr. Flynn," Ivanov vowed as the commandos dragged him and Kalishnik off into the fog.

Flynn slid his arms under Caitlyn and dug in to lift her. Unsteady on his feet, he carried her across the beach until he reached the long wooden staircase next to the boathouse. Every step up hurt like hell, the wound on his leg pumping out more and more blood. But finally, he reached the top, staggered past the Laundry House, and made his way through the main gates to the circular driveway surrounding the Fountain Court.

Glass shattered as the heat generated by the fire inside the castle blew out windows. The conflagration roared and crackled as the bottom floor burned.

The Russian helicopter roared as it lifted off. It flew over the castle and then over the sea. Flynn laid Caitlyn in the grass and sat down next to her. He took her motionless hand in his and held it to his chest. She still had a pulse, weak as it was.

As the sound of the helicopter receded, three Bushmaster armored troop transport vehicles rolled up into the circular driveway. Ten SAS commandos jumped out of each one. Four commandos surrounded Flynn and aimed their weapons at him. A fifth, a squad leader, addressed Flynn directly. "I'm looking for Caitlyn Valentine."

"You found her." Flynn tenderly smoothed the hair off her blood-spattered face.

A combat medical team rushed over and started treating her. One noticed the oozing between Flynn's fingers as he tried to staunch his own bleeding. They stabilized him and dressed the wound as a Black Hawk helicopter came in for a landing. Flynn felt lightheaded as they loaded Caitlyn onto the bird for an emergency medical evacuation. Then they helped Flynn aboard. He sat beside her and held her hand. The Black Hawk lifted off. Sirens fought with the growl of the chopper. Flynn looked down. The castle was in flames, now fully engulfed as a half dozen fire engines filled the circular driveway around the fountain.

CHAPTER FORTY

The bullet missed his femur and femoral vein and lodged in the meat of his right thigh. Even after six months of healing, the wound still affected his stride. He especially felt it walking up hill. The tiny towns around Interlaken were all connected by hiking paths. *Wanderwegs.* Prominent signs delineated all the trails and their difficulties with a color code. The yellow trails were easier, family friendly. Those marked red-white-red were steeper and more challenging. As Flynn recovered, he continued to push himself.

It was early spring, and the wildflowers were just beginning to bloom. Flynn enjoyed the cold, clean air and the snow on the distant peaks of the Eiger, the Mönch, and the Jungrau. Interlaken stretched below, sandwiched between Lake Brienz and Lake Thun. The warmth of the sun invigorated him. Cherry blossoms, lavender crocus, white narcissus, dandelions, and alpine wildflowers in a multitude of colors stood vividly against all the green. Stubborn clumps of ice and snow melted and flowed into a rushing stream next to the trail.

Flynn had been to Switzerland as a boy. The memories were vague, but he knew his mother was Swiss. His father Scottish. They spent much of their time abroad and many summers hiking alpine trails. Until his parents died in that tragic climbing accident in the French Alps. *Or was it a car accident near Bakersfield?* He could no longer remember their voices or even their faces. Childhood memories faded over time, and that part of his life felt dim and out of focus.

In the hospital in Glasgow, they put him under general anesthesia to remove the bullet. When he awakened, he couldn't remember where he was or how he got there, but he did remember the group home they put him in when his parents died. Somewhere in Riverside, California. He remembered the loneliness. Remembered the bullies. The ones who called him fat and stupid. The ones who gave him wedgies and noogies and flushed his head down the toilet. They called him Jimmy. They called him Dimmy. They called him Dummy.

But that wasn't him.

That was another person entirely. Someone sad and pathetic, and weak and alone. Someone who wasn't even sure he wanted to live. But when the anesthesia finally wore off, Flynn remembered who he *really* was. Someone capable and brave and resilient. Someone who fought the good fight. Someone the world needed. Someone who deserved to be here. And then a flash of fear as he remembered Caitlyn in his arms, limp and unconscious, her hair matted with blood. As soon as he awakened, he asked for her. They told him she was still in surgery and that she suffered a traumatic brain injury. A moderate one, but dangerous all the same.

Flynn spent three days recovering from his bullet wound. Caitlyn spent three weeks. They both were debriefed by MI5 and finally allowed to leave the country. Flynn arranged a stay for them at a luxurious private convalescent hospital in Interlaken.

The Burkhalter Center for Neurology and Rehabilitation sat on Lake Thun and specialized in patients suffering from strokes and traumatic brain injury. The institute catered to celebrities, the super wealthy, royalty, and anyone looking for privacy, luxury, and the best medical care money could buy. Flynn's old friend, Alessandra Bianchi, made a call and got them admitted. A major movie star and sex symbol in the 60s, she married one of the wealthiest men in the world in 1992 and still carried a lot of clout. Flynn swept her into one of his adventures two years back, and she had remained a close friend and confidant ever since.

The institute was connected to a five-star luxury hotel where friends and family members could stay. Both the hospital and hotel had magnificent views of the lake and the surrounding mountains. Flynn visited Caitlyn every day and worked with her every step of the way.

"Hey, yo! Hold up!"

Flynn turned slowly. Sancho tromped up the hill behind him, clearly struggling. "You all right?"

"This altitude is kicking my *ass*. I'm not used to it, dude."

Flynn stopped and waited for Sancho to reach him.

Red-faced and sweaty, his old friend couldn't catch his breath. "How high up are we anyways?"

"We're at almost four thousand feet. But when we climb the Jungfrau, we're going to be a hell of a lot higher."

"Is there really a restaurant at the end of this?"

"A country café. Traditional Swiss mountain food. Raclette. Fondue. You won't find better *Älper rösti mit schinken und käse überbacken* anywhere."

"I'll take your word for it, *ese*."

"You hungry?"

"Starving."

"Then we better keep moving."

Flynn slowed his pace so Sancho could keep up.

"You see the Times today?" Sancho asked breathlessly.

"I did not."

"A Russian court convicted Ivanov of embezzling state funds, extortion, fraud, espionage, and cyber-terrorism."

"Fitting, if a tad ironic."

"They're moving him from Lefortovo Prison to Black Dolphin."

Flynn nodded. He knew it well. "Penal colony No. 6 in Orenburg Oblast. One of the oldest prisons in Russia. They must have sentenced him to life."

Sancho nodded. "It's a step down from *Les Ambassadeurs Club.*"

"But in its own way…just as exclusive. I imagine Kalishnik is going with him."

"There wasn't anything in the Times about that, but it did say his wife now owns everything."

"Then Anya got what she wanted."

Sancho stopped to rest. "That is one scary lady."

"Not exactly trustworthy, but in the end, she did do the right thing."

"I guess."

"The one loose end is M. We still don't know who's controlling him."

"Oh, that's all settled now too."

"It is?"

Sancho hated fibbing to his old friend, but he needed to put an end to his paranoid obsession with Dr. Michaels. "Yeah, it turns out it was Ivanov."

"But Ivanov acted as if he'd never heard of M."

"Of course, he wouldn't ever admit it."

"What was he holding over him?"

"His…um…mother. He kidnapped her."

"The ruthless bastard."

"Well, she's safe now. It's over. Things are back to normal."

"Normal is a matter of opinion though, isn't it? Do you remember what Plato said about that?"

"I don't."

"All we can see are the shadows on the wall."

They continued and crested the top of the hill, reaching a view site that overlooked all of Interlaken. Sancho leaned on the black wrought iron fence and tried to catch his breath. A half dozen tourists milled about and admired the magnificent view. One of them was Sancho's wife, Alyssa. Baby Miguel rode in a front facing carrier.

Flynn reached out and shook little Miguel's hand. "Congratulations, little man. You beat us to the top."

Alyssa smiled and mussed his hair. "And I'm the one doing all the work. But you know who beat us all?"

She motioned with her chin towards Caitlyn, leaning on the railing, taking in the view. She turned and saw Flynn. Her face lit up with a grin. She jogged over. "Isn't this amazing?"

"You're amazing. But I don't want you to overdo it."

"I won't." She looked irritated. "I know I'm not a hundred percent, but I'm getting there." Caitlyn wore khaki-colored hiking shorts and a white tank top. She looked lean and strong and heartbreakingly beautiful. Her glossy black hair, cut in a pixie, was still growing out from the surgery. Her green eyes never looked more alive. "How's your leg?"

"Better every day."

She smiled at that. "Who's ready to eat?"

Sancho raised his hand. "I hear they make a great…" He glanced at Flynn. "What did you call it?"

"*Älper rösti mit schinken und käse überbacken.*"

"Yeah, that."

■　■　■

One-and-a-half year-old Miguel walked like a drunken sailor, teetering and windmilling his arms before landing on his well-padded butt. He grinned with delight as Alyssa helped him back up, happy to be upright on his tiny sneakers. She turned him around and pointed him at Sancho sitting in the grass about ten feet away.

Sancho beckoned him over. "Miguel! Walk to Papi!"

"Papi!" Miguel yelled and plodded for his dad, planting one unsteady leg and then the other, slowly tottering forward as he wobbled back and forth.

Flynn watched Miguel's progress from the first-floor balcony of his suite. He sat in a garden chair next to a small table topped with mosaic tiles. Caitlyn walked out with two drinks, a vodka martini, shaken not stirred, for Flynn and what looked like a Moscow Mule for herself.

Flynn regarded Caitlyn's drink sternly. "Is that?"

"A virgin. No vodka. No bourbon."

"I don't mean to nag."

"Yes, you do, but that's okay. No martinis for me until I'm fully recovered."

"You look healthier and happier than I've ever seen you."

"Well, you did meet me in a mental hospital."

"True."

Caitlyn smiled as she watched Miguel totter around. "I'm so glad they could come visit."

"They were worried about you."

"I was worried about me too." She laughed as Miguel landed on his little butt. "Is that the best age ever or what? I love it when they're just learning to walk."

"Alessandra told me she's coming to visit next week."

"Didn't she used to live here?"

"She did. She still has a house on Lake Como."

"I love it here. It's so unbelievably beautiful."

Flynn nodded. "Sometimes I wish we could stay here forever."

"Why can't we?" She reached over and put her hand on his. "I've been looking online at houses we could lease. Partly daydreaming, but partly not."

"Seriously?"

"I found a beautiful chalet in Unterseen."

"You want to stay here? Permanently?"

"Only if you do."

"You want me to stay here *with* you?"

"A little over a year ago you said you wanted to come with me. Be with me. Be together."

"And you weren't interested."

"I wasn't ready."

"And now?"

"Maybe."

"Maybe?"

Caitlyn squeezed Flynn's hand. "I don't know what the future holds or where this can go. But I'm not worried about tomorrow. All I care about is now. And right now, right here, being with you? That's all I want."

A wave of emotion rocked Flynn to his core. "That doesn't sound like *maybe* to me."

She grinned. "So, is that a yes?"

"Yes. Of course."

"I just want more time with you."

Flynn lifted her hand to his lips and gently kissed it. "We have all the time in the world."

ABOUT THE AUTHOR

Haris Orkin is a playwright, screenwriter, game writer, and novelist. His play, *Dada* was produced at The American Stage and the La Jolla Playhouse. *Sex, Impotence, and International Terrorism* was chosen as a critic's choice by the L.A. Weekly and sold as a film script to MGM/UA. *Save the Dog* was produced as a Disney Sunday Night Movie. His original screenplay, *A Saintly Switch*, was directed by Peter Bogdanovich and starred David Alan Grier and Vivica A. Fox.

He is a WGA Award and BAFTA Award nominated game writer and narrative designer known for *Command and Conquer: Red Alert 3*, *Call of Juarez: Gunslinger*, *Tom Clancy's The Division*, *Mafia 3*, *Dying Light*, *Evil West*, and *Resident Evil: Shadows of Rose*.

www.harisorkin.com

NOTE FROM THE AUTHOR

I was a shy, skinny, bookish, bespectacled, and insecure twelve-year-old living in the suburbs of Chicago when I first realized what I wanted to be when I grew up. I wanted to be Alexander Mundy in *It Takes a Thief*.

I wanted to be Illya Kuryakin in *The Man from Uncle*. I wanted to be part of the Mission Impossible team. I wanted to be Jim West, Derek Flint, and Matt Helm. I wanted to be James Bond.

Those men had no fear. They knew karate and could scuba dive and rock climb and skydive and ski and shoot the eye out of a flea at fifty yards. They were confident in any situation and were comfortable in their own skin. I think that was the biggest wish fulfillment fantasy of all for an awkward pre-teen struggling through puberty and that's what inspired James Flynn and his adventures.

At twelve I was terrified of girls. I was always picked last in gym class. I lived a life of perpetual embarrassment. In hindsight, that's probably how most twelve-year-olds feel, but at the time, I didn't know that. So, I started lifting weights. I became a gymnast. I boxed. I studied karate. I became a rock climber and learned to ski and scuba dive. I even studied in London for a year and traveled the world.

But I never did become an international super spy. Instead, I became a screenwriter and game writer, creating wish fulfillment fantasies for other nerdy twelve-year-olds. Thank you for indulging in my fantasies. I hope you enjoyed the journey. I do believe Mr. Flynn is just getting started.

Please connect with me on Twitter and Facebook and feel free to ask me anything. This is a two-way conversation.

~Haris Orkin

NOTE FROM THE PUBLISHER

Word-of-mouth is crucial for any author to succeed. If you enjoyed *The Spy Who Hated Me*, please leave a review online— anywhere you are able. Even if it's just a sentence or two. It would make all the difference and would be very much appreciated.

Thanks!

We hope you enjoyed reading this title from:

www.blackrosewriting.com

Subscribe to our mailing list – *The Rosevine* – and receive **FREE** books, daily deals, and stay current with news about upcoming releases and our hottest authors.
Scan the QR code below to sign up.

Already a subscriber? Please accept a sincere thank you for being a fan of Black Rose Writing authors.

View other Black Rose Writing titles at www.blackrosewriting.com/books and use promo code **PRINT** to receive a **20% discount** when purchasing.